BEHIND THE BEADED CURTAIN

Sophie tiptoed over and joined her. Never had the secret garden room seemed such a marvellous place to be, as the two excited and happy ladies settled down to watch and wait for the expected cabaret.

The Swedish lovelies had thrown off their outer garments and were reclining on a sofa in their underwear, struggling with their French language studies. It would be impossible, here, to reproduce their excruciating accents and their difficulties with the notoriously convoluted grammar. But it amused the two ladies for a while and gave them an opportunity to admire the couple's golden skin and almost-white hair, bleached by the Riviera sun. Soon Sophie got bored with their study and went to the console to pour large gins.

The couple were bored too, and Erik threw away his tome and yawned. 'We have better things to do, Kirsten,' he said as he slipped off his underpants.

'Ya, ya, I agree,' she said, following his example . . .

By the same Author:
THE SECRET GARDEN ROOM

BEHIND THE BEADED CURTAIN

Georgette de la Tour

NEXUS
A NEXUS BOOK
published by
the Paperback Division of
W. H. Allen & Co. plc

A Nexus Book
Published in 1990
by the Paperback Division of
W H Allen & Co plc
26 Grand Union Centre
Ladbroke Grove, London W10
Copyright © Georgette de la Tour 1990

Typeset by Avocet Robinson, Buckingham
Printed and Bound in Great Britain by
Cox & Wyman Ltd, Reading, Berks.

ISBN 0 352 32608 5

This book is sold subject to the condition that it shall not,
by way of trade or otherwise, be lent, re-sold, hired out,
or otherwise circulated without the publisher's prior
consent in any form of binding or cover other than that
in which it is puboished and without a similar condition
including this condition being imposed on the subsequent
purchaser.

Introduction

Readers of my earlier journal 'The Secret Garden Room' will already be acquainted with the principal characters of this narrative. It is to be hoped that, as their stories unfold, their all too human foibles and weaknesses will be understood and forgiven, in that generous spirit which should prevail between old friends.

This present diary records the happenings on the Riviera exactly twelve months later, the Season of 1929, the final, thrilling year of the decade of hot jazz, high jinks, fashion, daring and exhibitionism that constituted the Roaring Twenties.

It has been a privilege to undertake the necessary research into this fascinating era. My studies led me to private libraries in Monte Carlo, Paris, Florence, and London. I met countless survivors of the delightful period, and had access to their most private letters and papers, fragrant recollections and anecdotes without which this journal would not be possible.

It gives me great pleasure to record my thanks to these generous contributors who are too numerous to mention individually, and also to Madame Rosanne Poitiers of the Société Nationale des Auteurs Romantiques, who provided translations.

Chapter One

No-one on the coast could believe how fast the year had spun full circle. It seemed to have had the momentum of a whirlwind. Bernadette contemplated her diary and engagement book with an air that was a mixture of amused surprise and regret. The calendar had never been so full, the vicomtesse considered. The social gazette of the Cote d'Azur was always a scintillating affair, but the past year had been truly outstanding. The Ballets Russes and the Opera Du Monde had both played to capacity houses in the theatres of the Riviera, the casinos had had record takings, every hotel, apartment house and rented villa had been crammed to capacity, and the whole social scene had been a thrilling, delightful series of lavish events.

This stretch of coast along the Mediterranean, fabulously rich and exclusive, represented, in the public conception, a location where the upper echelons of society, the eccentric, the artistic, the hedonistic, and even the despised *nouveau riche*, could foregather in order to live life to the full. A perfect climate, warm sea, beaches, secluded coves for naked natural bathing, and a hinterland of precipitous mountains dotted with romantic ancient villages, combine to provide the perfect setting for lovers and escapists. The warm scents of the *maquis* of the interior float on gentle winds and mingle with those of the scrupulously maintained *Jardins Publiques*; oleanders, bougainvillaea, hibiscus, palm, geranium and a thousand other exotic varieties exude a heady intoxicating perfume.

No wonder, thought Bernadette, that the Riviera had become famous as the setting where scandal and outrageous behaviour were the norm. It was the jazz age, the end of the decade which was to become known in history as the Roaring Twenties. In its final ecstatic throes of wanton profligacy, sexual freedom, alluring fashion, and reckless hot-headedness, the Charleston era celebrated its existence with an extraordinary wild enthusiasm, dare-devil and sophistication. How could one possibly live anywhere else? What other place could offer such transport, delirium?

Bernadette remembered the fantastic party which she had given to mark the final performance of the ballet; the hot jazz, the dancing, naked swimming, fireworks and brazen couplings. It was the night she committed herself to her darling Marcel, the international couturier, and on which her cousin Sophie made up her mind to buy for Arthur, the well-endowed English army officer, his freedom from service.

The Ballet had packed their trunks the next day and left for an extended tour of Latin America, leaving behind them more than a few broken hearts. Angelique, the little chocolate shop girl pined languorously for Vladimir, the skinny Mongolian *corps de ballet* boy, and a score or more ladies of taste and fashion shed a tear at the memory of the sexual athletics of the remaining virile members of the troupe.

After Rio de Janiero, Mexico City, Lima, Caracas and Montevideo, the Company had gone on to conquer New York, Boston and San Francisco, before its triumphant seasons in London and Paris. The Riviera was now in a fever of excitement that the legendary ensemble was due to return to its spiritual home, the tiny gilded Opera House of Monte Carlo which had become its favourite harbour of repose in a life of permanent exile.

Sophie, Bernadette's cousin, had a collection of postcards, sent from all of the destinations mentioned above, written in a spidery drunken script which was the handiwork of Dhokouminsky, the chief character dancer who so adored her. 'It's no use, sooner or later he will have to know I have married Arthur,' she moaned as she lay in her *peignoir* in the secret garden room with Bernadette, enjoying a pot of hot chocolate. 'He's so crazy, he'll kill me, or even worse, emasculate my darling Arthur.'

Her hands roved to her loins and she trembled with delicious fervour at the memory of the giant Slav's onslaught of her plump little body. How he had ravished her at the tea dance in the shabby hotel at Roquebrune; full penetration no less as they gyrated to the passionate strains of a trio of elderly lady musicians in a crowded ballroom. And also she remembered, with a frisson that reached into her innermost recess, the incident of the journey, by horse drawn carriage, to the Hotel de Paris and a night of unsurpassed lust. She wondered if libidinous reminiscence counted as an act of unfaithfulness, but after a moment's consideration, dismissed the idea. 'After all,' she said out loud, much to Bernadette's amusement, 'I would be surprised if Arthur doesn't sometimes fondly linger on certain amours of his past, even perhaps when he is pleasuring me so ardently.'

'Quite,' Bernadette murmured. 'That is the nature of the beast. The male of the species is a hunter, a dominant, rapacious animal whose brain is centred on his scrotum.'

'And that is why we adore them, *non*?' Sophie winked, as she greedily tucked in to another slice of *millefeuille*.

The vicomtesse looked fondly at her attractive cousin. How gay, how sparkling, she thought, what an adorable companion. Really, one was incredibly lucky to have even one relative who was so charming. It was a whole year since Sophie had returned to the Cote d'Azur, widowed, but rich and beautiful. She had captivated society and enslaved the hearts of a considerable number of attractive men, but none was smitten as badly as the divine Arthur. Bernadette smiled as she recalled the early summer morning when she had first revealed, to her cousin, the secrets of the garden room—her legacy from her late husband, the vicomte.

She trembled as she remembered how they had observed Arthur and his friend Charles at the time of their *levée* in the adjoining apartment, through the secret peephole and two-way mirror. The spectacle of these handsome sleek men at their ablutions, semi-erect on account of their erotic dreams, had been powerfully moving. So was their deeply masculine gossip, as they recounted their sexual exploits to each other. Both women had had ample proof that Englishmen have been wronged when it has been suggested that they do not make good lovers.

'You remember the sight of Charles in the shower, *cherie*?' Bernadette asked Sophie.

'*Mon Dieu*, how could I ever forget,' Sophie replied, wiping a few crumbs from her creamy breasts which protruded from the lace of her négligé. 'How he struggled to have the cold douche control his massive organ.'

'Quite,' her cousin nodded. 'What was the point of spending himself when so many desirable women all over the Riviera were so greedy for him? An arrogant, but loveable boy.'

'And you remember my darling Arthur? How he was so overcome with frustration that he had to corset himself into a jock strap before he could go out with any semblance of decency?' Sophie recalled. 'But now that he is my husband, I think he no longer has that particular problem.'

Readers of the earlier journal will already be acquainted with the facts of the secret garden room where the pair of nubile and generously proportioned women were ensconced.

The late vicomte had restored the mansion, which was situated in the environs of Cap Ferrat, to a state of perfection for the arrival of his young bride Bernadette. For some years they had lived in this charming, large old house, in a state of complete rapport and mutual enjoyment.

Henri, for that was his name, had a monumental income, much of which was lavished on the creature comforts of the home; entertaining, rare foods and wines, and a host of brilliant visiting friends. The house attained a reputation for the extravagance of the hospitality it offered. Dowagers, deposed kings and defrocked priests gathered there for the Season, along with actors, painters, bohemians and writers. Some even said that the present fame of the Riviera was rooted in the social explosion that took place when the vicomte and his wife took possession of the mansion and initiated their much envied series of invitations.

Then, at huge extra cost, when Bernadette was away on an extended foreign trip, Henri gutted the interior of the ground floor and created a secret apartment which was invisible to the outside world. Windowless, save for a large domed roof of azure glass, and with access only from a door, in a small study nearby, which was operated by a secret button, the new apartment was totally unexpected, and unknown to their visitors. The outstanding inventions of the resourceful aristocrat, the two-way mirror system and the peephole, allowed full vision of a guest wing which occupied the corner of the building.

This accommodation was usually offered to young friends or relatives, bright holidaymakers in need of free lodging and comfortable surroundings. While Henri was alive, of course, the guests were female. How he adored to watch them bathe, dress and chatter. He savoured every item of their daring lingerie, their knee-revealing frocks, garters, suspenders and stockings.

Just before he sadly passed away he gave the key of this retreat to his wife, entrusting it to her for her lifetime. Sophie was the only other person privy to its delights; sworn to secrecy, and promised its exclusive use if and when Bernadette joined her darling Henri in the ambrosian fields. It was exactly a year ago when they had first spied on Charles and Arthur.

Charles had now left on a business trip, satiated in a physical sense from his series of affairs with forward women. (They included Angelique, the girl in the chocolate shop, and Edith, the Amazonian and aggressively lecherous voluptuary from Alabama who was an expert at the new Charleston dance.)

Arthur was currently serving the remainder of his commission, having been bought out of the army by Sophie, and was expected to rejoin his lovesick wife in a few weeks.

Bernadette stirred restlessly on her divan, toying with the ribbon at the neck of her lacy *peignoir*. She was wondering how the forthcoming Season could possibly approach the crazed amusement of last year's. Was she becoming dull and housewifely, constantly bound up with her new husband Marcel? He was kind, courteous, and a dedicated lover who applied every variation to his love-making technique, but she sensed a little of the nagging fear that can assail a woman approaching middle age.

She stood up and inspected her body in the full length art deco style mirror, allowing the lacy garment to fall to the floor. Bernadette was not displeased with what she saw. A mature woman, tall but rounded, with an ample firm bosom, long thighs and clear vibrant skin and complexion.

'You are like a ripe plum, darling,' said Sophie. 'Just like a fruit which is ready to fall from the bough. Any man would love to eat you.'

Bernadette was charmed by the comparison. It felt good to be at the prime of one's life, far removed from the stumbling inadequacies of gawky youth, and also from the first heart breaking agonies of young love. Sophisticated and elegant, worldly wise and humorous, she felt at that moment that she was the archetypal Frenchwoman, the symbol of Gallic femininity which, for many men, represents the most desirable goal of their psycho-sexuality. 'Not bad,' she agreed. 'It will be better for some sunbathing. The gardeners have prepared the swimming pool, thank goodness, and now the weather is so lovely we really must expose ourselves.'

'Quite', Sophie enjoined firmly. 'In the past, white flesh was much admired. In the old days men loved to fumble with petticoats, skirts and bodices, and rove their hands over marble white skin. Nowadays, the style is Health and Beauty. It's all because of the divine Isadora Duncan who threw away her constricting garments and danced in transparent gauzes, and the fashion for naked Swedish athletics. My goodness, how the Nordics and Germans cultivate their bodies.'

'And the Americans also,' added Bernadette, thinking of the corn-fed football players from Michigan who had dazzled everyone on the beaches the previous summer; and the muscular, nymphomaniac Edith whose breasts had developed to an enormous size from her endless pursuit of excellence in lacrosse and tennis.

'There is much competition from the young,' Sophie interposed, regarding her plump posterior in the same mirror, and then her soft curving belly. 'Arthur adores these,' she said matter-of-factly, cupping her well shaped breasts. 'But really, I shall have to do something about them, or I shall not be able to wear any of the new season's dresses which are meant to fit like a glove over a figure that looks like a boy's.'

'We shall begin a gruelling course immediately,' the vicomtesse announced, 'and exercise every day. Come, let us begin before our guests start to arrive.' The ladies lay down on the floor on their backs and energetically kicked their legs in the air. Pushing themselves so that their weight was taken on their shoulders, they propped up their bare bottoms and 'bicycled', panting with the effort. Next they stood with feet apart and did a series of toe-touching exercises.

Sophie noted the neatness of the triangle of hair at Bernadette's crotch and the tantalising way it lightly covered her mound of Venus. She made a mental note to attend to her own area when she was next in the privacy of her bathroom.

Then they rolled from side to side, exercising the muscles of their buttocks.

'Oh dear,' Sophie moaned as her generous breasts also rolled over one way and then the other, 'you see what I mean.'

'Darling, don't go too far. Some of the bright young things are so skinny they are like planks. I don't know of any man who wants to embrace a skeleton,' Bernadette laughed.

And so, in the peace of the secret garden room, the two cousins prepared for the forthcoming Season, toning up their bodies for what they each hoped would be a feast of the pleasures of love. Just as they finished their exertions the house telephone rang. It was her butler.

'The first guests are arrived, madame,' he intoned. 'A young couple, Monsieur et Madame Ormesby-Gore from England.' He had great difficulty with the pronunciation of this announcement, and save it to say that his phonetics could not be reproduced here.

'Ah, the young relative of Lady Letitia, and his new wife,' the vicomtesse said excitedly. 'Please take them to the small guest wing. Tell them I am presently occupied, but that after they have bathed and refreshed themselves, I shall meet them for cocktails in the *grand salon*, at about six o'clock. Thank you, Moutard.'

'Oh, what fun,' Sophie cried, 'people are beginning to show up. I know it's going to be a wonderful summer.'

Bernadette poured them cool drinks and indicated to her cousin to relax with her on the divan. 'Soon we shall take a look at them,' she said quietly. 'Letitia tells me that he is gorgeous, and the girl is supposed to be ravishing. It was the wedding of the year in *Angleterre*.'

The sunlight of that lovely afternoon spilled through the azure glass of the ceiling, and shadows of the leaves of jasmine and honeysuckle which trailed over it flickered in contrast. The naked ladies sipped their drinks in the cool sybaritic comfort of the stylish interior in anticipation of the young guests' appearance. Murmurs of voices were heard in the distance. Bernadette rose and drew away a rich brocaded curtain which hung over the two-way mirror.

The couple were indeed of surpassing handsomeness. Strangely matched in height, for the girl wore high heeled shoes, the red-haired couple seemed to these southern ladies to be escapees from the frozen North, like denizens of Valhalla. In fact they were Scottish, descended from a long line of kings, and now the heirs to vast tracts of Highland country dedicated to the rearing and killing of wild fowl. Indeed, they had brought with them the guns, fishing rods and tackle which their kind never travel without.

Bernadette commented that such equipment would be of little use on the Riviera, unless they were planning to hunt human quarry.

Though tired by the long journey from the ancestral highlands, the pair were thrilled to be there. As any traveller knows, the warm air and the scents which assail the nostrils when one alights at Nice, and follow one along the corniche, are intoxicating.

Fed on Letitia's stories about the brazen, louche behaviour of the *jeunesse doré*, and anxious to leap headlong into the frenzied round of pleasure which they had been promised, the relatively unsophisticated Scottish newly-weds could hardly wait to plunge into the maelstrom. They tore off their clothes and stood for a moment, toasting themselves with the malt whisky which they had managed to bring unscathed. Bernadette and Sophie were speechless on sight of the pair's nakedness.

The young wife, Cynthia, had Titian hair which fell far enough to cover her bottom, and a bright patch of pubis to match. Ian was thatched with the same colour, and in his case, the violent red hair covered his entire body, thicker in texture, over his wide chest and around the genital area.

'They are like ginger marmalade cats,' Sophie whispered to her cousin, grasping her arm to press the point.

'What an embrace,' Bernadette murmured as Ian closed Cynthia in a powerful squeeze, caressing her long tresses.

They watched as the lad rotated his hips against her slim body and she massaged the rounds of his firm buttocks. A few feet away from the ladies, in the quiet peace of the guest suite, the aristocratic pair had no idea, when Cynthia turned towards the bathroom, that the sight of her husband's thickened member, protruding magnificently from the auburn bush of hair, was visible to the watching women.

'You'll just have to wait for that,' they heard Cynthia call out gaily.

'What!' he yelled. 'After thirty-six hours on blasted trains, not bloody likely.' He followed her into the bathroom, going out of the range of the two-way mirror.

Bernadette and Sophie removed themselves to the intricately wrought Indian screen which contained the peep-holes already mentioned. Here it must be noted that, since the vicomtesse was invariably accompanied in her investigations by her cousin, it had been decided it was necessary to install a second hole in addition to the one provided by Henri. Sinking deep into the damask and silken cushions, they each applied an enquiring eye to the two lenses.

Cynthia and Ian were standing in the jet of the shower, soaping each other's body. They giggled like children let out of school. The Highland prince smoothed her freckled breasts lovingly with suds and then did the same to that part between her legs that was generously covered with silky red down. Cynthia stirred against his muscular body, relaxing and easing away the discomforts of the journey.

'What strong hands he has,' Sophie whimpered, one of her own travelling to her erotic centre.

'He clearly understands the technique of arousal,' her cousin breathed, feeling Sophie's warm breath on her cheek.

Part of the decoration of the Indian screen was an inlay of onyx and ivory, worked with precious stones and silver which depicted idyllic pastoral scenes of Eastern life. Nymphs and satyrs with enormously exaggerated genitalia were represented in the art nouveau style. The bas relief of the exquisite carvings brought these erotic aspects more into prominence. Much skill and labour had gone into their production, and much knowledge of those impulses which are the mainspring of carnal life.

Bernadette clutched the swollen tip of one satyr. It was wrought in fine detail and the patina was excellent, most probably the result of her caresses over the years. *This hardness must be the same as that which now surely infuses the boy, she thought.* The supposition was correct, as she saw when Ian turned his back to his wife, and Cynthia placed her arms around him.

First she washed his neck and chest. Sophie was entranced. It was as though the Scots maid was attending to a pet dog, there was such a tangle of wet hair, and she dealt with it with such loving care. Her small hands then slid down to soap the young laird's proud possessions.

His organ pipe thrilled to the music she played on it and on the sac underneath, easing every small wrinkle of skin, eventually peeling back the generous foreskin. This attention brought his member to an interesting tumescence, swollen and lengthened, but still not completely rigid.

Bernadette and Sophie gasped with pleasure as they watched the scene. Sophie turned briefly to her cousin and laid a hand on her forearm. It was a gesture of gratitude. Bernadette smiled by return. She was touched by this small act which told her how much joy Sophie took in being the sole other possessor of the key to the hidden chamber.

'They are so young and innocent,' Sophie whispered. 'It is really very moving watching them at play.'

Ian was certainly moved when Cynthia began her next caress. With a soapy hand sliding up one of his thighs and underneath the length of his stem she slowly raised it so that it was flat to his belly. Then, by continuing the stroking action over and past the exposed tulip of his glans, she let the partly sprung member fall back to its original angle. His eyes were closed, and his head hung back on his wife's shoulder. The watching ladies quivered, with a sharp intake of breath, as the muscles which controlled the descent instigated another levitation, this time unaided.

The member was now fully rigid and vertical, with its point reaching several centimetres past the husband's navel. Cynthia sidled around and placed herself on her knees in front of Ian. It was a charming composition, the long auburn hair touching the marble floor of the shower cabinet, her hands raised up in what looked like an act of worship. They cupped his scrotum and then closed firmly around the stem. The throbbing glans protruded, pointing upwards.

Cynthia began a slow, delicate manipulation of the skin that covered the shaft, sliding and pressing down on the rigid root then lifting up and squeezing over the bulbous end.

Ian's hands were now placed on her shoulders. In obvious ecstasy, he swayed slightly, and Sophie and Bernadette could see the powerful muscular contractions that surged through his abdomen at the end of each movement that Cynthia made.

He will spend any second, thought Bernadette, but her fears were unnecessary. The lad, knowing the depth of his arousal, turned from the thrilling attentions, and switched the water to cold. After scrubbing himself with much vigour, the organ seemed to be much less agitated.

He took Cynthia in his arms and felt for her hidden recess. She bent over, almost to touch her toes, with her saturated swathe of hair hanging down. Her posterior was presented to him for soaping and he gracefully obliged with smooth circular movements over her buttocks then with swooping insertions between the tops of her thighs. The observers both felt in their loins something of the sensation that was happening to Cynthia every time Ian's palm slid past and then between the lips which covered her inner sanctum. When he seemed to pause, they surmised that he was attending delicately to the small hardening button from where her most fervent thrills were aroused.

When the young laird turned for another application of soap, they saw that his contact with Cynthia's most sensitive area had brought him back, again, to a state of complete erection. Cynthia rose and recommenced her massage of this prize possession, but this time with more vigour.

'I die,' Sophie gasped harshly. 'How I would love to play this game with him.'

'*Naturellement, chérie*,' the vicomtesse whispered. 'Do you know that the Scots call it "tossing the caber"?'

This time it was too much for the rampant boy. Thirty six hours in trains had caused him much frustration. So many travellers were heading for the South at the start of the Season that they had not been able to secure a sleeping compartment. Ian had sat in close proximity to his new bride all this time without recourse to any release. The throbbing member which had pressed so uncomfortably into his tweed trousers throughout the interminable journey, now yielded to Cynthia's exertions.

He was young and strong, capable of instant arousal, and he knew, as did Bernadette, that it would be only a matter of minutes before he properly pleasured the ravishing Cynthia in the comfort of the vast double bed. Therefore his reluctance faded, not with a whimper, but with a bang, an explosion of animal force that ricocheted his pent-up juices around the shower cabinet to the hearty satisfaction of all.

Bernadette got up and drew the curtain back into place over the two-way mirror. '*Mon Dieu*,' she sighed, 'these amorous Scots have a certain primitive appeal, don't you think?'

'Darling, sensational,' Sophie agreed. 'And now we must leave them to their proper devotions'.

'I have a vision of them,' the vicomtesse said with some rapture, for she was a true romantic and, being a well educated person, had read in childhood the novels of Sir Walter Scott. 'When they retire to bed to continue this sensual experience, he will imagine that he is the legendary Ivanhoe, and that Cynthia is his immortal heroine. I see them rolling in the purple heather of the Scottish Highlands. There is mist, and their fiery red hair is damp, but they are ardent lovers, and couple ferociously. It is very moving.'

'Sweetheart, you are a poet. You conjure up a charming scene,' Sophie said as she poured fresh drinks. 'But the reality is that these frozen Northeners will bask in the sun, here on the Cote d'Azur, like lizards. They will soak up the heat and he will pleasure her behind every convenient rock between here and Menton.' Bernadette gave a tinkling little laugh. 'Of course, of course,' she said delightedly. She was in a rapture that the Season on the Riviera had got off to such an auspicious start. 'And I hope that one day, wandering along a quiet beach, we come across them.' 'Ah, yes,' her cousin sighed. 'Youth and love, sunshine, and sea air, the summer will surely be a perfect one.'

The hope expressed by the vicomtesse could be said to have a certain pertinence to another pair of lovers who met by chance in Menton.

'My dear darling Francois, how lovely it is to see you again. How long is it, let me see,' said Arlette.

'Years,' Francois replied. He was squeezing her hand, regarding his ex-lover with the devotion a St. Bernard has for his master. 'Years, absolute years, and I must say you don't look a day older,' he continued.

(She noted the fire in his eyes with satisfaction.)

'I should think not, *mon vieux*. We ladies have to look after ourselves or you rotten types don't give a damn for us,' she laughed with that same gay carelessness that had enchanted Francois throughout the delightful affair they had enjoyed sometime in the past.

'Must be five, maybe six, don't you think? Anyway, it's been a long time. And where have you been, what have you been doing?' Francois asked tenderly.

'Waiting for you, *cheri*,' she replied, giving him a warm damp kiss just behind his right ear. 'No, seriously, nothing much. My husband left me.'

'My God, did he find out about us?' Francois asked urgently.

'No, don't worry, sweet,' Arlette chuckled. 'I think his predilection for ladies of black complexion got the better of him. He ran away to Senegal with a dark princess who had gold rings in her nose and in her fanny.'

'You're joking,' he said. 'That's the best thing about you, you're such a sport.'

'Francois, you are divine, it's gorgeous to see you again. Give me a great big hug.'

He took up the invitation with enthusiasm. The time they had spent apart slipped effortlessly away. Here again was that same warm musky smell, the same comfortable breasts and the long deep cleavage into which he nuzzled as far as he dared for the sake of politeness in the Winter Garden of Menton where they had literally stumbled across each other.

'Lovely creature,' he whispered. 'I have missed you.'

'You made no effort to look me up,' she pouted.

'I thought you had done with me,' Francois said sheepishly. 'You always said I shouldn't get serious, that it was only a little affair.'

'Same old Francois,' she said fondly. 'Genius of the bedroom, and not an idea in his head.'

'Yes, I must admit my prick rules my mind,' he said, aware of the stirring in his loins that was sending a message to her belly, recalling past pleasures.

'You were the best lover I ever had,' Arlette asserted, holding both his hands and covering them with little kisses. 'Buy me a cocktail. We have a lot to discuss.'

Placing an arm firmly around her waist Francois steered her out of the building and towards a sophisticated bar in the Palace d'Hiver, the masterpiece of art nouveau which had become the rage with the Bright Young Things. It was lively and amusing there, a scene of gaiety and fashion which charmed them. Sleek haired young men and close-cropped girls wearing cloche hats, beads and feather boas, were engaged in jolly banter or dancing the Black Bottom to the accompaniment of a jazz trio.

'You needn't look at any of those little chits, my petal,' Arlette twinkled. 'From now on, you're mine.'

Francois grinned. He could hardly believe his luck and leaned over the table to plant a deep kiss on her luscious mouth. 'Kids like that mean nothing to me, darling. I like a mature woman like yourself,' he said meaningfully.

'Less of the mature,' Arlette riposted, pouting provocatively over the rim of her frosted cocktail glass. 'I'm only just coming into my prime, as you'll find out if you play your cards right.'

They joked and chattered like this for an hour, using a degree of intimacy which is only possible between a couple who have shared the whole catalogue of sensuous and erotic situations that is the norm of committed lovers. Between the moments of badinage and flirtation, without probing too indelicately, the couple managed to roll back the carpet of the last five years.

Arlette told him that she had taken a job with Monsieur Marcel, the great couturier, whose clients included many of the nobility, friends of his wife Bernadette, the Vicomtesse de Cliquot St. Maxine, and of course an unfortunate, but still profitable, number of the *nouveau riche* who were now flocking to the Cote d'Azur.

'I must tell you one day about some of the things he gets up to in the fitting room at the rear of the salon,' she confided. 'But what of you?'

'After that awful row, when I thought you were finished with me. . .' Francois began.

'How can you say that,' Arlette intervened. 'I was so exhausted, I didn't know what I was saying. Really, darling, you have no idea how much more demanding you are than other men. By the time you had finished with me, I was a wreck, in no mood for a lovers' quarrel.'

'So we were lovers, not just animals?' he murmured.

'Only real lovers could come to such a stormy conclusion,' she replied, stroking his thigh under the table. 'But if you are agreeable, now the intervening years have brought us to our senses, is there any reason why we should not pick up where we broke off?'

'Darling, take me home, wherever that is,' Francois implored, for the tremors and bursting sensations going on in his genitalia, caused by her fond looks and stroking action, helped to recall the quality of the physical perfection of their lovemaking in the past. 'I'll make it up to you, you'll see.'

He moved around the little table and pressed his lips to

her neck, breathing in the sensuous perfume she used to such telling effect, and ran a hand over her breast. She sighed and let her fingers rove to the area of his fly-buttons and found the familiar hard lump of flesh that had entranced her so completely in the old days.

'You're still hot,' she breathed.

'I'm boiling, let's go. I'll carry your bag.' The truth was that this courtesy was not inspired by any cavalier politeness, but he needed the handbag to cover the tell-tale bulge.

Outside, he hailed a taxi. It was a fair way to Arlette's new apartment. The driver drew a blind experienced eye to their lovemaking on the back seat. After all, amour was flourishing on the Riviera so prolifically that if he paid prurient attention to every fumbling couple, his driving technique would be so impaired that the gendarmerie would revoke his cab licence.

Arlette had two climactic moments before she got home, and Francois' underclothes were no longer pristine fresh, so of course they took a bath together when they arrived and toasted their fortunate meeting with a bottle of vintage champagne she brought from the refrigerator.

'I have almost no money,' Francois said truthfully on an impulse as he played with Arlette's breasts with his toes. He explained that he had finally become disenchanted with his job as a municipal officer whose duties involved street cleaning, sewage, waste disposal and other disagreeable activities. 'I quit. I have no work, no salary, no savings, no prospects. I can bring you nothing.'

'For the moment, until you find a more interesting job, don't worry. I shall keep you,' Arlette promised, ogling his attractive sexual organ which rose out of the foam. 'You will play me such wonderful tunes on that flute of yours I shall be inspired to drop you a few francs every time you perform. A satisfactory arrangement, *non*?'

They sealed the bargain with a passionate kiss and a coupling of remarkable vigour in the scented waters which were so agitated that Arlette was obliged to mop the marble floor afterwards as they had caused so many waves.

'I have enough for the two of us,' she claimed. 'I'm doing very well at the salon. M. Marcel has promoted me to be chief *vendeuse*, with a big increase in salary, and look here.' She showed him a well appointed room fitted with a sewing machine, irons tailor's dummies and rolls of expensive looking fabrics. 'He doesn't know it, but I have gained a clientele of my own, lately, and I copy his designs cheaply and well. A good idea, *non*? You see, I can afford you.'

Francois pondered the situation as he towelled himself dry. 'You're a marvellous woman,' he said, fondling her ripe mature breasts which were of a rosy hue on account of the bath. He placed a hand on the downy patch which covered her intimate region. 'So as long as I keep this happy,' he smiled, pressing his forefinger lightly on the small hard protruding nodule underneath, and then sliding the tip into her moist part, 'you'll cough up. Hm, not bad, but only until I get a new job, OK?'

With that he picked her up and carried her into the bedroom, where they continued their erotic play for many hours, savouring each other's bodies in a series of cataclysmic outpourings of passion, delighted to have rediscovered their libidinous friendship.

All was well for some weeks. Arlette would roll over on to his body as she woke drowsily in the morning and arouse him with licks and kisses in every part of his body. She particularly liked to nibble the folds of the skin which covered the pink tip of his glans, at the same time lightly pinching the nipples which nestled in the dark hair of his chest. Francois' organ invariably responded to this reveille and came to attention smartly, as every soldier who does his duty must. Then at lunchtime the *vendeuse* would return for a quick siesta, sometimes sprawling on the balcony with her lover, enjoying the heat of the midday sun, as their bodies entwined in further variations of coupling. In the evenings she liked to prolong their lovemaking by resorting to a slow massage, tickling, the intimate play of lingerie and deep kissing, with candlelight and wine, and sustaining suppers.

All this was to Francois' taste, physically speaking. He was a man of infinite sexual capacity. The one employment of his precious organ would stimulate him to another. He was not one of those unfortunate men whose ejaculatory ability is limited. There could be almost a ceaseless flow of his juices, so advanced was his carnal instinct. Hence Arlette's complete satisfaction. Customers in the salon remarked on her glowing health and shining eyes and some even brought her little gifts, they were so enchanted with her happiness. But, as in all the affairs of love, eventually some tiresome dissatisfaction crept in and for Francois, it was enough to unsettle him.

As explained, he was unendingly capable of obliging, and was happy to do so. What man would not be thrilled to have such an enthusiastic lover as Arlette, after all. However, he began to tire of the confines of the apartment. The unspoken terms of his contract were that he should be available at all times, so he felt he was cheating if he went out for a long walk, or went off drinking with a few chums, and missed her return. *I have fallen into the same old trap*, he thought one day as he lay on the balcony, recovering from a particularly fierce bout of passion. He was cradling his weighty scrotum as he pondered, and applying a little oil to his slightly bruised member. *My brain's in my prick. I need to get out and about*.

He thought of the relentless fun of the beaches and the promenade. Loads of entertaining young people playing games and swimming, bands playing, and dance halls echoing to the sounds of Dixieland jazz. *My friends will think I have deserted them, and they will accuse me of being a gigolo if they find out about my situation. I must get a job and my freedom from this place. I can still pleasure Arlette when she requires. That is no problem, I so adore her gorgeous body*. Thus declared, he dressed and made his way to the Croisette. After weeks of confinement his eyes were unaccustomed to the bright sunlight, so he purchased a straw boater and some dark glasses. A handsome man of refined appearance, he attracted many interested glances.

Strolling along, he came across a small tabac, a kiosk which sold cigarettes, magazines, postcards and newspapers. There was a sign saying it was for sale. *What an idea*, he thought. *Here I could watch life go by, chat up the girls, get myself a suntan, and make a reasonable income*. He telephoned the agent in charge of the sale, and was delighted to find that he had sufficient cash to put down a large enough deposit to secure the business. (Each time he had joined with Arlette in sensual play, he had been paid his wages as agreed, and the sum total was an impressive amount.) A few days later he was the new proprietor of the kiosk.

All his expectations were proved right. The cash came flowing in and crowds of pretty girls brightened his days. But the hours were arduous. He had not realised how early he had to be there to receive the delivery of the newspapers or how late he had to stay open in the evenings, selling ices and lollipops.

Arlette was distraught. The newly re-awakened lust that he had satisfied so well in the previous few weeks knawed at her loins with such frustrating intensity that she wept, waiting for her stallion to return to her. When he did, unaccustomed to long hours of commercial application, he fell asleep exhausted. In the morning he was off before she woke and she arose with unsatisfied fever in her parts.

'This just won't do, darling,' she said firmly, one evening as he lay crumpled on the carpet. 'look at that wretched object,' she flicked at his member with a feather duster, something that normally would have made the beast rear hungrily, 'there's no life in it at all.'

'Sorry, my sweet,' he replied, 'I know it's boring for you, but at least your purse is not getting emptier. Look here.' From his pocket he pulled a very large bundle of francs, the considerable takings of just one day at the kiosk. 'I don't need your cash any more.'

'That may be so, but I need your weapon between my legs, now come on, *cheri*, don't be so mean,' Arlette pouted. She lay on her back in an inviting manner, parting her thighs and then the small pink lips that covered her innermost treasure, pleasing for attention in her most seductive tones.

Normally Francois would have leapt upon her with alacrity, his organ primed for action, but this time his flaccid appendage lay tucked between his thighs without a glimmer of movement. 'I have no inspiration, sweetheart, how ghastly, I am a failure,' he moaned.

Lack of tumescence had never before afflicted him. All his

life, stimulated or not, his organ had remained in a semi-primed condition, waiting to spring to full size at the merest hint of arousal. He was now suffering the dreaded condition of impotence, that curse that drives men to drink or pornography.

Tears came to his eyes. Arlette, infinitely moved, brushed them away with consoling kisses, and then let her lips travel down his body, sucking and nibbling. She passed by the flaccid organ at first and, parting his thighs, played with her tongue at the sac of his scrotum and the strong muscle which had stayed unmoved so far, between there and the folds of his buttocks.

The slightest tremor coursed through his lower body, causing his abdomen to contract. The movement of Arlette's head as she kissed made the tresses of her hair fall on his belly, adding to the pleasurable sensation. Her fingers toyed at his groin and in the curling fronds of the nest of hair which covered his pubic bone. The limp organ was pressed against her cheek at that moment. Her caresses and movements travelled to it.

Francois watched, raising his shoulders from the floor, as she ran the tip of her tongue along its length and then imprinted the shape of her lipstick on the side of the shaft. More of the red cosmetic was then applied to the pink head of the dormant member, little sympathetic dabs of the mouth which transmitted such caressive, loving attentions that an inevitable stirring occurred.

In gratitude, as it were, Francois' dejected organ stretched out in length, eager to please his mistress. She smiled, cooed and encouraged, pinching with her white teeth every now and then as she noted the satisfactory progress of the desired tumescence. Gradually his member rose from its position of slumber, curling snake-like in a circular movement, thickening in girth as it travelled, until the tip of it faced him. Propped on his elbows, he watched the fascinating transformation.

Gorged with his blood, the fully protruding tulip waved in the air, moved by the impulses which stormed through the stem. A sparkling droplet appeared at the orifice, signifying that soon, more essential fluids would wish to follow. The entire member throbbed with a life of its own. Francois, without contracting a single muscle in encouragement had watched the generous Arlette restore it from passivity to a workable condition.

'My darling,' he gasped, 'continue. I am in your power, I am bursting.'

She was so thrilled with the mechanics of her successful arousal that she felt obliged to continue the play in order to discover any other interesting developments. First she tweaked the extended organ from side to side, and then, grasping it by the very base, twirled it in little circles, which brought gasps of delight from Francois.

More of the jissom arrived at the minute opening of the tulip-shaped hood. She licked at it, moaning with deep sighs of pleasure.

'Enclose it, I implore you,' Francois raged, beating his heels on the carpet.

She opened her mouth and took the tip inside, sucking gently, with both her hands clamped round the shaft. He called out, a long gasping throaty roar, as his raging palpitations thrust his hot juice upwards, his legs spread akimbo, and his back arched automatically in an abandoned posture of climactic satisfaction.

Later, wallowing in the bath, he said, 'Not so bad, that, makes a change.'

She smiled tenderly. 'You've been overdoing things. A tired man needs a bit of encouragement.'

'You can say that again,' he said, grinning. 'Hey, hand me my pants.' He fished in the pockets and pulled out a large bundle of francs. 'Fair's fair,' he said, peeling off quite a good number, and handing them to her.

'You used to pay me, now it's your turn.'

And so, yet again, love found a way. Arlette and Francois lived in peace, contentedly, for many years in the same apartment, sharing their money and comforts. It was a good and sensible arrangement. Neither took the other for granted, and each of them was always prepared to pay the price of love.

Chapter Two

Frederick Fanshawe, the failed drunken American novelist, often used Francois' kiosk. Every morning, when he dragged himself from his bed, he took a stroll along the promenade to cure his hangover and refresh himself enough for another bout of drinking. Francois' stall was the only one to stock American papers, and Frederick needed the information they contained concerning Wall St. and the stocks and shares that provided the income he was currently squandering.

One morning after purchasing this necessary news, Fanshawe retreated to a low bar in the market area where he knew he would find a contingent of his friends. They were mostly foreigners like himself, writers, painters, bohemians, hangers-on, and derelicts generally. Usually they had to club together to pay for drinks, but this time Fanshawe had received a cheque from his wife, the Lady Letitia. She had, in an uncharacteristically generous moment probably deriving from a large intake of alcohol, decided to share with her decadent husband part of a bequest from an elderly relative recently expired.

The fat waiter perspired as he served a continuous flow of drinks. When word of Fanshaw's bit of luck spread, the bar became packed with thirsty comrades. He had never had so many back-slapping friends. He cried a little when they told him how nice, how generous he was, and drooled bleary-eyed into his glass of Pernod contemplating his failure as a novelist.

What initial promise there had been, he sighed, what opportunities at Harvard and Yale; his first novel had been hailed as a minor masterpiece and he had secured a contract with *The New Yorker* magazine for thousands of dollars. Alas, everything else had failed. His inability to keep to deadlines had earned him the ignominy of having his contract cancelled, and besides, rejection slips for his tawdry books came crashing through his letter box.

'Cheer up, darling, it's not the end of the world,' cried a tousle-haired girl who threw herself on to his lap, squashing his unshaven face with her large pendulous breasts. 'My, my, what a face you've got on today. Anything I can do to help?'

Fanshawe was vaguely aware of the groping she was giving to his genitals and smiled forlornly. It was a long time since he'd been sober enough to get an erection and he didn't suppose there would be one now, no matter how hard she tried. 'Life's such a bloody mess,' he intoned mawkishly. 'I often wondered why we artists are put on earth to suffer like this.'

A sentimental tune of the day emanated from the wind-up machine on the zinc bar. A throaty Parisian sparrow gave her soul to the melody and the unashamed bathos of the lyric. No matter that the record was heavily scratched, and the music barely audible over the animated conversation and clatter of the café, Fanshawe found it intensely moving—especially when the needle got stuck in a groove and all that could be heard, until the *garcon* moved it on, was, 'de la vie, de la vie, de la vie, de la vie . . .'

'I'm a failure,' he cried.

'Oh no you're not,' insisted the girl in his lap. 'What do *you* think, dears,' she asked the crowd. A raven haired beauty who studied Art, and between canvasses was freely available to anyone with the price of a drink, sidled round and threw her arms round Fanshawe, easing the other girl to one side.

'You've got everything, honey,' she said, because she was thirsty again. 'You've got imagination, more than most folk have, and that's a great gift.'

'Imagination is a curse,' Fanshawe yelled, hoping at that moment that one of the aspiring young writers at the table would take a note of this immortal saying and use it later in a profound and praiseworthy article for a learned journal, or in a full length appreciation of his literary talents. 'My days are a torment. All my life I have suffered this way. Plots and characters come floating into my brain, confusing the reality, and the nights are anguish, one movie scenario after another. I wake exhausted.'

'Pissed,' a bohemian whispered.

'Imagination is nothing. It's those guys who have none, but a lot of guts when it comes to promoting themselves and arseholing publishers, who make it, I can tell you,' Fanshawe continued.

'Oh, yeah?' said a young writer who had just had a piece accepted by a publisher of cheap paperbacks, and thought the jibe was meant for him. 'I don't think you got any stories, I think you're a load of bull.'

'Bullshit,' said another, because the drink had made him brave.

'He does so,' the heavy breasted girl exclaimed. 'Go on Fred, tell 'em one. You just go ahead and make something up right now.'

'OK, ma'am,' Fanshawe slurred, pouring himself another shot of Pernod, for he knew what reputation he had left was at stake. 'Are you ready for this you guys?'

'Two young farmers are walking down this path, see. It's in the middle of the country, miles back in the mountains . . .'

'Here in France?' asked one.

'Yeah, up in Provence,' Fanshawe continued.

The assorted crowd gathered in close to hear the ongoing narrative which the writer told as if he were reading prose from a novel. Sometimes they marvelled at his fluency and the boldness of the imagery he invoked.

'They were young and bronzed, walking the path with a kind of swagger, secure in their masculinity and content with their situation in life. One carried a sack over his shoulder, and the other had a large leather satchel strapped to his back.

'They stopped for a while to smoke cigarettes, lying in the sweet smelling grasses. The conversation turned to girls. Strong and girt like young bullocks, they had more desire than experience, and much of their talk came from speculation, rather than from knowledge of the opposite sex. They excited each other with their talk, and had part erections when a pair of pretty girls came their way.

'They made a perfect picture in their anemone-coloured clothes. One wore a shantung dress of pale cream with a border of mauve at the hem, and the other wore darker cream, the shade of butter, with a collar of dark crimson. Both had straw hats over their blonde heads, and both wore white lace gloves and white heeled shoes. Their skin was of the palest colour and not freckled. The boys rightly supposed them to be from a town, since in that region all the females had suntanned complexions and rough skin on account of their labour in the fields.

'The blood in the boys' veins ran amok as the girls approached. They stubbed out their cigarettes and then rearranged the bulges in their trousers before standing up, holding their hands in front of their parts.

'One winked at the other before speaking. "*Bon jour, mesdemoiselles*, what a fine afternoon."

'The girls smiled but moved on.

' "Wwhere are you going?" the other lad asked.

' "None of your business," said one of the girls, over her shoulder.

' "Oh, it is miss. There's some pretty wild cattle about these parts, I wouldn't want you to get a fright, or get chased."

'The girls ran towards them.

' "Oh, where? They're not bulls are they?" one asked, quivering.

' "Yes indeed, miss. Great big brutes that would kill you as soon as look at you," a boy said, nudging his friend.

' "We'll have to show you the way, or you might get lost. Sometimes the mist comes down in these mountains," the other lad said gravely.

' "We'd be very grateful," the girl with the mauve collar murmured, blushing.

' "Better get started then," the boy with the knapsack said, hoisting it up on to his back.

'The four proceeded up the bank and across a meadow.

' "My name's Isabelle, and this is my cousin Stephanie."

' "I'm Guillaume, and this is Pierre."

'The introductions having been made, the boys were

emboldened to ask where the girls were making for.

' "To our aunt's house, the Chateau de Brazande," Stephanie smiled. "We are taking a little holiday there."

' "We know it well," Pierre assured them, "and will escort you there."

'The girls stepped out in front. It was amusing to see the way they picked their way through the tussocks of grass and the cow-pats. Also to see the way their little bottoms swayed from side to side in their tight dresses.

'Guillaume nudged his friend and pointed down with one hand to his crotch which he was squeezing with the other. "Nice bit of stuff we've found, eh?" he whispered.

' "They wouldn't want anything to do with common gawks like us," Pierre said under his breath, "though I bet they open their legs for city slickers."

' "What do you think?" Isabelle asked her cousin, *sotto voce*. "I think they're rather interesting." A smile hovered around her mouth like a butterfly hovers round a flower.

' "Well, in a rustic, heavy booted way," replied Stephanie, "though I couldn't help noticing the tantalising bulges in their trousers."

' "Perhaps they are not so well endowed as you think, cousin. The trousers look like hand-me-downs which have tended to squash their parts into such prominence," Isabelle opined.

' "Let's take a better look," suggested Stephanie. "I say, boys, we're awfully tired. Do you think we could sit down and have a rest for a while?"

'The lads gladly complied. They had finished their tasks for the day and could think of nothing nicer than dallying with two such spring-like lovelies.

'The girls noticed what dark lashes both boys possessed, their sun-tinted skin, and glossy ringlets of hair. When they lowered their eyes, in a gesture of mock modesty, they discovered that underneath the flies of their trousers, the boys did indeed seem to be blessed with generously sized genital organs which seemed to be straining to be released from their bondage.

'The sturdy country lads took note of the girls' milk-white

skin and gleaming teeth, the rise and fall of their creamy bosoms in their shantung dresses, and the graceful shape of their slim legs which were stretched out in the grass.'

'Do stop, I'm getting a hard-on,' one of Fanshawe's drinking partners interjected.

'Quite right, that's just what those boys are up to,' the bohemian painter exclaimed. 'Go on Fred, I'm on tenterhooks.'

The large bosomed girl who originally sat on Fanshawe's knee moved around to the chap who had made the interruption and sat on one of his knees, allowing one of her hands to trail downwards towards his crotch. She was not going to let such a tumescence go unappreciated.

Fanshawe proceeded. 'Pierre lay back and pretended to close his eyes, but in reality he was peeping up Isabelle's skirt. He caught a glimpse of stocking top and the clasp of a suspender. How his hands longed to rush and ping it open and draw the stocking down her fine leg. The thought caused a disconcerting flow of blood to his already swollen organ and in order to conceal the resulting protuberance, he turned over on to his belly from where he could make, he found, even less detectable inspections.

'Guillaume was more bold. He plucked a piece of grass and stroked Stephanie's arm with the end of the stalk, causing slight little goosepimples to appear among the fine down that covered it. He had lit a tiny fire which burned slowly in her loins and started a flow of her juices as sweet as that of the grass which Guillaume then popped into his mouth and sucked on, smiling cannily at her.

' "Where do you come from?" he asked.

' "Paris, of course," she answered.

' "I suppose you go to big parties and have loads of boy friends, eh?" the cheeky boy asked, drawing closer so that his face was near to hers. "I wish I knew a girl like you."

' "Well, now you do, don't you," Stephanie blushed, feeling the hot breath from his mouth so close to hers.

'Pierre, in the meantime, had squirmed his way towards Isabelle's head, where it lay among the meadow flowers. She had tossed aside her straw hat and her long blonde tresses were spread about in enticing array. He took a few strands and wove them into a curl, sniffing delicately at it. "I expect you think we're nasty boring louts," he murmured softly, "but let me tell you, even a dumb country youth knows a good thing when he sees one. You're prettier than all the flowers in the field." Her blue eyes widened with pleasure at this compliment and she patted his hand by way of thanking him for it.

' "It's a pity we look so messy," Guillaume said earnestly, looking deep into Stephanie's equally blue eyes. "You might think better of us if we weren't in our working clothes." He rolled over and pulled the sack towards her. "Look," he said, "we've been out rabbiting," and pulled out a pair of the brown animals tied together by a thong.

'At the same moment Pierre tore open the satchel. "We got a brace of pheasant as well," he exclaimed.

'The two girls were as dumb as the dead prey. They stared at the carcasses in mute horror and fascination, cringing as the boys pushed them closer for their inspection.

'After the first initial shock Isabelle stroked the fur of the rabbits. "They're so soft and beautiful," she crooned. "What poor little darlings." She gazed at Pierre with admiration, impressed with his obvious strength and the hunter's cunning he clearly possessed.

'Guillaume spread out the wings of the pheasants and swooped them through the air. "I snatched them up with my own hands," he said, standing confidently with his feet apart over Stephanie's body.

'She looked up to where he was framed in the hot afternoon sun and felt her limbs quiver. His raw brute force, tamed by an indefinable gentleness, moved her profoundly.'

'Get on to the dirty bits,' one of Fanshawe's cronies cried, 'and *garcon*, if you don't bring some more drinks, we'll have your guts for garters.'

'This all sounds very sub D. H. Lawrence to me,' the boy who had placed a minor book with an even more minor publisher groaned. 'I suppose you'll be saying next how those lads' hands smelled of the fur and feathers of the poor creatures they'd killed.'

'Exactly,' Fanshawe retorted. 'The girls were ravished by an animal instinct . . . nature in all its wonderment and power . . . the lure of the hunter . . . the fear of his prey . . . they both felt trapped and at the same time possessed . . .'

'Did they open their legs, I want to know,' a rough voice interrupted.

'I'm coming to that,' Fanshawe said, 'if you behave. Anyway,' he continued, 'the truth was that the moment held such a gripping force that Stephanie and Isabelle both experienced a contraction deep in their beings. Flirtation of a mild variety had led to a brief scene of dalliance, and then the glorious manhood of the two country youths, proud in their innocence, struck a chord in the souls of the girls. Both wondered why their underclothes were damp, when there had been no sensual play of any significance. Their legs trembled, and they licked their lips, feeling dry in the throat.

'Both were ready to be taken there and then, but the simple lads, used to the lengthy courtship that is required in rural surroundings, did not realise this fact. They had no idea of the impression they had made, moreover, and soon suggested that the four walk on.

'They came to a muddy section of path and offered to shoulder the girls through it, but the girls, hooting with laughter, and not entirely unaware of the effect they were having on the boys, peeled off their shoes and stockings and walked through the mire which came up to their knees. They pulled their dresses up to their hips to save splashing them, and rolled gaily on to the next bank.

'What a sight of suspender belts and silk knickers, wide in the legs, allowing tantalising views of their little blonde bushes. What a scene as they ran to a small pool where they washed their legs in the cool water and then came back nearer to the boys to lie down and dry them with bunches of sweet smelling herbs and grasses—a task in which the lads assisted, naturally, stroking tenderly and going up their thighs as high as they dare. What a surprise when first one, then the other, parted her legs, softly sighing in gratitude for these attentions, reclining further back into the bank in invitation.

'Guillaume could hardly take his eyes off the gusset of the

camiknickers behind which, he knew, Stephanie's private parts were hidden but he managed a quick encouraging grin to his friend.

'Pierre reached for the elastic of the drawers that clung to Isabelle's white flesh and pulled them down to her knees. He stared unbelievingly at the treasure he had uncovered. He turned to see that Guillaume had done the same and already had his face over the triangle of hair that was revealed.

'The young flesh smelled fresh as spring, gorging the boys' senses. They drank the perfume as deeply as they could that of a bunch of wild flowers, but the headiness of the scent caused a sensation in them which was more profound than anything that mere blooms could engender. The rabbit catchers burrowed their noses into the girls' objects of desire, tunnelling with their tongues into the lovely orifices.

'Stephanie and Isabelle, splayed on the grass, were open-eyed with wonder, staring up into the fading sky of the late afternoon as they received this devastating benediction. Their blonde heads turned and rolled, and little sighs and moans of ecstasy escaped from their lips.

'Close contact not only with the prime object of their desire but with the underwear of such exquisite artifice drove Guillaume and Pierre to near madness. They simultaneously reached under the girls' hips and released the catches of the flimsy suspender belts, then tore them away, revealing more belly flesh. The next garments to be removed were the camiknickers which were caught about the girls' knees. In one jerk they were hoisted away in movements that sent their legs flying in the air. Both pairs of limbs came back to earth in that inviting and universal position which is favoured by all lovers. The youths struggled feverishly with belts and buttons. It seemed to both sexes that it took an inordinate time to unbuckle and open the flies.

'The girls marvelled at the proud engorgements that sprang to view when the lads' trousers had been pushed hastily down to their knees, and screamed in fantastic pleasure when the two organs plunged deep into the waiting recesses.

'These couplings were of ferocious intensity. The girls flailed their legs in abandonment, heaving their hips upwards from the ground as the hunters drove their weapons in mad pursuit of orgasmic release. Wave after wave of incredible satisfactions came pouring forth for each of the quartet, who, in this natural surround, and being in the advanced throes of arousal that the afternoon had produced, suffered no inhibitions.

'Stephanie, indeed, was relieved that her cousin was with her, and vice-versa, and it is doubtful if either of the two shy country boys would have involved himself in such carnalities if he had been unaccompanied.

'Time and time again the boys rose to further attacks, thrilling the girls with their primitive, unsophisticated approach. Their virile young manhood kept their weaponry in fine upstanding order. The maidens gurgled with pleasure as the lads picked them up, rolled them about, and disported in every conceivable kind of coupling in that dappled glade.

'Each fresh entry, as ardent as the previous, brought Isabelle and Stephanie to yet another dizzy peak of lust and then the quenching of its fire, drowning them in waves of delirious happiness. After two hours of these athletics, the four lay kissing and cuddling in the lengthening shadows brought by the setting sun. All was peace in the world. An owl hooted as it set out on the chase, and flocks of birds, returning to roost, sped away over the tree tops to evade the predatory hawk which hovered still in the orange sky.

'A bargain was sealed over loving kisses that the shattering experience would be relived, the sooner the better. Dressed as tidily as could be managed, the girls were escorted to the Chateau de Brazande by the dutiful, smug, grinning boys whose loins ached and thrilled from the pleasures of the afternoon.

' "Tomorrow, then," they whispered at the gates of the great house where a dog barked and lights twinkled in windows.'

'I can't stand another dose of this. They're not going to go through it all over again, surely,' moaned the heavy breasted girl who was so erotically influenced by the tale that she had brought the painter to climax by massaging his crotch with great vigour during the story.

There were a dozen other besides the aroused girl with Fanshawe. Quite several more of the group had been affected in a sensuous way by the story. Other hands had strayed, to groin, to breast, and lips were wet from licking as well as drinking. The *garcon*, who had hung about waiting for the juicy bits was glad his apron covered his little hump of hard gristle.

The tables involving the group were littered with glasses and full ash trays, spilled liquor, the remnants of croissants, and crumpled newspapers.

In all it was a scene that the social-realist school of painting would have adored. The overhead green-shaded lamps, trimmed with a fringe of glass beads, threw circles of watery colour on to the group, isolating odd figures slumped in their chairs, or head in hands at table; differing perspectives and groupings that, in their raffish charm, would appeal to an imaginative artist. But the indolence of posture, casualness of bearing and juxtaposition of varying masses were not artfully wrought—rather the scene came together naturally. The models, with their total lack of self-consciousness, plied so freely with drink by their host, fell into the apt composition with spontaneous ease, creating a scene that would take many hours to achieve in an artist's studio, or on a film set, where even the curling wreaths of cigarette smoke must be provided by machinery.

The painter sketching in a corner of the cafe, who had been ravished by this composition, shed tears of frustration when it was broken by the arrival of the bill. The *patron* himself brought the addition. It was an extremely long piece of paper tape with an amazingly large total. While the rest of the gang shuffled their chairs and made to exit, Fanshawe cast a drunken, bleary eye down the row of barely legible figures printed in faint violet coloured ink, and capitulated in despair to the final amount. He threw a large wad of francs on to the table.

'Is that it, then?' the young writer asked him. 'You said they were going to meet up again the next day.'

'They sure are,' said the storyteller.

'Same action?' asked a leering crony. The story had given him the best sexual thrill he had had in weeks.

'There's a twist at the end. You gotta have a twist,' Fanshawe said groggily, rising to his feet. Even as he thought about it, the germ of an idea swelled and flowered in his mind. 'OK, you kids, it's time for lunch. Whaddyersay we mosey over to the Bistro Latouche for a bowl of chowder?'

The gleeful hungry crowd roared their approval of the idea. Such largesse was not common in the bohemian world which was centred in this old part of town, and their bellies were empty. 'Lets go,' they cried, shambling out into the hot sunlight.

Under the awning of the bistro Fanshawe took up his story again as the company quaffed *vin rosé de Provence* which was served in large earthenware pitchers at the check-clothed refectory table which could accommodate them all.

He began as the *sardines au beurre* arrived. 'The two lads spent a feverish night. Not only did they rub their hands with glee, thrilled with their good fortune coming across such a pair, they also rubbed their troublesome organs which kept on rearing up in rigid form, obsessed with the built-in memory of the day's delicious traumas.

'The girls giggled and tossed and turned in their shared bed, reminiscing and comparing notes. They were hot in their cambric nighties and went to the casement window for fresh air. It was cool and refreshing. They bared their breasts to the moon, and then lifted their gowns to cool their fiery bellies, dreaming in a welter of hot anticipation of the pleasures to come.

' "Oh, Stephanie," Isabelle whispered, clutching the window sill to steady herself, "the memory of that hard stiff shaft is something that will stay with me all my life."

' "Me too, darling. Look my legs are still trembling," Stephanie gasped. "They were so powerful, weren't they? Not like those weedy boys in Paris who are only interested in one quick jab."

' "Ravishing, literally," agreed Isabelle. "I'm bursting for another go, aren't you?"

' "I'm on fire—desperate," Stephanie murmured. "I want to try the other one, though. Do you mind if I have yours?" she tremulously enquired.

' "I was thinking the same. Oh I adored the way he thrust at you, those hefty buttocks crashing up and down . . .," Isabelle's voice trailed away.

' "Yes, wasn't it exciting, having one perform, and seeing the other in action. We must swap over so we see how the other one gets on . . ." and Stephanie's voice petered out as well.

'So Stephanie dreamed that night of Guillaume who had ravished her on the grassy slope, and also of Pierre whose thick stem she now desired to feel in her body, while Isabelle suffered a nocturnal reverie concerning the reverse situation.

'The four met at the appointed hour under a large oak not far from the gates of the Chateau. They kissed their partners of the previous day, and then for the sake of general friendship, or so the boys thought, the other of the opposing sex. But the girls lingered at the greeting.

The second set of kisses progressed from a little peck on the cheek to a full kiss on the mouth, their hands closed round the boys' necks. They explored with their tongues and took the lads' hands and placed them around their plump bottoms, sighing and fluttering their eyelashes but in between stealing glances and winking conspiratorially at each other.

'The novelty of this fresh pairing was not lost on the lusty pair of farm boys. Each new sensation was grabbed quickly and returned in full measure. Pausing for air, Guillaume's eyes sought Pierre's. Both boys registered bewilderment, but also delight, for variety is said to be the spice of life.

'After much of this fascinating foreplay, when all four were in a state of trembling agitation, Isabelle told the boys that today, instead of going further into the country in search of a nesting place, as the original plan had been, they could go back to the house, as the girls' aunt had left in the gig for a shopping expedition in town. The boys were horrified at the notion.

' "Suppose she comes back and finds us," asked Pierre. He had visions of the rich landowner beating him with her crop.

' "Oh no, she will be away for several days. She has much to do," Stephanie crooned, leading her new partner towards the gate, followed by Guillaume intertwined with Isabelle.'

The diners in the bistro had arrived at the main course, a simple *steak avec pommes frites et petit pois*.

Pausing with a piece of the grilled meat half way to his lips, one of the company said, 'Oh, this is the twist is it?'

'I like it, it's cute,' one of the girls threw in, sensing that the approaching diversions would stimulate her as much as those in the first episode did.

'Oh, no,' Fanshawe drawled, 'this is only the start—change partners and dance—the big twist comes later.'

The crowd didn't mind the convolutions of his plot at all as long as the carafes kept coming, and who knew, the erotic thoughts which were aroused by Fanshawe's inventions might lead to some couplings within the group later in the afternoon. It was an ideal way to spend a boozy lunchtime.

Fanshawe continued with his story. 'Just inside the main gate stood an old barn of enormous proportions, creaking with age and covered with lichens. The tall double doors stood invitingly open, revealing a dim interior, piles of new mown hay, and bales of yellow straw. Pierre drew Stephanie inside, beckoning the others to follow.

' "It's alright," Isabelle purred, "we can go in the house. There's no-one there. Aunt Berthe has given the servants the day off."

'Guillaume pulled her to the floor of soft hay. "We'd be much more cosy here," he said, "more like what we're used to."

'Pierre meantime drew the doors together and then led Stephanie to a similar spot nearby.

'Ready for action, the girls today wore no underclothes and their bodies were fresh from the bath. The boys had scrubbed at the wash-trough in the yard of their homestead and shaved and pommaded themselves with lavender-scented hair oil. Perfume, proximity, novelty and desire together conspired to bring about a double conjugation of awesome lust.

'The well matched pair of lads, whose sexual parts had often been compared and found to be of similar girth and length when the two were engaged in adolescent games of sexual discovery, matched the intensity of the previous day's assault on the girls' willing mounds. While they were both in the position favoured by the missionaries, they grinned wolfishly at each other, timing their strokes together. First long, slow and deep, and then accelerating towards joyful conclusion, the more intriguing as they knew exactly what yesterday's girl felt like in response to the thrusts of their members. Equally, Isabelle and Stephanie were each ravished by enjoying what the other had savoured before.

'Several momentous and simultaneous climaxes took place within these parameters, followed by grateful kisses, and ardent expressions of tenderness. And then eyes roved across the floor and memories of the previous day's activities burned across the space. Unspoken assent led the boys to detach themselves from their partners and sidle over to a fresh one, the object of past desire. They kissed breasts, and plunged their tongues anew, and the girls thrilled to the new attentions.

'There was suddenly a great roar and a flash of light as one of the enormous doors was thrust open. Bright sunlight blinded the boys who were at that moment on their knees, each intending to enter the space so amicably vacated by his friend. A figure, that of the returning aunt, was outlined by the brilliant wave of light. Crop in hand, as imagined by Pierre earlier, she presented a terrifying sight. In a second she was on them, beating with the short whip.

'The boys rolled away, smarting from the pain in their buttocks, and the cousins ran crying from the barn.

' "Come here," she commanded to the lads whose distended organs showed, by their very size, the extent of their lustful intentions. She threw her whip down and grasped the quivering, well lubricated pair of shafts, one in each hand, and squeezed them tight, yelling, "How dare you, filthy bumpkins. How dare you play around with my precious little nieces in this disgusting filthy way. I'll show you."

'With that she squeezed harder as if to inflict pain and teach the lads a lesson. The boys winced and gulped to her satisfaction, but the reason they did so was that both knew an enormous ejaculation was due. Try as hard as they might to resist, the incredible pressure on their inflated shafts completed the circle of stimulation, and led to them both shooting a large dose of their orgasmic juices towards the enraged matron.

'A strange fascinated expression came over her face. It was a long time since she had witnessed the ejaculatory phenomenon. Memories stirred in her brain. She watched the semen slide to the floor from her riding skirt, and then brought her eyes level with those of the flushed, shamed youths. A greedy look came into her face as she squinted at each in turn, and then a sly smile spread across her mouth. "You bad lot," she said, lightly manipulating their slackening implements. "And to think I wouldn't have found out about these goings-on if I hadn't forgotten my shopping list. It's naughty of you coming sniffing round my girls, they're too young, far too innocent. But I'm a woman of the world, I know what tricks you boys get up to."

'Pierre and Guillaume hung their heads, muttering inaudible some sort of apology.

'She raised their chins slowly. "But never mind, you can come here again. There's always some work that needs doing, and I'll pay you well . . . the girls are going back to Paris next week. I could use a pair of strapping lads like you." '

A roar of applause and banging on the tables greeted the end of Fanshawe's story.

One of the women was in tears. She thought it was wretched that the pastoral had to end in such a way. 'What a rotten old bitch,' she cried, 'taking those lovely boys from the girls!'

'Bravo,' others shouted. 'What invention, surely there's more.'

Frederick, slumped over the remains of the crème caramel, smiled wanly. The narrative and the endless flow of wine had exhausted him.

'You should publish it immediately,' said the girl with the heavy breasts. 'People would pay a lot for that story. *Mon Dieu*, it was evocative.'

'Strong stuff, *mon vieux*,' one of the artists grinned. He intended to start tomorrow on a series of large oils depicting such a foursome in the meadows, lyrical pictures that would not offend good taste, but would sell for large amounts.

'Seriously, why don't you go home and put it down on paper. It's all there. You see how impressed we all were,' the bohemian girl urged, hoping Frederick would call for a round of brandies.

'No, my darling. It's what I was saying earlier on; inspiration, imagination, ideas, plot, they are nothing. The real horror is facing a sheet of blank paper and a typewriter ribbon. That is for hacks.'

'I don't understand you at all,' she murmured sweetly, lying through her teeth, because she knew that Fanshawe would prefer to be in a café getting plastered, rather than face the lonely writer's task.

The bill for lunch was preposterous, and added to that for the drinks earlier, completely swallowed up Letitia's timely gift. But Fanshawe paid up happily because he had enjoyed having an audience.

The young man who had placed a minor novel with an even more minor publisher scurried to the stationers and bought a large packet of typing paper. *What a waste of good material if I don't do something about it*, he thought. A few days later he delivered a manuscript to the very same publisher. The material was perfectly remembered, and rendered on to the page with some style.

The publisher thoroughly enjoyed reading it. 'My boy, you're on to a winner with this one,' he said, the next time they met. 'I know just the right kind of arty magazine that will go for it.'

He rubbed his crotch thoughtfully. 'I got a hard on twice, going through it. That's not bad for a short story.'

It was the worst act of plagiarism to hit the publishing scene in years. Someone brought the magazine to Frederick's attention. At the time was in a bar, blind drunk on absinthe, the deadly drink that was banned but which you could still buy if you knew the right place to go.

'Well, shit, man,' he grinned. 'So the little bastard wrote down my work and earned himself a few bucks, and do you know, I just don't give a damn. Didn't you know that imitation is the sincerest form of flattery.'

Chapter Three

Bernadette, comfortably ensconced in the glamorous secret garden room of the mansion, received a telephone call from Sabine, an old friend who was in some distress and needed a confidante.

'Tell me all, *cherie*,' the vicomtesse purred. She was reclining naked on a gilded *chaise longue*, having discarded her flimsy négligé on account of the heat.

All about her were strewn papers and drawings, materials from the collection of her late husband Henri, which she had been perusing with a view to cataloguing correctly. They were part of his precious hoard of erotica; an heirloom which she decided must be preserved and tabulated in a manner of which the vicomte would have approved. As Sabine talked, Bernadette idly inspected a sheaf of Japanese prints from the last century. There were at least twenty varied postures, out of the hundred or so depicted, that she had not tried; sexual couplings of such imaginative dexterity that she felt obliged to suggest some of them the next time she found a suitably athletic lover.

'Time is slipping by,' Sabine wailed, as Bernadette savoured a particularly outstanding example. It involved a complex system of pulleys and counterweights which effortlessly levitated the female and lowered her over the prostrate form of the male. Bernadette was consumed with a vision of the carnal pleasures that could be derived from the use of such a machine; what a series of insertions and withdrawals, prolonging, teasing, so utterly original in concept.

'My darling, you are only thirty five,' the vicomtesse consoled.

'Thirty two, my sweet,' Sabine corrected untruthfully. Bernadette laughed into the telephone receiver, '*Mon dieu*, you should go to a contemporary for advice. *Alors*, I am far too old.'

'Don't joke. This is *trés sérieux*. I am *desolé*. Why does no man wish to take me?'

Bernadette composed in her mind a picture of Sabine. Tall, incredibly elegant, well-boned, and of flawless complexion; her aristocratic good looks should hold appeal for any man. Wealthy, chic, with a breeding of impeccable origins. She was a catch indeed, but the truth was that men steered clear of her as if she were an iceberg. 'Tell me how you spend your day,' Bernadette suggested, 'give me some background. I want to know how you approach the subject.'

'I rise at six and drink a glass of lemon juice, without sugar, and take a cold shower. Then I exercise for an hour, bicycling my legs, touching my toes, bending my waist. For half an hour after that I stand at the window doing deep breathing and bust shaping exercises. My maid runs my bath, sponges me, rubs me with a hard towel, massages me with creams and oils and helps me to dress. I take a cup of *tissane* and one small piece of toast.

'When I have dealt with my correspondence, my chauffeur takes me to the chiropodist or chiropractor, then to the *coiffeur* where my hair is arranged and the girl manicures and lacquers my nails. Then I visit the dressmaker or milliner, shop for shoes, lingerie, a new handbag and by then it's time for lunch—a small salad and a glass of mineral water.'

Bernadette sighed and rolled her eyes at this catalogue. It seemed, even though she herself was a fastidious woman and groomed every aspect of her body daily, that the system of purification Sabine described could be tedious to a degree.

'In the afternoon I treat myself to a session with the acupuncturist, or sometimes the aromatherapist, and maybe a brisk walk along the promenade,' Sabine continued. 'Then perhaps a cup of English tea and a long rest before dinner.'

The vicomtesse's attention at this moment was drawn to a print which depicted two Japanese sumo wrestlers of enormous girth, in simultaneous conjugation with a diminutive geisha. *That little girl knows a thing or two,* she reflected. *What a sensation it must be for her, containing two prodigious martial instruments.*

'But it's all to no avail,' Sabine cried. 'I make myself look as adorable as I can, I try to ensure that my body is a temple at which gentlemen can worship, but, my dear, they are all pagans. Why do I bother?'

Bernadette listened to her sobs. She thought the time had come for Sabine to mend her ways. 'Listen, darling' she breathed with some emotion, for the Japanese rituals were stimulating her naked body to lustful sensations, 'it's all very well turning yourself into a bandbox—deodorising yourself to a state where you could be mistaken for an advertisement for shampoo or perfume—but men want something a bit more womanly when they're on the scent. Your daily *toilette* does seem rather rigorous, my pet. Has it not occurred to you that men can be put off by perfection? I am sure that, to many, the thought of assaulting a female form such as yours, prinked and perked to such sanitary correctness, would be akin to desecrating the Holy Grail. Relax, get a little tight, let the wind blow in your hair, go without make-up . . . men will come running . . .'

The vicomtesse's eye was caught by another picture. Drawn with economy in fine strokes of black ink on yellowed rice paper, it showed a harmonious composition of a tea-house. In the centre of the room a girl touching her toes with her fingertips had been entered by a customer from the rear. A second girl was in a hand-stand on her colleague's back, with her parts proffered to the client's mouth. In each of the four corners of the room equally acrobatic entanglements were taking place. The most impressive was a trio in which a geisha, hanging with flexed knees from a man's shoulders, had taken in her mouth the entire shaft of his friend's member.

Bernadette was riveted by this and other depictions. 'Sabine,' she said sternly 'loosen up. Men are not interested in saints. I shall send to you a certain young man I know. He has great charm and will make you laugh. Do everything he says. Don't argue, I will help you only if you cooperate to the full. Goodbye.' She put the receiver back and began the long and difficult task of cataloguing the collection.

Sabine was mystified and of course a little curious until, a few days later, a handsome buck knocked at her door and presented both his and Bernadette's calling cards. She was dismayed he had called so early. Her *toilette* was in no way complete. The young man, whose name was Alain, would take no argument. He grabbed her coat and bag, placed his arm round her waist and led her to his bright red sports car.

It was one of those sparkling windswept days of brilliant sunshine and little showers. They sped along the corniche, in and out of tunnels and along hairpin bends, tooting and waving at other cars, in a heady delirium.

At first Sabine had struggled to keep her hat on, and then tied a scarf over her hair, but soon she abandoned all attempts to stay *soignée*, and unpinned her long black tresses which went streaming out in the wind.

Alain laughed and joked charmingly. He looked like a head choirboy or server, youthful and enthusiastic, more like a handsome brother than a potential lover. Sabine was captivated by his easy charm and infectious behaviour. She laughed gaily at his jokes and dare-devil antics and felt more relaxed than she had in ages.

They pulled up at a small café overlooking the bay of Antibes and ordered drinks. Sabine was so happy that even when a small shower occurred she had no desire to go inside, and they sat on the terrace watching the waves sparkle on the rocks below.

'You have done me a power of good,' she cried happily. 'What have I done to deserve an outing with such a nice boy?' Her hair was now tangled, and her silk blouse damp and not quite tucked into her waistband. Her mascara had run, making black smudges round her eyes, but for the first time in years she did not fish in her dorothy bag for a mirror.

Later, many more miles along the enchanting coast, they dined at a small establishment in a rough fishing village. They ate prawns and lobster with pink mayonnaise and drank a large carafe of *vin rosé*.

Sabine mopped up the last dregs of sauce with bits of bread, spilling some down her front, but she giggled and poured herself another glass of wine as she was so infected with the day's happiness.

They took a stroll along the cove, side-stepping the fishermens' nets and tackle. Tar stuck to her shoes, and her silk stockings were wet from the tide, but the magic was so strong she did not care. In a secluded corner of the bay they fell on the sand and basked in the warmth.

Sabine felt contented. She felt like a gift that had been unwrapped of its ribbons, paper and cellophane. Sea, sun, and air and the presence of the vibrant happy boy, combined, lulled her into a rare joy.

At that moment she looked adorable. Alain could not resist passing a hand through her tangled hair and touching, with a fingertip, her mouth which was now devoid of lipstick. Her eyes opened wide in surprise, for it was a long time since such gestures had been made to her.

She sat up and began fidgeting with the unruly locks. He begged her to ignore them as he loved her windswept appearance, and when she opened her vanity bag, he took it away from her and placed it out of her reach. Then he kissed her smudged eyes and laid a hand on her stained blouse, murmuring sweet endearments. The wine had loosed his tongue, and her warm closeness stirred him.

When his mouth closed over hers and his tongue gently penetrated it, shivers ran down her spine and shook her limbs. Years of denial and frustration melted away. She wished this boy to possess her, to ravish every part of her frustrated body. Her thighs fell apart, inviting Alain to rove a hand over the silk of her skirt, brushing lightly over the slight mound at the base of her belly and then the well shaped curves of her breasts. She could feel the hardness of his swelling part on her thigh as he delivered these caresses, and pressed her leg closer to it, sensing the throbbing energy that had entered it.

Now he was at her throat, sucking hard at the concave hollow which is one of the most powerful of the erogenous zones, with his hands kneading into the nape of her long slim neck. Sabine turned towards him so that they faced each other and slid a hand between them to explore the stiffness that now urged against her belly. *What years I have wasted*, she thought regretfully. *Bernadette is so right. This boy wants me because I smell of the sea and salt-spray.*

Alain lightly lifted the hem of her skirt and circled her knees with a fingernail. He then traced the same figures upwards over the insides of her thighs, coming to rest at the little mat of hair that he found when he passed a hand through a leg of her camiknickers.

A frisson shook her body, and warm lubricating fluids were transmitted to the orifice underneath the curls. She gasped when a finger tip eased down to the moistened lips of her part and surely, but gently, parted them and found the central nerve. Electric shocks and waves whirled through her body. Since she began her self-defeating and over emphatic campaign of vanity, no man had dared to touch her in this way. The newness of sensation made her throw her arms wide, open her knees, and thrust her pelvis forward towards the handsome smiling boy whose breath now came in short pants, warm and insistent in the ear he was biting.

It was as if she were a tube or a tunnel widening impulsively, wanting to shallow and trap him in the dark recess of her body. She sucked greedily at his mouth and clasped that part which she longed for him to lunge into her.

The crunch of pebbles nearby brought them to their senses. Two gnarled fishermen, pushing their boat towards the shoreline, nodded and pointed in their direction, then called some humorous, lewd encouragement.

'Come,' Alain said, 'there is a very nice hotel at the back of this village, very quiet and discreet. I shall go mad if I don't have you in bed soon.'

As he spoke he pressed a finger into her inviting opening. The firm, brief entry brought Sabine, in one roaring flush of pure pleasure, to a climactic height of passion. Pressing down on the finger, she abandoned herself to the extremities of the surge, gasping her pleasure as quietly as she could muster, as the fishing boat slipped into the water and the old men laughed, looking backwards over their shoulders.

Several hours later (after Alain had slaked his thirst on her body, and she lay drained on the crumpled bed in the small hotel, remembering such exquisite moments of their love-play, each fresh simultaneous and orgasmic explosion, and the tenderness and vigour the boy had applied to his courtship) Sabine vowed to cancel all her appointments; couture, manicure, coiffure she could do without. *I shall be a child of nature*, she thought *and run barefoot on the rocks. I shall wear no make-up, and the only exercise I shall take will be in bed*.

She telephoned Bernadette.

'Your advice has paid off. I am now a satisfied woman.' She told the story at length, thanking her confidante profusely, and gurgling how she adored the boy.

'There will be others now,' the wise lady told her. 'I prophecy that you will be a raging success, the toast of the Riviera. You were far too perfect before. Goodbye, darling, *et bon chance*.' Sabine turned from the telephone box in the lobby of the hotel and took a chair to wait for Alain to descend from the bedroom.

A good looking man in the corner of the hall turned his head and stared with open admiration. He saw a woman in her prime, at ease with her body. Its most natural posture stimulated him greatly, as did her black tresses of hair which fell, unhindered by pins, in a sweep down her back. He noted her glowing eyes and clear complexion, uncomplicated by artificial aids, and her long slim legs, bare of stockings. That muscular urge between the tops of a man's thighs which travels on through his stem, and repeats itself a great deal, according to the extent of the amatory arousal, did its work.

He rose to his feet and advanced towards Sabine. He was charming, suave and handsome. He bowed, smiling. '*Bon jour*, madame. I am new at the hotel. My name is Sombert, Georges Sombert.'

'Sabine Dulac,' she answered, extending a hand which he kissed.

'*Enchanté*,' he said, devouring her with a glance. 'The little bar is open, may I buy you a drink? Such a lovely lady should not be alone, not for one instant.'

'*Merci*, monsieur, you are charming to be so gallant, but

I am waiting for a friend.' She spied Alain coming down the staircase, and also her reflection in a mirror. She thought she looked happy and wholesome and was more delighted with herself than she had ever been. Turning back to Sombert she smiled expansively, capturing his heart, 'But if you are here tomorrow . . . around lunch . . .'

If Monsieur Sombert took up the implied invitation from the liberated lady they may have been just about ready to climb into bed when the Paris Express roared by on its way down the coast and into the platform of Nice Central to disgorge a variety of passengers.

Grossly porcine Germans barked for porters and trolleys, jostling with pale Swedes and Finns; lithe American athletes carrying tennis rackets, golf clubs and hockey sticks, marched cheerfully along singing jolly college anthems; wispy-looking English nannies made shrill attempts to control their boisterous charges and their perambulators with little success; Buckets and spades, kites, fishing nets and bowling hoops went flying in all directions.

All of the above were shoved energetically aside by a wild horde of dancers—the returning Ballets Russes fresh from their headline-making foreign tour—who were in a delirious state of excitement to be arriving again for the long-awaited season in Monte Carlo.

Dhokouminsky strode ahead, dragging a large theatrical basket behind him; his first assignment, after a refreshing bottle or two of pastis, was a telephone call to his beloved, Sophie, cousin of the vicomtesse.

Vera Lidova, the prima ballerina, impressive in sables in spite of the warm weather, stood aloof while the company *regisseur* Borzdoff essayed to have her vast quantities of baggage removed. She waved elegantly to the crowds and offered her autograph, but there were no takers. Everyone scurried to battle for taxis to take them to their hotels and villas. It was the annual headlong rush to the south and the magic of the Riviera.

Vladimir, the slant-eyed Mongolian *corps de ballet* boy looked healthier and had more weight on his slim bones than last year. His soaring technique had been rewarded by Borzdoff. Promotion to the coveted status of junior soloist had brought a little extra money from the cheating manager, and at last, he almost had enough to eat. His first thoughts were centred on half a dozen croissants and an assortment of gateaux at the station buffet, followed by dinner with the skinny Angelique. It will be remembered that last year she warmed her way into his heart and body with boxes of reject chocolates from the *confisserie* where she worked.

Galina, the blonde soubrette of the company glared at Lidova, her arch enemy. She had not forgotten how the seductive siren had tried to lure Arthur, the well-endowed British army officer, from her grasp. She would show her who would take possession of the giant phallus this year. Of course both she and the over-virile Dhokouminsky were unaware that the officer had meantime married the rich widow Sophie. In her blissful innocence she imagined that soon she would be conjoined with the possessor of that amazing organ whose onslaughts had ravished her so satisfyingly in the latter part of the previous Season.

The principal conductor of the ballet, Igor Polovsky, eyed Galina with a lascivious air, remembering a certain encounter with her on the ocean liner that had sped the company to South America last autumn. He followed her cab so that he could register in the same hotel.

The poorer elements of the company of dancers piled into charabancs for the alluring drive along the coast to Monte Carlo. They cheered at the first sight of the sun-drenched sea, rocks, and bathing coves, and made a large number of assignations, pointing to particular favourite spots; the shade of a tamarisk, or under the lee of a cliff, for instance, places which, in their experience, made perfect locations for al fresco couplings. They all agreed it was going to be a delightful summer.

The main body of the *corps de ballet* lodged, as always, at the charming if shabby Hotel de la Poste; a raffish little establishment situated in an alley only a stone's throw from the Opera House. Not only was it cheap with a dining room where vast quantities of nourishing foods were dispensed, but it was also so close to the theatre that the dancers could potter to and fro in their practice clothes. The bizarre promenade at various points of the day was a highly entertaining feature for local workmen who gathered to watch the raggle-taggle collection in their torn tights, sweat-stained leotards and worn out ballet slippers.

There was another bonus at the Poste—the elderly *patronne* was not only deaf but extremely short-sighted. She had no idea, when she handed over the keys for a dozen or so rooms, that they would soon be occupied by at least thirty struggling artists. Sleeping two, three, or even four to a bed made for some interesting situations and varied the social patterns in an agreeable way.

Even Dhokouminsky lodged there. The small weekly rate appealed to his practical mind. It not only left more in his pocket for boozing, but also on those occasions when he did not manage to find a suitable love partner among the crowd of fans at the stage door, or a local rich hostess to invite him home, it was simple to barge into one of the rooms on his corridor. There were rich pickings among the strong-thighed ladies of the *corps*.

Polovsky had followed Galina to the Caprice, not nearly as grand as the Hotel de Paris where Lidova stayed, but more in keeping with her status as a soloist than the overcrowded hotel favoured by her inferiors.

Vladimir ran up the stairs and knocked at Angelique's door. He could hear her canary singing in its cage and could smell the perfumes of the flowers she so carefully cultivated in her window boxes. A tear rolled down his expressive hollow-cheeked face as he remembered the simple bohemian nature of their love in the enchanted attic. The great Puccini knew something of these charms when he composed the immortal work in which Rudolpho, Musetta, Marcello, Mimi et al. sing of the youthful ardour of their poverty stricken lives. Moved with longing for the little chocolate seller, Vladmimir entered the small café downstairs, moodily contemplating a cheap glass of red wine, to await her return.

Dhokouminksy raged in a taxi towards Bernadette's mansion

in search of Sophie. Monsieur Moutarde, on instruction, had told him on the telephone that the lady was neither at home with the vicomtesse, nor expected. the great Slav dancer rang at the gates and when there was no answer crossed the street to a nearby *épicerie*, where he purchased enough wine to see him through the seige he intended to make at the locked entrance.

It was an awful day. Tradesmen of all kinds were turned away, and visitors who were expected to lunch or dinner were telephoned and had their invitations cancelled. The staff were instructed firmly not to approach the great wrought iron gates in case the savage Slav choked them to death through the bars.

Inside in the secret garden room, Sophie wept inconsolably, and Bernadette paced in a distressed state of agitation. On sudden inspiration she went to her escritoire and wrote the following note,

Cher Monsieur Dhokouminsky, how kind of you to call at my house. It would have been delightful to see you. I remember with enormous pleasure your performances last Season, and the warmth and gaiety of your visits here to parties and dinners. Unfortunately I am indisposed today. My cousin Sophie, who also would adore to greet you if she were here, is detained elsewhere, and does not arrive to the Riviera until next week. Please do me a favour however of meeting me tomorrow at the Auberge des Amis du Vin at one o'clock and be my guest for lunch. I die to meet you again. A thousand kisses,
La Vicomtesse de Cliquot St. Maxine.

She showed the note to Sophie who by now was red-eyed and trembling. 'Don't worry, darling,' Bernadette pleaded. 'Go to your room and take a long nap. Dry your tears. I have a little plan.'

She called for Yves, the bootboy, to take out the missive, but on another inspiration, sent for Marietta, the full-breasted Corsican maid. Naturally the vicomtesse addressed her in the outer small study, in order that the secret of the garden room was not given away. 'There is a madman at the gates,' she said, 'take him this. In no way let his hands touch you through the bars.'

The inspiration paid off. Dhokouminsky's enraged lust for Sophie was partially assuaged by the maid's appearance on the staircase outside the mansion. He saw a young, thickset, dark haired beauty. Her breasts, encased in her starched apron were impressive, and her plump posterior extremely interesting. She smiled as she advanced towards him with her full hips swaying. When she smilingly handed him the note he noticed her almost black eyes and long lashes. For a few moments he was so obsessed with her peasant beauty that he did not read it. Marietta dropped a deep curtsey and ran back to the house.

The dancer squatted on the pavement and opened another bottle. When he read the note his eyes widened. The tall, elegant widow who had provided the most lavish of last Season's parties and was obviously rich as Croesus, was madly in love with him. Or why a thousand kisses? Thoughts of Sophie came floating back into his brain, but on the walk back to the Hotel de la Poste, other thoughts of a more libidinous nature, concerning Bernadette, her luscious body, and her undoubted wealth, stole in as well.

The next morning he strolled to the Caprice and knocked on the door of Igor Polovsky, the ballet conductor. It was answered by Galina who was limp from the night's entertainment with the maestro. Dhokouminsky demanded to borrow one of Igor's natty suits. When it was refused he threw the naked musician across the room and pinned him against the armoire. 'You no give suit, I dance like a pig. I go slow when you go fast, I go quick when you go slow, you look like peasant waving stick at donkey. You get fired, no?'

So, suitably dressed, for Polovsky cared greatly for his appearance, Dhokouminsky repaired to the Auberge des Amis du Vin to meet the vicomtesse. He was already in a state of tumescence. Over-lusty to a degree, that was his normal condition, but the thought of meeting the attractive lady added to the agitated state of his member. He pushed it aside in his pocket and tried to disguise the bulge by clinking his small change.

'Allo darling,' he said, rising to his feet gracefully when she arrived. 'I kiss your hand.' He noticed the deep cleft of her *décolletage*, and the heady sweetness of her perfume. Also the vast diamond rings, bracelets and brooches that adorned her person. Her hair was sleek, dressed in an interesting chignon and held by valuable matching brilliants.

'*Mon cher garcon*,' she breathed, 'how *ravissant* to see you again.'

Their conversation was fast and witty. Bernadette, the perfect hostess, entertained him with many slightly *risqué* stories, increasing his sensuous expectations to a troublesome degree. He wished to call a taxi and return with her to the mansion at once, so great was the lust that, always dormant in his loins, was aroused. He made several indecent propositions as his tongue warmed on the fine wines she ordered, and pawed at her hands with his normal indiscretion. They were attacking a plate of *salade des fruits de mer* at the time.

Bernadette thoughtfully chewed on a lobster tail. 'But, *cheri*,' she murmured, 'it's not I who desires you. Of course I find you, well, devastatingly handsome, and I adore your ravishing dancing, but there is another who is in love with you.'

By now Dhokouminsky was a little drunk. He thought tearfully of Sophie. 'Where is she?' he demanded. 'Why is she not here in Monte Carlo to meet me? Has she gone with other man? I kill him.'

Bernadette laid a consolatory hand on his knee. 'I have bad news for you, *mon cher*,' she murmured, 'but I know you will recover.' She pulled from her handbag a gold cigarette case which was studded with gems of such rarity and perfection that their value would pay for the entire season of the Ballets Russes. 'There are many other attractive women on the Riviera,' she said soothingly. 'I am spoken for, and my cousin Sophie has had to enter into a marriage of convenience.'

The Slav's eyes narrowed to slits of ferocious intensity.

'Any scandal will cause tragic results,' she continued. 'It is a union decided by the families concerned. Have no fear, cousin Sophie admires you enormously.'

In a sudden powerful contraction of his hand Dhokouminsky crushed the wine glass he cradled into a thousand splinters, without even breaking the skin of his palm.

'But there is a friend of mine that I wish to tell you about,' Bernadette whispered, giving him a glance of such intense salacity that he melted forthwith. She told him of Sabine Dulac, the sanitised paragon of beauty who had mended her ways recently. Ravished by Alain, the carefree driver of the red sports car, and the next day by the casual visitor to the small hotel in the fishing village where Sabine had finally been seduced, her friend, she told him, was ready and available.

'She adored you in the wild dances of the Tartars last season,' the vicomtese related. 'Your use of the whip enthraled her.'

The idea of such devotion in one so relatively unspoiled appealed to the lecherous athlete. 'What does she look like?' he demanded.

Bernadette painted a picture of a paragon, a wit and beauty that he would find enthralling.

Dhokouminsky massaged his groin with feeling in anticipation of meeting this beauty.

Bernadette rose after paying the bill. She excused herself for a moment and made for the telephone booth. She made two calls, the first to her cousin. 'You can come out of hiding,' she said, 'and tell the staff to unlock the gates. The Russian stallion has got the scent of the luscious Sabine in his nostrils.'

The next call was to her friend Sabine. 'I am having a small cocktail party tomorrow. There will be a person there who I know you will adore meeting. I am sorry that Sophie and I are committed to dinner with other friends, but please feel free to use my house and the principal guest room afterwards as you wish. Moutarde will serve dinner promptly at eight thirty. Goodbye, darling, *bon chance*.'

When she got home she carefully placed the folder which contained the collection of Japanese erotica on the pillows of the aforesaid room. *I don't think Dhokouminsky will need these aids, but at least it will amuse them*, she thought. Cocktails were served at five in the following afternoon.

Monsieur Rognon was there with Camille, the leonine mannequin who, the reader may remember, was afflicted by a rare condition (a form of female satyriasis which induced in her a plethora of involuntary orgasms; it was an incurable kind of autoerotism that many eminent phsycologists and sexologists affirmed was indeed a blessing rather than a lamentable ailment).

Frederick Fanshawe, the drunken failed American novelist lay slumped in a corner. His wife, Lady Letitia, flushed with the success of her major work, a photographic survey entitled *The Penis in Life and Art: limp and erect*, was fresh from the launches of the book in London and Florence, the latter city being the source of her inspiration. She was accompanied by Paolo, the young art student who became her lover and was promoted to be the principal model for the work, so handsome and prodigious was the member that had given such pleasure to the author.

Letitia chatted gaily with the small gathering, but kept an eye on the number of cocktails her inebriated husband consumed. It was not that she disapproved; on the contrary, she encouraged him, in order that Frederick should arrive back at the Hotel de Paris in a comatosed condition severe enough to let her slip away for a night in the arms of her doe-eyed Paolo.

Carlotta Bombieri, the Neapolitan dwarf who owned a flourishing brothel in Marseilles (this fact unknown of course to the vicomtesse), made a brief appearance. She had made an earlier arrangement to escort one of her old clients, Borzdoff, the manager of the Ballet, to her establishment for an evening of pure unalloyed joy.

Marcel, the grand couturier who Bernadette recently married, was charming to all, especially to Vera Lidova, prima ballerina of the company.

Vera looked radiant in the new gown she had purchased at Marcel's establishment in Monte Carlo that morning. It had the new short length, falling to the middle of the knee, and was cut with the most daring neckline. Made of the sheerest peach coloured chiffon and totally unlined, it completely revealed her uptilted breasts and dancers thighs. An ingenious drape across the front hid her pudendum, but clearly the implication was that the wearer sported no underclothes. Sequins and bugle beads, arranged in a pattern which was obviously of art deco origin, and a hem of swansdown completely the delightful creation.

Lidova piroutted gracefully about the *salon*, revelling in the general admiration, and kissed Marcel two times too many for Bernadette's taste. The vicomtesse had a shrewd idea, knowing her husband's rampant profligacy, that the dancer had paid a very cut-price rate for the dress after spending an hour in the fitting room, on the divan, with the couturier.

Dhokouminsky had conveniently forgotten to return the borrowed suit to Igor Polovsky, therefore he presented a handsome picture. His dancer's frame and flirtatious grins had captivated Camille at once and caused one of the aforesaid emissions. If the libertine had known, he would have taken her there and then on the sofa, but he just followed her sniffing at her neck, whispering the most stimulating endearments.

Arriving just in time, luckily, to save the poor mannequin any more flushes, Sabine joined the party. To say her appearance was stunning is an understatement. When Bernadette introduced her to the Slav stallion, for once he was speechless.

Sabine's hair had been cut in the latest fashionable Eton crop, and was glossy black, the fringe falling provocatively almost to her lashes. The extremely short style bared her long slender neck. Her costume, which perfectly reflected her new outdoor-girl image and suntanned looks, was what was known in the trade as a sailor suit. Made of sparkling white lawn, trimmed with blue bands and piping, it was worn with bare legs and sandals. Sabine was the picture of Modern Woman, athletic and vibrant, just the girl to grace a yacht party or a beach picnic, freshly wholesome and gamine.

The fact that she already admired him, from last season's performances, was also a spur to Dhokouminsky, for he was incredibly vain as an artist. He stroked her sun-ripened bare arms as he led her to a discreet corner, and later fingered her tanned calves and knees. The seduction was patently obvious to all, but no-one cared. Each of the party was concerned with his or her own arrangements for the evening.

Vera Lidova, for instance, was looking forward to seeing

the Greek millionaire Voussoudossoulos at dinner in Antibes. The thought of his generous patronage last season had already caused her to start a mental shopping list. Rognon was hoping Camille might relent at last, and Letitia knew, from Fanshawe's condition, that her night of lust with Paolo was assured.

Marcel had joined in the conspiracy concerning Sophie. In a few minutes from now Bernadette would effect her cousin's escape via a rear exit and whisk her along the coast road for dinner at Cap Ferrat.

'My darling,' the vicomtesse breathed in Sabine's ear, 'I can see you adore him, and he is insane for you. The house is yours.'

Dhokouminsky was so struck that he barely noticed the others leaving, and by the time the limousine which stole away his past love Sophie crunched down the gravelled drive, his lascivious tongue was deep in Sabine's welcoming mouth.

Moutarde, the butler, announced that dinner was served at exactly eight thirty. Dhokouminsky was ravenous, and Sabine welcomed the diversion as the Slav beast had barely given her time to breathe since the departure of the rest of the party. She looked at herself in a mirror as she rose and was pleased with what she saw. No smudged make-up, no tousled long tresses, just healthy skin and eyes fresh from the life on the beaches of the Cote d'Azur.

The dancer's underclothes were already damp from the arousal of his enflamed parts. He took Sabine's hand and rubbed it over his groin, meantime nibbling one of her earlobes. She was thrilled with the long hard truncheon-like apparatus she found there and gave it an appreciative squeeze. Here was truly a man of power and effective equipment.

'We must go in,' she said reluctantly. 'Bernadette has been so kind offering us this hospitality, I would not like to upset the servants by arriving late at the dinner table.' She walked from the *salon*, closely followed by Dhokouminsky, who had a hand up the rear of her short skirt, playing at the cleft between her buttocks.

Moutarde was not surprised when they entered the dining room thus enjoined. Bernadette's house had entertained all kinds before, and anyway he had learned quite a few tricks from the more outrageous of the guests.

They sat side by side at the long table instead of taking the chairs indicated by Moutarde and fed each other with dainty morsels.

The vicomtesse had ordered a delightful meal and the talented chef and kitchen staff had worked miracles. There were oysters of course, and phallic-shaped fat asparagus, slivers of *crudités* to dip into a variety of beguiling glazed sauces, sweetbreads served on heart-shaped rounds of pastry, and juicy strawberries of gigantic size to roll in sugar and cream. The whole meal was conceived as carefully designed platters, easy on the palate and digestion, perfect for a couple who intended to take another dessert of a more carnal kind afterwards. The vintage champagne was delicious and heady, and a far more suitable accompaniment than heavy clarets and burgundies would have been.

They sat for a while savouring the pleasures of the meal, Dhokouminsky staring ardently at his new beloved. Sabine reflected what a good friend Bernadette had been, first the charming Alain who had stormed her senses on the beach and in the small hotel; then the kind considerate lover she had taken the day after, the handsome Monsieur Sombert, whose telephone number was newly inscribed in her address book, with an accompanying star for excellence.

The Slav thought to hell with dumpy little Sophie. If she wants an anaemic Englishman so what. Had he known anything of Arthur's phenomenal skill as a lover, his staying power, and the size of his appendage, envy would have set in, but for the moment he was happy, with his lusty animal instincts poised and alerted.

Soon he led Sabine upstairs. They were shown the way to the principal guest suite by Mariette, the maid who delivered the note from Bernadette the day before. He could not resist a pinch at her cosy rump when Sabine's head was averted and promised himself to look her up on her next free evening.

The vast bedroom was in an entirely different style to the remainder of the house. What small areas of wall remained, for the principal parts were taken up by mirrors of enormous size and tinted a smoky shade of pink, were pitch black. The ceiling was also mirrored completely and a talented artist had painted on it the barest and most suggestive outlines of coupled figures in the throes of sexual union. The deeply sprung mattress had been lowered into a pit around which little fountains played, the waters springing from the diminutive sexual parts of cherubs who sprouted wings. More vintage champagne was placed in an ice bucket at the side, and on a gilded table stood a row of sweet-smelling unguents.

After the perfect epicurean repast, the pair were now presented with an apartment that even the ancient Sybarites of Rome would have envied.

In a similar pit in an adjacent chamber, a warm bath had been run, with foam and perfume. Dhokouminksy and Sabine lowered themselves into it after undressing each other, slowly and caressingly; it was clear they had the whole night to enjoy, and could afford a leisurely approach. Her breasts were smooth in the silky water, as was her firm belly. She groped his sensitive parts as he smoothed his hands over her mounds and the rising nipples. She could feel the surge of muscular tension in his member, and the swelling it brought. The delicate ovals contained in his sac shifted lazily as she massaged, suggesting the rousing collection of juices, and the hood of his shaft came to a throbbing hardness.

Dhokouminsky lay back in a trance as she expertly drew on her knowledge, sliding the skin that covered the imposing shaft towards her where she lay opposite him, until the skin covered the head again. The reversal of her movement, causing a slow uncovering in the warmth of the bath, caused further impulsive beatings in the length of the fiery dancer's instrument.

He reached down her body and gently washed the part between her legs that now tingled and dilated. His fingers played at the short dense matt of hair and the lips underneath. She pushed at his fingers, guiding them towards the extra-sensitive hard little nerve centre that was available to the touch when her willing lips were parted.

'Aah,' she gasped, pressing her own hands to her breasts as he played on the button, 'you are a wonderful lover. Ah, you know exactly where you are going.' He pressed downwards and into the very opening of her cleft, stirring with a finger, then inwards until its length was taken up.

'Oh, oooh, I am faint,' Sabine moaned as the Slav worked his way seemingly into her very soul. 'Take me here in the water.'

'Dhokouminsky pulled her towards him and twisted her round to face him. He had an extraordinary strength, having spent the most of his working life throwing the likes of Vera Lidova over his head in ballet performances. He lifted her up and placed her so that her part slipped over and engulfed his vertical member in one sliding downward thrust, with her legs splayed out to the side. He placed his strong hands underneath her rump and squeezed.

'Now I help you ride me like horse,' he grinned.

Apart from the movement of his forearms he was perfectly still in this show of brute strength. Only his closed eyes and the width of his smile conveyed the ecstasy that throbbed through his body as she rose and fell on his hugely swollen hammer-head and rigid shaft with a more urgent and thrilling action.

Sabine came to a fast conclusion on this ride, jabbing and tensing with an ever increasing fervour until she cried out, arching her back and locking Dhokouminsky's pole in a dynamic hold that almost brought him to conclusion at the same moment, but he held her firm, with her tunnel of love in a thrilling spasm of enclosure, until she subsided and sank forward with her breasts on his chest.

She felt the still unsatisfied rigidity throb inside her, but still the Slav's hips were motionless, and she marvelled at his control. To her surprise, for she knew that certain signals in his brain must be screaming for ejaculatory release, he rolled her to the side, then lifted her bodily out of the sunken bath.

He tossed her over his shoulder as if she were a small child and took her through into the mirrored bedroom. The wily dancer slipped a hand between her buttocks and stimulated her enflamed parts as he carried her round past the pink mirrors, each in turn revealing a new aspect. His fingers slipped easily into her interior, knowingly arousing further lust, and he bit with some force on her nearest buttock. He stopped in front of the gilded table and unstoppered several of the phials which rested there. Her eyes glazed over as he anointed her lavishly with handfuls of the powerful sweet smelling oils and she shivered with delight as he roved his hands over her lubricated body. They were now in a corner of the vast room, a dozen metres from the sunken bed.

Sabine quivered at the sight of the myriad reflections in the mirrored room. Dhokouminksy's tanned muscular body towered over hers like a powerful Tarzan. His hands squeezed her buttocks and her breasts, and his legs, wrapped around hers with the grip of a viper, pressed against her thighs alternately with a strength that amazed her.

He nuzzled into her oiled breasts with avarice, glancing at the effect in the mirrors, and caught Sabine's wild expression as she tossed her head in her delirium. Their lubricated skins moved against each other so easily, it was almost as if they became one. She crooned in her devastating pleasure, and Dhokouminsky took up the theme, whistling his favourite Argentinean tango.

He bent his knees and rubbed the tip of his monstrous glans at her centre, and found the hard little fulcrum with it. Circling carefully at first, and then more tantalisingly, he titillated the sensitive button with his enterprising equipment until the delirious Sabine parted her legs and implored him to enter once more.

But Dhokouminsky teased her again. With his arms akimbo, and now singing the tango out loud, he locked his very orifice on to Sabine's clitoris. The length of his stem created a distance between them, and acted as a guide, as with a slow, slow, quick quick slow, he danced her backwards to the foot of the bed. Visions of this exotic *pas de deux* sparkled from every mirror, but though the image of the dominant organ which propelled them was certainly a novel one, Sabine wished the gap to close so that she could once more be in thrall of the massive penile weapon.

The Slav arrested their progress for a few minutes and held her still, while with clever thrusting little jabs of his pelvis, he expertly inflamed the small button to such a degree that Sabine gushed her love juices again. They fell on the bed and Dhokouminsky's member hurtled into her waiting chamber with ferocious speed, thrust to the hilt with an abandon that brought him instant release in a flow of passionate intensity, and Sabine, now reduced to wailing like a feral cat, experienced the most overwhelming sensation of her life.

Bernadette paid them a social call the next morning. The night had been a cornucopia of lustful events. The pair were sprawled naked on the vast bed as the vicomtesse entered bearing coffee—a rare treat for a guest in her house.

Dhokouminsky and Sabina rolled over from where they were lying on their exhausted bellies, and lay on their backs without shame.

'My little love birds,' Bernadette murmured as she poured two cups. 'I suppose you had a wonderful time?'

'Dhokouminsky taught me his latest piece of choreography,' Sabine answered drowsily. 'I am now such a fine dancer, I think I shall audition for the Ballets Russes.'

Letitia woke in a cold sweat after the night of love with Paolo in her room at the Hotel de Paris. She was trembling from the emotions which a tortured dream aroused in her breast, and searched in vain for her lover. He, of course had fled early before Frederick Fanshawe, whom Letitia had locked in the adjoining dressing room the night before, could wake and discover him.

The dream had been fearsome. Lady Letitia, in an open-topped Bugatti, was being conducted on a cultural tour of the art treasures of northern Italy by a chauffeur who bore a striking resemblance to Jean-Paul, Bernadette's driver. The townscape of Florence was a vista of rose madder, umber, burnt sienna, terracotta, amber and cream. The car sped from one great gallery to another, to palaces and churches, and through lavish gardens furnished with monumental marble staircases and fountains. Everywhere she called out for her darling boy, the handsome youth she had immortalised in her newly published survey of the male anatomy. There were fleeting visions of him in the dark shade of cypresses, but when she called, they vanished into thin air. Once she ordered Jean-Paul to stop in front of a life-sized bronze of a Roman gladiator, but as the car drew up to a halt, the verdigris of the metal turned to livid green and the sculpture broke up into a pile of dust.

'Take me to Perugia,' she commanded, 'he will be there in his favourite bar with his friends.' But when they got there after dashing along the banks of the Tiber, the town was deserted. A crone sitting on the steps of a tenement cackled at her and told her Paolo had been raped and abducted by a posse of witches.

The nightmare drive took them on to Spoleto and thence to Assisi where a hooded monk shook his head sadly and showed her a sack of bones, human relics, and the gold necklace she had given to her lover in appreciation of his worship of her body. Then as if by magic, over the mountains to Bologna where they found a chanting brutal crowd attacking a stone statue on a plinth in the central square, hammering away its genitals and trampling them to small fragments.

In panic Lady Letitia telephoned Bernadette and told her of these horrors. 'What can the dream possibly signify?' she implored, but Bernadette could not help. She merely told her to visit M. Galantine, the eminent physchiatrist, which she did immediately.

His answer was brief, but terribly expensive, when the bill came later. 'Madame,' he said, 'there is nothing to worry about. Like many other women before, and like many more to come in the future, you have lost your head over a bit of cock.'

Chapter Four

Vladimir, you will remember, had repaired to the Café de la Colombe to await his darling Angelique. *Madame la patronne* was not too pleased that he only took one small glass of wine during the tardy period he spent mooning at the window table. At first she had tried a little conversation, but the Mongolian's facility in French was, to say the least, limited. The fat old lady cheered up when Gavroche and Josette entered. The painter and the bohemian girl were thrilled. He had just sold the first of a series of erotic oil paintings which were inspired by Frederick Fanshawe's improvised novelette at the Bistro Latouche a few weeks earlier. Seeing there were only a few customers Gavroche called for drinks for everyone.

Vladimir asked for a brandy, and the painter made it a double, such was his glow of success. Josette smiled expansively at the skinny dancer. She wondered if, within his bony frame, lurked the wild variety of sensual longing that appealed to her. There were many indications that she may be right. His long legs were placed wide, at right angles to the chair, in that extraordinary turned-out position which comes naturally to dancers; and when, in his boredom, he stretched, the sinews of his neck and wrists suggested a pent-up wiry strength and elasticity which fascinated her.

Gavroche beamed happily at the *patronne*. He was remembering, with a mild stirring in his groin, how Josette had hurried home with him to the rooms he occupied, by coincidence, on the floor below Angelique's attic apartment. It was the first time they had come together sexually. Their love-making was athletic, abandoned, almost brutal, but spiritually uplifting. Fanshawe's lyrical and provoking tale about the country boys conspired to make Josette desire the stiff organ of Gavroche. She had massaged it with such vigour, under cover of the table at the bistro, that he had already been relieved of a considerable amount of his love juices, but the fantasy of the American's licentious story lived on in his brain causing him to reproduce some of the more powerful images of the quartet's couplings in the ensuing hours on his rickety bed. He had no idea that Josette's cries and groans were heard so distinctly in the attic above. Angelique, awaiting Vladimir's return, cried in frustration and misery, fearful of his reaction to a certain turn in events.

Josette's large breasts and loosely-hinged thighs provided his libido with further stimulation, if that were needed, as did her fat belly and curvaceous buttocks. She rolled and flailed her body and limbs with inspired fervour at each new onslaught. Gavroche surprised himself at the extent of his powers, but the admixture of his partner's lust and the memories of the abandoned foursome in the mountain meadow, and then in the barn of the Chateau de Brazande, fired his sexual drive like never before.

Josette could not believe her luck in having found such a randy chum. She became the perfect model for his work. Her generously covered frame glowed after their early morning lovemaking when he set up his easel, and her eyes showed him that warm, satisfied enigma with which an artist seeks to enliven his canvas. The resulting works were spontaneously alive, with a sensuous feeling that vibrated towards the viewer, and became instantly saleable.

Gavroche thought that he owed Fanshawe a great deal in return for this inspiration; perhaps one of the paintings, later, when enough had been sold to put him and Josette on a firm financial footing.

Vladimir's eyes roved about the walls of the café which were decorated with cinema posters supplied by the manager of the house nearby, and displayed by the *patronne* in return for two weekly complimentary tickets.

He reflected that the stars of the silent screen seemed to be from another world, and of a glamour far removed from the daily grind of his dancer's life. But to him, the faces of the ravishing film stars were an alluring vision of some kind of paradise—one he would enter with his beloved little chocolate seller when he became famous and rich.

A strong tremor shook his body. He saw her suddenly pass the window of the bistro, and raced outside to embrace her, crying out incomprehensible declarations of love and longing. When she turned on hearing her name, the look on her face, and the sight of the bundle she was carrying, drove into his soul.

'It is our *enfant, chéri*,' she said, with tears pouring down her pale cheeks.

Time stood still for those few moments, even though a taxi flew past, and the great bell in the belfry nearby chimed the hour. An old crone dressed in a black shawl brushed between them, and a string of school children skipped along on their way home.

'Come,' Angelique said, leading the way into the shabby hallway, smiling shyly. 'I have waited so long for this moment.

Vladimir's heart pounded as they mounted the steep staircase, each tread creaking painfully. It was not until she opened her door and they stepped inside that he caught his first sight of the child.

He cried, with strange confused emotions of pride; the shock of surprise, and fear. Instant ownership of an infant who was so recognisably the product of his loins almost caused him to faint. The baby was so like any other born in his village in a far-flung department of the Steppes, it could belong to no other father. She had slanted eyes like his own, a pale, sallow skin, long delicate fingers, and lashes long enough to beguile a Mogul emperor.

The emaciated dancer laughed and seized the child, to whirl it around the room in his arms. Angelique stood trembling, hardly able to contain herself. For months she had feared his return. Perhaps he would be furious. At first, when her belly swelled, she was afraid that the child may have been seeded by Charles, the English yacht-broker who had taken his pleasure with her before she came across Vladimir. But the child's foreign features had reassured her. It belonged to her beloved *corps de ballet* boy; the half starved Mongolian lad who earned a pittance from the greedy Borzdoff.

Her own earnings were small enough, supplemented by selling programmes and manning the ladies' cloakroom at the Opera House, and she knew that the child's father would not be in a position to provide for her.

However, Vladimir was delighted. He grabbed Angelique and hugged her, planting a hundred kisses on her willing mouth. With his poor French, sign language, and incomprehensible babblings in his own tongue, he explained that when the company of the Ballets Russes went on tour, after the season in Monte Carlo, they would travel with the baby in a basket, and Angelique could be employed in the wardrobe. There would be many hands to help; the ballerinas would nurse it with love and affection, and he would take the baby out for walks between rehearsals.

Angelique was happy suddenly. Madame Larousse, the proprietor of the chocolate shop had been very kind and had allowed her to keep the baby in a back room during working hours, and indeed had bought its first layette. Surely she would allow her to go on tour with the ballet at intervals, and then return to her employment when the company played in the theatres of the Riviera.

And so we leave the little pair in the attic high over the rue Lefêvre. Vladimir kissed Angelique's breasts after she had fed the infant. Her nipples tasted sweet, and a little of her milk trickled into his mouth. He was contented as he watched her nurse the child and sing it to sleep, and afterwards he made love to the mother, fondly, with warmth, and a deep gratitude. It was the most tender scene to take place on the Cote d'Azur in that entire season.

In the immediate *quartier*, for it was in these narrow streets that the bohemians, writers and painters resided, the news of Gavroche's success spread like wildfire and a throng of acquaintances began to assemble at the Café de la Colombe. Josette was happy enough to receive a few fond embraces and sly manipulations from old friends, but the artist, remembering the bill Frederick Fanshawe had had to pay, wisely took the view that since the cost of friendship can soar alarmingly when one has a bit of luck, it was expedient to beat a retreat before the entire purchase price of his first sale was swallowed up in drink. Besides, he had to effect some more research on Josette's body if the canvas he intended to attack the next morning were to glow with the erotic content he had in mind.

'Come, darling one,' he said firmly, steering his model to the door through the crowd of disappointed chums, 'we have work to do.'

Over their heads, when they embraced in the rickety bed, they could hear the rhythmic pounding of the equally antique mattress upstairs in Angelique's attic. Josette knew that the instigator of these percussive effects was the slim Mongolian youth whose bulging crotch had protruded so interestingly from his slim frame when he had sprawled in the chair in the cafe below. She gathered that her surmise as to the extent of his lust had been justified.

Each time the sounds came to an end, and the lampshade in the ceiling of Gavroche's room stopped swinging, Josette marvelled at how soon, after laughter and happy cries, they resumed. She nudged Gavroche repeatedly, pointing upwards at the swaying light-bulb. He also was fascinated. Carnal images raced through his mind.

There can be, when members of the human race intrude on the love-making of others, feelings of either revulsion or absorbtion, but rarely, if ever, attitudes of indifference. The prudish and the coy will claim the latter, naturally, since, in their hypocritical fashion, they deny that the sensual joys of union are the mainspring of human life. Wholesome individuals will allow that a degree of interest is not unnatural. That is why the stimulating arts of literature, the theatre, cinema, painting and sculpture are so widely appreciated and understood. A truly enlightened sexologist would therefore have made no condemnation of the interest shown by the artist and the model on that warm night.

Gavroche was so enthraled by the noises from above that he paid small heed at first to his partner. Prurient curiosity led his hand to stray to his thickening organ. His concentrated aural efforts had caused an unconscious arousal in his member that surprised him. He took hold of the swollen stem and squeezed it appreciatively. Each thud of the bed upstairs was echoed in a vibration in the article in his grasp.

Neglected, Josette drew his other hand towards her private part and spread his thick, paint-stained fingers over it. At first Gavroche was so intent on his own sensations that they remained there inactive, until she stroked and pushed them into a position where their tips brushed against the damp lips of her orifice.

The magic of the lubricity of this region did its inevitable work. He marvelled at the ease with which a finger slid open the little pink flaps of flesh and found the tight nerve-case which throbbed to his touch. Gavroche thrilled also at the delicious way in which Josette lifted her groin, presenting her awaiting channel at such an angle that his whole finger became submerged in her juices. He found a thread of his jissom at the orifice of his enlarged, throbbing glans and transferred it to her private parts, making the area even more damp and lubricated.

Josette moaned now that both his hands were employed at her mound of Venus and the sensitive places underneath and sought the satisfaction of holding her lover's mast. Turning towards him she placed both hands around it and squeezed gently, trying to draw it towards her nether regions.

'*Attend un moment*,' Gavroche whispered, as a new approach had begun upstairs. This time it was of short duration. He counted only ten thrusts, but they were obviously of sufficient dynamism to bring both the lovers in the attic to yet another orgasmic burst, as they heard Angelique and Vladimir cry out in unison, a long ecstatic and thrilling sound which rang down the intervening staircase.

The effect on Gavroche and Josette was so powerful that they both yielded to a premature ejaculation of great force, the more satisfying since they shared the carnal moment with the one which happened overhead.

Gavroche was elated as he drew himself over Josette to properly continue. The intimacy of the close couplings reminded him further of Fanshawe's al fresco love scene and inspired the dawning of several compositions of great beauty which would grace future canvasses. Josette accepted his entry with gratitude, clasping the walls of her love-passage around his still-tormented stem with a muscular contraction that throbbed a message of her devotion to it.

He began with firm, slow strokes, almost withdrawing and pausing before again seeking the depths of her moist interior with the hard-nosed tip of his member. Each move cost her a sharp breath and the arch of her back. In the moments between she sunk her lips into his neck and bit fiercely, and pressed her fingernails into the muscles on either side of his spine.

Shudders ran through Gavroche's torso and clenched buttocks and transmitted themselves to Josette's body underneath. Her legs parted wider, and as she lifted her knees he plunged even further. He held her by the nape of the neck, pulling her more closely towards his bursting stem.

Her next emission was awesome, slow and lasting. Gavroche felt devoured as she reared herself from the bed, offering herself to his thrust which now gained in pace, excited by Josette's foaming and galvanic orgasm to a speed which shook the bed on its old springs.

The noise, which was as great as that from the attic earlier, somehow added to his enjoyment. Each powerful rapid thrust was matched by a springing sound as the old bed crunched and swayed.

Upstairs, the satiated Angelique and Vladimir smiled at each other, wrapped in each others arms. He kissed her eyelids and whispered thanks to her. She crept from the bed and crossed over to where the infant lay in its bassinet, and was joined in a moment by the Mongolian youth. Both gazed at the child and each in turn planted a small kiss on her forehead.

As the night sky darkened to an ultramarine of great glamour, pin-pricked with stars, they rocked the child, and downstairs Gavroche rocked Josette until they finally fell asleep exhausted.

Vladimir went to the window and looked out. There were

tears in his beautiful slanted eyes. He no longer felt an alien.

In the morning, while the bright little canary bird trilled in its wire cage at the casement, Angelique, almost swooning in her joy, raced round to the *patissier* to buy fresh croissants while Vladimir made a large jug of coffee. He was nursing the baby on his knee when she returned, a gesture which moved her greatly.

'Can we go to the beach?' she asked. 'It will be good for her.'

The company had two weeks of long-awaited holiday before rehearsals started in earnest, though dedicated ballerinas such as Vera Lidova were already in daily practice at the *barre*.

Vladimir thought about his new promotion and the roles it would bring him, but eventually relented. Getting back into shape could begin later. So they repaired to the rocks by the sea not far from the Opera House.

Most of the company were already there, toasting themselves in the hot sunshine, relaxing their tired muscles which ached from the punishing tour which had just been completed. The dancers gathered round Angelique, Vladimir, and the baby girl in her bassinet, cooing and gurgling.

How the boy was teased! The boys who shared dressing rooms with Vladimir made dreadful jokes, blaming his legendary appendage which they had always said would get him into trouble one day.

The girls adored the child and were enchanted by the slim chocolate seller who had the figure of a dancer. Some envied her lustrous eyes, and others her long shining hair.

All agreed that the Mongolian had done very well for himself, not only in finding himself such a pretty girl, but in providing yet more proof that, far from being the hothouse of depraved homosexuality that it is often accused of being, a ballet company is a fortress of natural behaviour, especially when it is composed of virile Russians.

As if they were yet another assertion of this claim the soubrette Galina and the conductor Igor Polovsky, after joining in the familial congratulations, had retired to the privacy of the cover of two large bath towels, where they continued, as discreetly as they could manage, the love-play they had been enjoying in the hotel on rising that morning.

The ladies of the ballet were incensed, as always, that they could not join in the sun worship of the men. Their contracts stipulated instant dismissal for the sin of reddened, burnt, or sun tanned skin.

'I do not want brown or black swans in my company,' Borzdoff always raged at the start of a tour away from the Motherland, 'only white, or else you going, pretty fast.'

To be sure, the white foundation which the girls used on their bodies in *Swan Lake*, *Les Sylphides* and *Giselle*, would only cover the lightest of suntans. The stage lighting would turn any other shade of brown into purple, an unthinkable skin tone.

The boys on the other hand, usually being required to appear as warriors, golden slaves, hunters, oriental seducers and the like, could get as bronzed as they wished.

So the boys raced around the beach and the rocks, swimming, diving, and showing off generally, while the girls lay under beach brollies or improvised coverings. Even swimming for a few minutes under the hot Mediterranean sun could result in a tan and incur the wrath of the company manager.

Nevertheless, the girls enjoyed themselves. Old rivalries and fresh ambitions were aired that morning, as they would be throughout the holiday period, and they loved the attractive spectacle of the menfolk disporting themselves. They tittered about the goings-on in the Hotel de la Poste, wondering who would be their next lover.

A favourite amongst them all was Paquin, a star of the Paris Opera Ballet who had been engaged as a guest artiste for the season by Borzdoff. Tall and elegant, with an easy smiling way, the hand kissing Adonis, who came to the company with a formidable reputation for being an irresistible seducer, was even now cloistered behind a rock with the young Ivanova, the most recent addition to the *corps de ballet*. There was some fury already that the new apprentice had been promptly cast in some enviable roles, namely several important fairy variations in *The Sleeping Princess*.

Anna Galinkova, the *jeune premiére* who felt most aggrieved, made an instant decision to lure Paquin to her room that very night with the promise of supper in bed. She also had a nice way with foot massage, something no dancer can resist. *That will fix the silly bitch*, she thought.

There was a general consensus that it was time for lunch. The baby agreed and set up a lusty bawling. Angelique obliged. It was so handy having the child's food to hand, so to speak, and when she exposed a full breast to its mouth, the enchanted company gathered round to watch.

It was all so blissful, lying in the shade, munching at baguettes with cheeses and salads bought in the morning market, and drinking from bottles of wine which had been cooled in rock pools. Afterwards the boys played cards, eyeing the girls and trying to decide which they would try to take back to the Poste for the inevitable afternoon siesta.

Galinkova's burning glances had already begun to make their mark. Paquin detached himself from Ivanova and strolled towards her. She could not but notice the considerable bulge in his bathing drawers and wonder if it was she that inspired it, or whether it remained from his closeting with the new member of the troupe. She was pleased to see that it did not seem to decrease, rather more to grow, as she stole into place by her side and whispered a few endearments in his mother tongue.

Lunch, and the conversation, was gay and uninhibited. They spoke of last Season's triumphs and the wild parties, especially those given by Bernadette, the vicomtesse, and hoped that she would repeat them this year.

Soon they noticed an amazing sight far out in the sea. It was Edith, the charleston dancer from America who most of the boys of the company had enjoyed on the island in the middle of Bernadette's swimming pool the previous year.

Edith flailed through the waves at the rate of knots, using a variety of strokes; breast, crawl and butterfly. It was an Amazonian display which the company rose to cheer. 'Hi, boys,' she called as she emerged from the water. 'I sure am glad see you again.' And so they were to see her.

She was followed at a distance, because he could in no way match her speed, by Charles, the English yacht broker.

Vladimir was the first to recognise him. It was Charles who had taken flowers to Angelique's apartment in gratitude for her favours, and in anticipation of a renewal of their affair when it became obvious that he did not have the stamina to withstand Edith's nymphomaniac onslaught on his genitals. It was Vladimir who had gracefully accepted the bouquet, thinking that it was a tribute from a fan of the ballet.

He rose and greeted him like an old friend. Charles stared into the youth's slanted eyes, and recognised them as belonging to the boy who had supplanted him in Angelique's affections.

The sounds of a baby's gurglings caught his ear. Heavens, there was the elfin chocolate seller herself, cradling an infant. Angelique glanced at him, her cheeks burning, then lowered her head. Charles stood perfectly still—fear and worry torturing his brain. He tried counting the months since their separation, but in his confusion could not manage the sums, only the vast amounts that he might have to pay if a French court awarded Angelique a handsome paternity award.

Vladimir was now at his side, holding the baby up proudly for Charles to see. The relief was instant. He saw the same hollow cheeks and the same Mongolian slanted eyes, the dark pupils and long lashes. For once in his life, the arrogant but charming ex-public schoolboy made an impetuous gesture; something without regard to thinking what he would get out of it. He bent down and kissed the young mother on the cheek and sad, 'Well done, congratulations. Haven't you done well.' Then he shook Vladimir by the hand and hoped his envy would not show.

He strolled off with Edith to the beach café where they would lunch, wishing this summer would bring him the same happiness as he saw back there on the rocks; his eyes were clouded with tears when he tried to read the menu. It was the salt from the sea, he explained to Edith.

'Let me order, big boy,' she grinned, slapping him heftily across his shoulders. 'I see I'm going to have to take you in hand,' she added with a salacious wink.

Soon the raffish troupe wandered into town to their various lodgings. Galina and Polovsky paused for a glass of lemon tea at Chez Fifi, a small elegant salon, and Paquin took Anna Galinkova on the autobus to his rented villa at Roquebrune. Vladimir and Angelique did a little shopping on the way to the attic, and most of the remainder went to cause more havoc at the long suffering Hotel de la Poste.

Dhokouminsky was just leaving from there with Sabine. She looked extremely weary, a fact which caused some merriment among the group. The Slav winked knowingly. He was no fool to have taken his new lover there when the hotel was mostly empty.

Sabine had heard from Sophie of his wonderful way with a whip in the barbaric Tartar Dances, and implored him to show her his tricks. The sight of the naked figure of Dhokouminsky leaping around the room cracking the fearsome bull whip had provoked her to even more adoration, even though he cracked a large mirror and broke a porcelain vase.

Later as he tantalisingly flicked the tip of the leather thong over her belly and teased her breasts with it, rather like a snake might relish a morsel of food with its darting tongue, Sabine had melted for her savage and he had taken her with an ardour which entranced her, with her wrists tied to the bedrail by the leather thong.

They were on their way to the mansion of Bernadette. Sophie, his love of last year had officially come out of hiding now that Dhokouminsky and Sabine were openly knotted together, as it were, and kisses of a friendly nature could now be exchanged all round. How marvellous it is when common sense and rationality prevail and the affairs of the heart can be settled, and love can flourish!

Edith tried very hard along these lines with Charles. She lay her cards on the table, as it were. They were sitting on high stools at the beach bar. She thought he looked terrifically handsome in his wet bathing suit. It was full length and made of striped cotton in red and white. The material was just thin enough, in its damp condition, to make the shape of his genitals visible. She sported an orange one-piece, offset with purple bands, with a matching mopcap and swimming sandals which were cross gartered up to her plump knees.

The setting was perfect. A striped awning over their heads provided welcome shade, and the thoughtful proprietor had created a miniature garden around his booth with troughs of bright flowers and hanging baskets.

Edith was thrilled to be back on the Côte d'Azur. When she could tear her eyes away from Charles's crotch, she waved expansively at the scene ahead. 'Ain't it deevine, honey? This place is just so cute and cultured. My daddy is so pleased his little girl's in Europe, soaking up this civilised atmosphere!' At that moment she downed a large Martini on the rocks in one gulp.

Charles, even in his depressed condition had to agree. As far as the eye could see, the vista of rocks, waves, palm trees and little beach establishments presented the prettiest and jolliest scene one could possibly imagine.

The bright young things bobbed about in the sea playing with giant rubber balls, and in the distance sleek yachts, some of them his own hired craft, sailed from bay to bay in an elegant and colourful display of seamanship.

'Why you so glum, sweetie?' Edith asked, prodding him in the ribs flirtatiously with a cocktail stick. 'You got everythin' a guy could want: your own business, you live here through the summer in a perfect climate, you got loads o' friends, and best of all, honey pie, you got me.'

Charles moodily contemplated his tall glass of vermouth. The business was certainly an enormous success. He now managed, for his father's company, a whole fleet of yachts, both small and ocean-going. He had facilities for sale and hire at all the major centres; Nice, Cannes, Menton, and Marseilles, as well as the smaller harbours such as Monaco, Villefranche and Antibes. Money rolled in, as did social invitations. Sleek girls were in plentiful supply, and the best of his English men friends were down on the coast whooping it up with abandon. Even his very best friend, the army officer Arthur with whom he had shared Bernadette's guest apartment last year, was due to arrive any day. It was true that Edith, greedy for physical contact and insatiable in her lust, would open her thighs for him at the drop of a hat. Last season indeed she had almost crippled him and he had been obliged to pass her on to Gus, the American football player, in an attempt to stave off complete neurosthenia and exhaustion of the libido.

But something was missing. Was it his English sensibility that stopped him from enjoying himself to the full? Or a feeling of guilt that he possessed such wealth, and like the rest of the *jeunesse doré*, spent so much time in the pursuit of pleasure?

'Chin chin,' Edith whooped, knocking back the next Martini. She adored the life down here in the South. The previous evening she had been the star attraction at a Grand Charity Ball where she had been cheered to the roof for her performance of the latest dances. Her repertoire included the Charleston, naturally, but she had delighted the crowd with the Black Bottom, the Bunny Hop, and the Suzie Q. 'Aw, come on, dinky doo, cheer up. It ain't the end o' the world,' Edith cried.

She leaped up on to the bar and began to dance wildly, throwing her long legs higher than her head, bobbing and dipping, and gyrating her large behind in a most obscene manner. A crowd of bathers gathered and clapped out a rhythm for her, whistling and singing the latest rage jazz tune. Her breasts shook violently and threatened to pop out from the top of the bodice. She sang raucously,

> 'Slap your bottom, shake a tit,
> the shim shim shammy is a great big hit.
> Do it to me baby, with a voh de oh doh,
> gimme the hots babe, come on lets go.'

She matched her actions to the words; sexual innuendo at its most flagrant was hurled at the crowd as she shook and stomped. Her finale was a huge leap into the splits with such force that the bar collapsed with a great deal of crashing of glasses, ice buckets and bottles. She clutched at the awning for support, but this came tumbling down too, and she landed in a heap on the sand.

The crowd cheered ecstatically, for this was the age of the

raver, the 'I don't care' culture, slap happy kids with time on their hands and everyone out for a lark.

Charles paid up of course, a very large bundle of francs, and the free loan of a jolly little yacht for the next weekend thrown in for good measure.

It was a hoot, a jolly good show, razzmatazz, and whoopsy-day, they all cried, and ran back leaping into the foamy waves, cheering Edith who was carried aloft by two strong chaps before being unceremoniously chucked into the briny. All save Charles who walked slowly back to the spot where he had left his clothes, trying desperately to shake off the glooms.

He strolled back to the main road, taking a short cut through the gardens of the Casino, and stopped to buy a copy of *Le Monde*. While he was reading on a wayside bench, a large Rolls Royce cruised by.

'Stop the car,' the vicomtesse ordered, and rolled down the window. 'Yes, I am sure it is him.' Jean-Paul reversed gently until the car was directly by Charles.

Bernadette leaned out. '*Bon jour, jeune homme.*'

Charles leaped to his feet, doffing his straw boater. 'Hello Bernie, how are you?' he asked warmly.

The English diminutive had always pleased the vicomtesse. The familiar address made her feel young. Charles kissed her hand and then leaned through the window to place two affectionate kisses on her cheeks.

'You bad boy,' she said. 'You have been here two weeks already, I know because friends have seen you, and so far, not even a telephone call.'

Charles blushed a deep pink. 'I know you won't believe me, but I was going to call this evening.'

'Of course, *cheri*,' she replied, a little coquettishly. 'What are you doing right now?'

'Just taking a walk.'

'Well please join me. We can go to the house and, later, when you wish, Jean-Paul will drive you home.'

Charles jumped in smartly. He was always pleased to see his beloved Bernie.

'Where are you staying this Season?' she asked. 'Is it comfortable?'

'Sharing a villa with a couple of chums, chaps actually,' he answered with a grin. 'You must come to dinner when we are more prepared.'

'*Enchanté*,' the vicomtesse laughed. 'I adored the flowers you sent me when you left last year, and the lovely cashmere jumpers from London,' she said, patting him on his knee.

'You were very kind to Arthur and me,' he answered, 'letting us stay in the guest suite.'

Bernadette quivered internally at the memory of the boys waking with quite alarming tumescences, taking showers, exchanging salacious gossip, and in the case of Arthur, seducing the debutante Annabelle. Charles would die if he knew that all this was revealed by the two-way mirror and the special peephole in the secret garden room, and that she had invited Sophie also to feast her eyes on them.

'I love having young people about me,' she smiled. She noticed Jean-Paul smirking at the driver's wheel, so with a quick click of a button she closed the internal window and cut him off from their conversation.

She had to admit to herself Charles looked quite appealing. He had grown a much heavier moustache since last year and had slightly thickened in appearance. His white flannels and striped blazer were immaculate. The thought of the unusually large organ between his thighs unnerved her.

'How is your love life,' she asked.

'Non-existent,' he replied truthfully.

The candour of his eyes touched her, and in truth she had never seen the boy so downcast, though his well trained politeness had tried hard to disguise his mood.

'You were so successful last year, my darling,' she teased, 'all the girls were after you.'

He grinned sheepishly and hung his head. 'What people don't know, they'll make up,' he said feebly.

They were soon at the mansion. Bernadette ordered tea to be served in her small *salon*. *What a charming boy*, she thought as he performed little courtesies for her such as fetching and lighting cigarettes, arranging a cushion behind her and helping with the tea things.

'I remember you when you were a child,' she said fondly.

As she sipped her favourite imported Earl Grey she had a picture in her mind of a lad eight years old, making sand castles on the beach at Portofino, or was it Cassis, she pondered. While the boy was at play, his father, Sir James had made passionate love to her in the changing cabin. She had been barely sixteen and it was her first experience of carnal gratification. Here she was now, about to behave like a young girl and flirt with that same boy twenty years or so later. 'Ridiculous,' she exclaimed out loud.

'I beg your pardon,' Charles said, surprised.

Bernadette quickly pulled herself together. 'I was just thinking how ridiculous it is that a handsome man like you is not in love. What is wrong?'

Charles poured out his soul to her. He told her about a young girl he had been mad about last summer, the lovemaking in the attic, and how she had gone off with a boy from the ballet.

'I know all of that,' she said. 'It was the little girl from the chocolate shop.' He looked embarrassed, but she took hold of his arm firmly and stared straight into his eyes. 'She was a charming girl. I went to the shop myself to take a look at her. Everyone knew about her.'

'They were all laughing at me?' he groaned.

'Don't be a snob. I was a laundry girl and a tailoress myself, you silly boy. Love makes no distinctions between the classes.'

Charles passed the room, puffing nervously on a cigarette. 'I treated her badly, I'm afraid,' he admitted. 'I only thought of myself. We made marvellous love, but sometimes I was like a beast. I didn't care how she felt.'

He was tortured with images of the small attic and his ravishing attacks on the limp, pliant girl. He had sometimes sat on a chair with his eyes closed and commanded her to pleasure him, and then gone off to a smart lunch with his society friends, leaving her alone and unsatisfied. How often, too, she must have gone hungry because he was ashamed to be seen in restaurants with her. He thought, as well, how greedy he had been, in what a hurry to enter her the moment he came to her room. He wondered if she had been in pain on account of him.

'And then?' Bernadette enquired.

'You know everything, Bernie. I might as well tell you and get it over with,' Charles said simply. 'It was the American girl. I thought I was pretty hot, but, my God, she nearly finished me off. It's hard for a man to say this but I just couldn't keep up with her, she was so sex-crazed. The truth is, she sickened me.'

'*Mon cher garcon*,' Bernadette murmured, 'there is a parable here: it is a question always of two minds and bodies, two sets of needs, two hungers . . .' her voice trailed off. After a moment she began again. 'My darling Sophie is in rapture with your good friend Arthur. They are soul mates. My friend Sabine, who thought she would never be loved, is ravished by that crazy Russian dancer. I myself am lucky to have my darling Marcel. We are a true pair. You on the contrary, used the little Angelique as a masturbatory article. I will say no more. And then the huge American girl used you in the same way. You were the abuser and then the abused, *non*? Soon you will find a girl who is your equal in every way, and I mean that only in a sexual sense.'

While Charles pondered these words of wisdom, she wrestled with the idea of revealing to him the secret of the garden room. Both she and Sophie had been privileged to observe, after the initial hurried play in the shower, the most tender lovemaking scenes of the Scottish aristocrats Cynthia and Ian. How instructive that could be, she considered, what a manual of technique he would gain. But no, she decided, it would be a betrayal of the vicomte's wishes. Instead she decided that if she could organise such harmonious arrangements for Marcel, Arthur and Dhokouminsky, she could do the same for Charles, and when he left to return to town she began to consult her telephone book.

It was a few minutes after midnight when Yves, the vicomtesse's boot boy, stole down the corridor and let himself into Mariettes' room. Everyone in the house had retired late because Bernadette and Sophie had given a small dinner party for Vera Lidova which had got rather out of hand. The ballerina was eventually detached from Marcel's lap. She had been raving drunkenly about his couture creations for hours, and it was getting tedious as everyone had to rise early the next morning. Arthur was expected at midday, and there was much to do.

The Corsican maid stirred in her bed crossly and pleaded to be left alone. After all they must be the first to rise in the morning, and she was tired. But through half-closed eyes she watched Yves drop his trousers. The moonlight coming in the window illuminated his half erect apparatus, and then his chunky body, when he tore off his shirt. Involuntarily she licked her lips with a moist tongue. From that moment on there could be no return.

Yves peeled back the coverlet and stared at Mariette's marble white breasts. They seemed even larger when she lay, like this, on her back than when she was constricted in her uniform dress and apron. Even in the darkened room he could see the trace of blue veins that patterned the skin, and the brownish aureoles that encircled her nipples. He leaned over and pressed his lips into the creamy flesh of the mounds, and ran his tongue around the little pointed protuberances which hardened to his touch.

Her legs stretched out in the bed and her feet arched with the pleasure. She turned her head and saw that his pendulous tool now throbbed up and down, thickening in girth by the second.

He climbed on the bed, hurrying before his member became completely erect, and squatted on his knees over her chest. Taking his proud possession in his hand he squeezed a drop of his jissom on to each of her upstanding nipples and drew circles with the tip of the organ in the lubricant. She moaned, but he placed a hand over her mouth and begged her in whispers to be quiet. Sophie's new maid was installed in the next attic room, and the walls were paper thin.

He placed his hands underneath her buttocks, kneading the flesh for a moment and drew her further down the bed so that he had enough headroom to lie over her with his member between her ample breasts. He held them together close to his gristle and throbbed a silent message to them, pressing them in time to the muscular surges which coursed through his now rigidly stiff piece. When he moved his pelvis, the member slid between the two mounds easily, as her cleavage was now well moistened with his flow of love-juice. Between his abdomen and the soft flesh which engulfed his organ, the bulbous head moved in and out of its casing of foreskin, causing a sensation to the frenum which was so delightfully moving that a long stream of emission coursed outwards, every muscular contraction bringing fresh pulses of the hot liquid to pour over Mariette's skin as far as the nape of her neck.

The power of Yves' orgasm enthraled her and she was in no way disappointed that it was premature. She knew that the thick member would stay erect as long as she were still interested in its function.

As he slid his body downwards in a slow tantalising fashion, edging a few centimetres at a time, her thighs parted in anticipation. When first the hairy scrotum and then the thick organ passed over the bush of her pubis, she writhed ecstatically and clenched at his firm buttocks in an agony of desire, wishing for the pumping action she adored to begin. But he rested at the point where the tip of his member touched the throbbing little button where her very libido seemed to be centred.

He pressed with small stabbing thrusts, and circled his hips, meantime massaging her breasts and sucking at all parts of her neck or mouth until she was in a delirium of sensuous fever. She begged him to enter and although she spoke *sotto voce*, he folded both of his palms over her mouth when he detached himself briefly, and by arching, eased the iron rod she desired into the awaiting passage.

Even though her lips were covered, a long gasp escaped. He lay prone without movement, whispering urgent instruction to her to be silent. The conspiracy added to the rich enjoyment of the moment, and the pulsating energy of the trapped organ beat its own message. He marvelled at the silkiness of the hot chamber and the titillating sensations like electric shocks that emanated from her interior and trickled the length of his stem.

The house was completely still and quiet. There was only

the sound of their agitated breathing. He dipped his tongue deep into her mouth and sucked hard. It was as if he wished to devour her. She was ravished, and spent in a long series of waves that thrashed through her body and rocked round his perfectly still, trapped organ.

When he began a pelvic thrust of some force, moved enormously by the extent of her passion, she came again, writhing and twisting in a delirium of carnal transport. The power in her strong frame surged as she took him by the shoulders and pushed him bodily away from her. She flung herself over him and sucked greedily at the member which she had given her such transports and he gave himself up in totality to her gratitude.

Mariette remembered the first time Yves had stolen into her room, soon after she came into the employment of the house. He had been drawn towards her in a state of aroused sexual curiosity when he heard her moans from the next room. He told her how his rod had stiffened when he heard her little whimpers and sighs; sounds which could only be inspired by a happening of an erotic nature.

She had been stimulating herself when Yves, aroused by the sounds from her room, and in a priapic condition, had dared to enter her room in the hope that she would agree to amorous play. After all, what is self-abuse compared with the real thing, he—and then she, when she saw his massive organ—had asked.

Their play had gone undetected in that accommodating house. It was not that the owner, the kind vicomtesse, was careless of her charges, however. It was just that she, her husband Marcel, and their guests were far too involved in sexual dalliance themselves to be worried about what the servants got up to. It was a splendid arrangement. Of course Mimi, Sophie's new maid, had heard a few disturbing sounds in the night, because Mariette and Yves were naturally, on account of their youthful lust, bound to engage in many further bouts of erotic splendour. As the night wore on they became less inhibited, reckless one might say. Mimi was thrilled at such a clear indication that her room neighbours were having such a good time. *Eh bien*, she thought, *if the little mice next door can play like this, so can I.*

She had a plan in her head which concerned the dark, handsome chauffeur, Jean-Paul, and tactical play would begin the very next day.

The mansion was in uproar. Sophie was in a fever of excitement at the prospect of Arthur's return from England. It was six months since their marriage, six long months which he had spent working out the final part of his service as an officer of the British army.

At first Sophie had repaired to London, to be available when he had an occasional furlough, but the climate, the food and the service in the hotels had appalled her. She had telephoned Bernadette. 'I must return, my darling. I shall die otherwise. Every day there is fog or snow, or else it rains in torrents. The bath water is cold, and the soap is something terrible called carbolic. I am given awful things to eat; overcooked beef, watery cabbage, and a dreadful wedge of pudding from Yorkshire. Also here they think a woman is depraved and a seductress if she takes a glass of wine.'

And so she left her beloved and spent the winter on the Riviera. He had phoned four days ago from London, then a few hours later from Dover, then from Calais when the ferry boat arrived. The next day he called from Rouens, and the one after from Lyons. Yesterday she had listened, breathless with excitement to his call from Avignon. The progress from the land of mist and mellow fruitfulness to the blazing Cote d'Azur was almost complete. He was expected at lunch time.

M. Ratatouille, the new chef, and his staff created havoc in the kitchens. There were birds to be plucked, fish to be scaled, sauces to be glazed; roasts, vegetables, salads, tarts, and cheese platters to be prepared; wine to be brought up from the cellar, and scores of extra tasks in order to provide a proper welcome.

Monsieur Moutarde supervised the setting of the table, with orchids from Bernadette's hothouse, gleaming silver service, and buckets of champagne.

Yves, exhausted but happy from his satisfying night, was despatched to prepare the changing room suite at the side of the swimming pool, and to re-stock the bar there.

Mimi assisted Sophie with the final arrangement of the new and devastatingly expensive wardrobe she had purchased for her returning stallion; silk shirts from Italy, suits from Saville Row, shirts from Paris, colognes, emerald cufflinks, tie pins, a new cut throat razor, and a dashing malacca cane.

The bed was furnished anew with the finest cambric sheets. Sophie had placed vases of intoxicatingly scented lilies about the bedroom, arranged cheval mirrors in strategic places, and now lay soaking in her bath to await the arrival of the beautician and hairdresser who would create the final transforming effects on her person.

Sophie tingled as she recalled the amazing morning when she and her cousin had discovered the well-endowed Arthur exercising in the swimming pool and had, together, seduced him, both in and out of the water. What strength and staying power he had demonstrated, what rigidity and stamina, as he pleasured them both equally. The al fresco coupling had been followed by an afternoon in the changing rooms which were luxuriously appointed with day beds, showers, and all kinds of creature comforts.

Sophie imagined that the retired officer might well like to take her first at the scene of their initial embrace and conjugation.

The vicomtesse entered Sophie's bathroom only to excuse herself. She wanted to drive into Nice, to Marcel's boutique and pick up an ensemble she intended to wear for the luncheon party she was providing. As it was still early, there was plenty of time for the trip. She kissed her cousin, who was up to her chin in bubbles, goodbye. 'Bless you, *ma chére*,' she said fondly. 'Soon he will be here,' and with a dainty wave of a silk hanky, she was gone.

It would not be an overstatement to say that Sophie was in the grip of lurid sexual expectation. It was six months since Arthur's giant member had last penetrated her luscious body. She had been utterly faithful to her absent husband, and had not once yielded to the self-stimulation to which even the most ascetic must have occasional recourse. Even at this moment, her private parts quivered and throbbed in anticipation and her handsome breasts heaved up and down in the foaming bath water as she contemplated the joys that would assail her on Arthur's return.

Mariette could not bring much energy to the polishing and dusting tasks that had been allotted to her. She sighed often, thinking of the night she had spent under and over Yves' body; the catalogue of his inventions, and the number of times he had brought her to cataclysmic joy. He was a dear boy—thick of girth and thick of stem—and she could not wait to do it again. She crooned in tired contentment.

Mimi watched from an upper window as Jean-Paul opened the car door for Bernadette, and waved seductively with a feather duster. The chauffeur read the message in her lustrous eyes, even at that distance, and spent the time on the journey into Nice planning a few diversions to entertain her.

The beautician and the hairdresser were admitted at eleven by Moutarde. He was impressed particularly by the swaying gait of the former, and her arrogant thoroughbred looks. Her arched eyebrows shot up as she appraised his person and her tongue protruded the merest fraction from her painted mouth. The moment was brief and cruel; the butler should have known by now that there exists a species of woman whose mainspring intention in life is to tease or provoke. Such a lady gains greatly in self-esteem by arousing lust and this is why she teases so frequently. Pity the poor man who is left perspiring and hopeful when she swivels on her heel and sticks out her bottom in a movement that is artfully designed to be both erotic and insulting.

Both of the experts fussed over and pampered the scrubbed, scented and well-powdered Sophie. The *coiffure* was *soignée* and completely modern, with its sleek waves and crimped curls. Tendrils of her hair were teased into child-like wisps at the nape of her neck, softening the sophisticated, sculpted effect; and the beautician used her cosmetics with such subtlety that Sophie's complexion seemed genuinely youthful.

She was so rapt at these attentions that she did not really

notice when Moutarde lightly knocked and entered with a tray of refreshments, ostensibly to sustain the artistes in their work, but in reality the butler wanted another glimpse of the exotic beautician. In spite of the revelation of Sophie in her camiknickers and brassiére, his eyes alighted greedily on the object of his desire. She was tracing a fine line around one of Sophie's eyes at that moment, and gave Moutarde the merest sneering glance, but, fool that he was, he went on smiling: such idiots are men.

The great preparations continued, with the clock ticking towards the expected time of Arthur's arrival when Bernadette hurtled into Sophie's room. She was ablaze with anger.

'I found Marcel in the fitting room with that bitch Vera Lidova,' she screamed.

She was so furious that she seemed not to care that she was spoiling the last delicious moments of Sophie's anticipation. She was in her underwear, and his fly buttons were open,' she continued, weeping wildly into her silk hanky.

'Do you suppose they had consummated their lust, or were indeed just about to begin?' the practical Sophie asked. 'If it was the latter, they have committed no offence, darling, eh?'

It had not occurred to Bernadette that she may have arrived at Marcel's boutique just in time to stop an act of unfaithfulness. She presumed that one had been completed: *un fait accompli*.

'Ah,' she beamed, 'if you are right, perhaps they were just about to start their little deception. I can understand why. She is a wily seductress, and my husband, besides being a philanderer, is very handsome.'

'You have stopped an affair beginning,' Sophie said confidently. 'He will never dare to make love to her in the fitting room again, now he knows you are alerted and liable to pop in at any odd moment.

'Thank you, my darling,' Bernadette gurgled with pleasure. 'What a woman of the world you are. You deserve great happiness with your wonderful Arthur.'

At that moment there was a great tooting of a car horn, and raised voices of greetings down below in the courtyard.

'He is here,' they screamed, and ran downstairs and out on to the marble steps that led to the drive.

Arthur was getting wearily out of the vast car which was piled, on top and in the open trunk, with baggage and trunks, fit to bursting. A young woman was standing by his side.

'Hello darling, hello Bernadette,' he cried, rushing over to kiss his wife fervently on the mouth, and her cousin on her proferred cheeks. Sophie sank into his arms. The relief was stupendous. How she loved him. He turned and indicated the waiting young woman. 'You remember Annabelle, don't you?'

It was at that moment that Sophie fainted. Jean-Paul ran over in time to stop her falling down the steps, and it was he, assisted by Mimi at Sophie's feet, who carried her into the *grand salon* and laid her tenderly on a sofa.

The vicomtesse was outraged by Annabelle's presence. The shock arrival that had caused her cousin's fainting fit. How dare Arthur bring his ex-lover to her doorstep, she raged inwardly, and how dare Annabelle accompany him on his return.

'Leave this house immediately,' she commanded imperiously, pointing towards the massive wrought iron gates. 'Your baggage will be sent to you later.'

The distraught debutante fled, scarlet faced and weeping, ashamed at this reception.

Bernadette stalked into the house and confronted Arthur, who was on his knees patting Sophie's hands. 'How could you, you monster,' she implored.

Arthur trembled at her fury. He had no idea that she and her cousin, being guardians of the key to the secret garden room, had observed him ravish the besotted English girl last year when she visited the guest apartment. They had seen every detail of their lovemaking, tender and explosive by turn, multi-orgasmic and prolonged. That was before he had parted with Annabelle, preferring to comfort Sophie. The poor girl had returned to England. He had not seen her since, until they met for the car trip to the South.

Sophie's eyes opened with difficulty. She looked deathly pale, and began to cry inconsolably. In her delirium, she too had a vision of Arthur at Annabelle's knees, with his head buried in her fur, and then of the debutante's lips caressing the tip of that massive organ which now rightfully belonged to her, his wife who had waited so long for his return. Images of the happenings seen through the two-way mirror and the peephole surged through her brain. She also imagined frantic, lusty couplings in every hotel in which Arthur and Annabelle had stayed on the journey through France.

Arthur kissed her tear-stained eyes. He was perplexed at such a home-coming, and desolated by his wife's sudden collapse. But she pushed him away, her bosom trembling and heaving with emotion.

'I thought you loved me but you have come here with your little English hussy. You have made love to her for days. Yes! That is why you took so long to arrive. And these last six months while I waited in agony for you, she has been your mistress.' Sophie turned her head and sobbed violently.

'I say chaps, there's been a frightful misunderstanding,' said Arthur, rising to his feet. 'Annabelle's married, you know, to my brother, actually. We're all great chums, its jolly super, and all that.' He laughed nervously. 'Nigel couldn't come down yet. He's engaged on business. So when they suggested I bring Annabelle, I thought, jolly hockey sticks, why the devil not? She's a super gal.'

The mist in the ladies' minds began to vanish. This was clearly a case of that almost incestuous interbreeding for which the English aristocracy were framed. Arthur, tired of Annabelle's wimpish charms, had passed her on to his frustrated brother. Naturally, after such a takeover, his brotherly love, a quality for which the English were also celebrated, would automatically rule out temptation between Arthur and his ex-lover. *In a curious way, the British manage to settle their amours with a sanguinity that the hotheaded French should envy*, Bernadette thought.

The ex-officer stood perplexed as these reasonings and others beset the practical and resourceful French ladies. Sophie dabbed her eyes and looked at him reproachfully.

'How do I know that you still don't love her?' she asked.

'I will show you how, he said firmly as he hoisted her in a fireman's lift and ran lightly up the stairs with her on his shoulder. 'Like this.

He threw her on the beautifully prepared bed. His nostrils were full of the scent of great vases of lilies and the costly perfumes which she had anointed her body. He cared not for the cost of the garments he tore from her body, nor the dishevelment of the careful *coiffure*, or the onslaught he made on her carefully painted face.

'Do you believe I love you, desperately, without reserve; that I love no-one else; that I have been faithful to you for a whole year; that Annabelle and I, for heaven's sake, we parted a year ago, are just good friends? Do you believe me?'

'Why should I?' Sophie asked, with just a hint of her normal coquetry returning.

'Because I am an officer and a gentleman,' he replied.

'You are no longer an officer,' Sophie pouted, a little more teasingly.

'But I am a gentleman, and what's more, an English one, and surely you have heard that an Englishman's word is his bond?'

At that moment his wonderful English organ sank into her depths, and made music that would have moved a packed congregation to tears.

Bernadette, meantime, had retired to her small *salon* where M. Moutarde poured a fortifying drink for her. She pondered the problematic nature of love for a while, and then rang a bell and sent for the chef.

'Monsieur Ratatouille,' she said, smiling graciously, 'my cousin Sophie, Madame Forbes-Dalrymple apologises. She is a little indisposed, and also her husband, Monsieur Arthur is a little *fatigué* from the journey from England. I do not wish your splendid lunch to be spoiled by waiting. Please serve it to the staff, with my compliments.'

Chapter Five

Lidova was not at all put out that she had been discovered, almost in flagrante delicto, by the vicomtesse in the dressing room with Marcel. If anything, scandal added to her reputation, and she was hoping that if the Greek millionaire Vossoudossoulos heard about it he would be jealous and try to reclaim her. For he had been very cool when they had dinner together in an intimate restaurant in Antibes a few evenings before. It was odd how he had not responded to her usual smouldering looks and wilful gropings under the table.

Mere sexual satisfaction was not enough for the great ballerina. If that were all she required, there were plenty of lusty boys in the Ballets Russes who could more than satisfy her needs; what she needed desperately was cash, or at least, expensive presents. Borzdoff was a stingy soul, hard pressed to pay up usually, and whenever she asked for a rise, he simply threw his hands in the air and told her there were lots of other principals available, which was true: emigré Russians who had fled the Revolution were dancing all over Europe and America.

Lidova had considered simple prostitution in Paris, but turned the idea down. The pickings might be good, but to be a successful lady of the night, she would have to give the job her full attention, and she loved dancing too much. No, her legs were meant to be in the air, and her feet on pointe. A prima ballerina could not surrender—she would fight to the end.

It was while she was in this truculent mood, and worried about her bill at the Hotel de Paris that she came across Frederick Fanshawe and M. Rognon. They were on their way to the Casino for a flutter. They bowed low, murmuring a few delicate compliments, and asked her, if she was doing nothing, to accompany them. The great ballerina accepted graciously, but added the proviso that, as she was extremely thirsty after her practice at the *barre*, a drink first would be a good idea. A lady of her rank required champagne, Rognon surmised, and to his horror, she managed to down several bottles by herself in the bar of the Hotel. He and Fanshawe stuck to cheap aperitifs, but the bill was astronomical.

The effect on Vera was startling. She rose and gave an impromptu rendering of the Dying Swan there in the crowded lounge. Even though her costume was inappropriate (she was wearing her sable coat turbaned hat and high heeled shoes), the tragic languor and expressiveness of her arabesques and *bourées* infected everyone with such enthusiasm that they rose as one man and gave her a huge round of applause.

The success of her dance went to her head. Calling for more champagne, she led the way into the ballroom where a negro trio was playing dance music. They had reached the point of their repertoire where they concentrated on the blues from the deep south of America, and were joined by a handsome dark singer dressed in immaculate tie and tails. He sang of St. Louis and Chinatown; soulful melodies that captivated Lidova so much that she advanced on to the dance floor.

Her first move was a serpentine glide towards the singer, stretching out her incredibly elegant feet, with her hips thrust forward in her tight dress. As she vamped across, she slid off the sable, and with a careless gesture, threw it behind her. With her hands on her slim hips, she girated and bumped her behind, to the wail of the saxophone, and pouted her lips at the band with an air of total lasciviousness.

The dancers watched agog from the circle they had made round the floor. To their amazement, she slipped off one of the shoulder straps of her dress, then the other, and ran her hands down over her bosom and crotch, where they lingered while she leered provocatively. Then her fingers went to the hem of her dress and edged it up, revealing her black silk stockings and suspenders. A gasp went up from the watching crowd. Monsieur Rognon started towards her as if to restrain her, but Fanshawe held his arm.

'Don't bother. These rich bastards have come to the Riviera for fun and sex. For Christ's sake, let the bitch give 'em some.'

The music took a wilder turn. A trumpet blasted out the slow, but hypnotic beat of the blues, and the drummer beat on the cymbals with wire brushes, an insistent rhythm which Lidova took up, twisting her thighs and hips from side to side while she pulled the dress up and over her head. The crowd cheered at the sight of her camisole and drawers, vivid red satin creations which looked fantastic next to her white skin.

The music was approaching its coda; a crashing, thumping sound, which drove Lidova right up to the singer. She threw her arms round him and embraced him, rubbing her groin against his. As the band struck its final chord, she fell at his feet, her back on the floor of the rostrum, and her right leg elegantly extended vertically, with her foot accurately placed at the centre of his private parts.

The crowd, the members of the band, and the waiters went wild, stamping and clapping with huge enthusiasm. The singer drew her up to her feet and kissed her. The manager of the ballroom was inspired to send her a bottle of vintage champagne, and of course, Vera was in a state of rapture. Her transformation from classical ballerina to musical comedy vamp was complete.

M. Rognon was devastated. His knees were still trembling. She could have anything, anything at all. He must have her body, at any cost. 'She is a siren, Fanshawe, and I am lured to my fate,' he gasped, puffing nervously on a cigarette. 'What can I do?'

Frederick was unimpressed. He had often seen men in this condition before. 'Calm down, you silly old fart,' he drawled, 'you're screwy. She's half your age. Why should the goddamn hoofer take off her drawers for you?'

'Age has nothing to do with it. I adore her, I shall be her protector and keep her in the style that a great artiste deserves,' Rognon enthused. 'I have never been moved by woman in this way. She is wonderful, marvellous.' His voice trailed off as he contemplated a vision of Lidova performing for him in a similar manner in the privacy of a bedroom, and the joyful copulation that would follow.

Fanshawe glanced at him sourly. It was only a day or so ago that Rognon had been babbling like an idiot about Camille, the leonine mannequin, and the involuntary ejaculation he had enjoyed in her presence. The man's a fool, he thought. At his age he should be happy with his memories instead of paying out good cash for sex.

'What's a geriatric like you doing, getting his cock in a twist over a strumpet like her? You're mad, she'll have your guts for garters, and she'll take you for every penny you got. Come on, let's go, I'm not going to let you make a fool of yourself,' he rasped, taking hold of Rognon's arm and trying to drag him away. But the art dealer was rivetted to the spot, gazing in adoration at the ballerina, who was now surrounded by a crowd of sycophantic admirers begging for autographs. 'Come on, the bitch has already cost you a fortune,' urged Fanshawe, but Rognon had already broken from his grip and was running like a madman towards the object of his desire.

Fanshawe left in disgust and made his way to a little bar where he knew some serious drinking would be taking place. He was annoyed on two counts; first Rognon would be taken for a ride and make a fool of himself; and second, having lost every franc he possessed, he'd be no good any more for a touch, or even a round of drinks. It was a case of good money going to waste. Thank the Lord, he thought, that he himself had gotten over all that juvenile rubbish called sex. It was messy and untidy, and moreover exhausting. When he looked back at his earlier life, he was amazed that so much of his time had been spent in its pursuit. Letitia was still at it, crazy woman, running around sniffing at anything in pants, especially if it was young, Italian, and arty. The silly old tart seemed to think he didn't know about her latest affair, the nifty little stud from Florence, Paolo; but if that was the way she wanted it—playing games of hide and seek, sneaking the little bastard in and out of the hotel at all times of the day and night—well so be it, and good luck to her. He was going to have a damn good drink.

Back in the Hotel de Paris, Vera Lidova was posed cunningly at the foot of the great staircase in the main lobby. The nonchalance of her demeanour was artfully contrived, and came from a lifetime's study of body language. Her long eyelashes were lowered demurely, and the crook of her black-stockinged knee seemed innocent enough. The sable coat was draped along the lower stair tread, its casual treatment seeming to represent that its owner was so rich she had forgotten its value.

Rognon eyed this vision with a lascivious gleam, licking his tongue over his bristly moustache.

'Darling, I had a wonderful time,' she said, pouting her cerise painted lips, 'but you know, even great ballerinas must go to bed. Take me to the lift.'

Rognon shook as he escorted her through the lobby. She leaned on his arm, and he smelled her luscious perfume, heady and musky. The lift was crowded. She pressed closely up to him, her pudenda in close contact with his groin. He quivered as a hand stole into his trouser pocket and played with his small change.

'You very kind, Rognon,' she breathed, 'so generous, you make Vera feel very happy.' His member rose to the occasion with gratitude and throbbed its message to the inserted fingers. 'Vera very tired, darling. Must rest before ballet class tomorrow,' she whispered in his ear. When the gates of the lift opened at her floor she said, 'Meet me at stage door at one o'clock tomorrow, you nice man. We have good time, *non?*'

In a trice she was gone, leaving a trace of her scent behind her. Rognon's head was reeling. He felt three metres high as he walked back to his home, and dreamed that night of the explosion to come.

It was a brilliant day, the Riviera at its finest. Mother Nature had done her very best here, thought Rognon, as he promenaded in his best suit along the principal boulevard. He stopped at a florist and bought a giant bouquet of gladioli. The colours were gaudy and gay, the perfect reflection of his mood.

No-one was walking alone, he observed to himself; everyone was in pairs, strolling hand in hand. They had obviously all been engaged in the pursuit of love; maybe even that very morning after rising. The thought of so much lovemaking going on in every hotel and rented villa stimulated him vastly.

He imagined also that behind every set of closed shutters, the remaining residents of Monaco were similarly occupied. Lust was everywhere, he thought, and looked about him for further evidence. Yes, here on a bench in the municipal gardens a young man had his arms around a girl's waist, and quite clearly, his tongue was down her throat. And there, another had a hand across his partner's bottom, no doubt in an attempt to stimulate her to further activity after lunch. Overhead, leaning over a balcony, a brazen pair still in their night clothes, with their hair still ruffled from the night's excesses, were fondling each other as they looked out at the day.

His turn was coming shortly, he reckoned, with a tightening in his loins, and Vera would not be displeased with him as a lover. It was so long since he had been involved in regular lovemaking with a permanent partner, that he had plenty of the essential essences stored up to satisfy her. Yes, life was good. Why, only this morning he had sold two large canvasses by a young painter, Gavroche. The stupid boy was so grateful to have his work exhibited that he had settled for ludicrously small prices, and he, Rognon had made ten times those amounts without any effort at all. The pictures were so inspiringly erotic, they had sold like hot *gateaux* as soon as they had been put in the window. So now his wallet was stuffed with francs, he could afford to take Lidova to a very impressive lunch. Not so much that she would only want to sleep afterwards, he reminded himself, but just enough to whet her appetite for a little dessert with him afterwards in the Hotel de Paris.

He was admitted to the stage door entrance of the Opera House by an obsequious little man wearing pince-nez.

'Madame Lidova say's, sir, that she will be down in about ten minutes. She is taking a shower,' he said, with the hint of a leer. 'Please take a seat in the *foyer de la danse*.' He indicated a practice room nearby where the morning class had just ended.

Rognon was fascinated by the sweating dancers. Some were on the floor in splits; others had their legs pressed in a stretch so high up the walls of the room that their feet were much higher than their heads. In the centre of the room a male dancer was practising lifts with one of the *corps de ballet*. The most spectacular, and to Rognon, the most interesting, was a one-handed lift. The boy's right palm, inserted under the girl's crotch, with his thumb, placed for balance, directly over the area of her clitoris, was extended skywards. The girl sat cross legged on this hand, seemingly oblivious to the sensation, or that of the boys fingertips being pressed into the crack between her buttocks. *My God,* Rognon thought, *these dancers must have an interesting personal life.* He doubted very much that he could do anything so athletic, but he anticipated that Vera would show him a few interesting things.

Two girls were gossiping nearby. He strained to listen over the excruciating sounds of the pianist who was practising in the far corner, trying to make sense of the latest score by Mr Stravinsky that the new choreographer was to turn into a ballet.

'And do you know, he did it right there and then—he was only wearing a jock-strap. He tore it off, and had her on a pile of tutus on a skip behind the backcloth,' one of the girls said breathlessly.

'Not in the middle of a performance?' the other asked incredulously.

'Oh, yes, that Dhokouminsky is a dirty old man. It was *Les Sylphides* that night. They'd just got to the prelude when he had his way with her, and she couldn't shout out, or hit him, or anything. So just you watch out. Don't go behind the cloth in a show, whatever you do.'

The salacious tale warmed Rognon, as did the spectacle of all the girls in their semi-transparent tights and bust-revealing tops. As the legs flailed all round him, he thought of the joys to come with Vera and by the time she appeared, his member was ramrod stiff with anticipation. He beamed, and handed her the gladioli which she accepted gracefully. 'Darling,' she said, bestowing on him several damp kisses, which he took to convey a meaning more sensuous than platonic. 'I am ready. I am in your hands. Take me where you will.'

Outside he hailed a taxi. Her hand was immediately on his knee, and her mouth at his ear. She told him fondly how happy she was to have found a new friend.

'Boys in the ballet so boring,' she said. 'Only thinking of dance.' Her fingers strayed further up his thigh. 'You very nice man. Me, I like older type, more mature, you know.'

Rognon's rod almost burst with pride. He stirred against her hand and slid his bottom along the seat until her fingers rested on the hard lump in his trousers.

'My, my what a big boy, and so quick. Maybe you much younger than I think, she murmured, fluttering her eyelashes.

'You are so ravishing, how could any man not get into this state when you are so near,' he said, his voice thick with emotion. 'I adore you, may I kiss you?'

'Just little on the cheek, darling, as Lidova must look good for public. No mess with lipstick.'

So Rognon leaned over and kissed her tenderly where she indicated and then on her slim neck, which she did not seem to mind either—especially as her fingers had closed in a vice-like grip on his tortured shaft. He was in a delirium by the time they reached the restaurant, and his draws were just a little sticky from the liquid she had caused to flow. Rognon gazed into her eyes as he adjusted the bulge, and hoped it would not be long before they were in a more suitable location. She held his arm tightly, with that fervour that lovers reserve for each other, and insisted that they dine in the small private room at the rear.

'I want only to be with you, darling,' she whispered.

Lidova could not contain her excitement when she saw the menu, especially as such divine smells were issuing from the kitchens. There was a choice of grilled lobster thermidor, fillets of sea bass with broiled fennel, squid with ink sauce, sole veronique, and many other seafood specialities. To follow, marinaded venison, breasts of pidgeon, *chateaubriand aux truffes*, and saddle of hare cooked in Beaujolais.

She chose a mixed platter of fish and crustaceans, reasonably surmising that it would give her something of everything, which it did. Rognon, who had ordered a simple fillet of trout, gasped at the size of Vera's dish, and was desolated to think what torpor she would suffer afterwards.

'Think of your wonderful figure,' he pleaded, but to no avail.

The platter was demolished at speed, and a dozen more oysters ordered in a twinkling of the eye. Soon she was tucking in to a large bowl of *fraises du bois*, liberally topped with *crème chantilly*, and then a fat slice of chocolate and almond gateau.

She was wise enough to keep his crotch on the boil between mouthfuls however, and by the time liqueurs and coffee were served, she had sneaked his fly buttons open. The large menu card propped open on the table gave some cover from the prying eyes of the waiters, and of course, in the private room, there were no other diners.

Vera wiped her mouth with her napkin with a satisfied grin. 'Food makes me sexy,' she giggled as her hand slid into his flies.

Her fingers went immediately to the tip of Rognon's organ, and thrilled it with her exploration. The juices she found there were warm and viscous. She rubbed them around in little circles, each tiny movement sending tingling vibrations through the stem and into the heaving thick muscle between his legs.

As she applied these ministrations, she drank from her liqueur glass using her free hand, licking her lips lasciviously between sips. When it was empty, with her eyes fixed on Rognon's, she dipped the tip of her tongue inside the glass and wiggled it in the most suggestive manner. The lubricated touch of her fingers, now tweaking at his frenum, and the simulation of oral sex with the last dregs of chartreuse, drove Rognon to an extreme. He had barely finished a magnificent discharge of his precious element when the head waiter came in with the bill.

Rognon was so glazed with partly satiated lust that he did not care if he seemed flushed and perspiring and, after all it, was warm enough in the enclosed little room for him to have achieved such a rosy glow.

'Have another liqueur,' he urged, wishing for another round of pleasure. He pushed her hand further down until it enclosed his scrotum. She could begin there this time, he thought.

'Oh, no, darling, we must go. I am expected at Marcel's. Come.' With that she stalked imperiously from the restaurant, nodding to the other diners in the principal room, some of whom rose to acknowledge her, and hailed a passing cab.

Rognon had fastened his buttons in a trice and was soon pawing at her breasts in the back seat.

'Thank you, wonderful lunch, darling,' she said, giving him a seductive glance, for she knew what a bill she was going to run up that afternoon.

Arlette welcomed Rognon and Lidova at Marcel's boutique. She could hardly keep a straight face. It was only a few days since Bernadette had insisted on interrupting Lidova's fitting with the grand couturier and found him in a compromising position with the almost naked ballerina.

'Marcel is not here today,' she said, smiling, 'he has business in Paris.'

'No matter,' Vera winked roguishly, 'another time I see him. This is my friend Monsieur Rognon. He comes to help me choose some underwear. He has the good taste,' the ballerina murmured, nudging the chief *vendeuse*. 'He like only expensive things.'

'I expect, monsieur, that you are expert in the matter of ladies' underwear,' Arlette breathed, only too willing to join in the conspiracy because her main earnings came from commission. 'Please sit here, sir, and I will see what I can find to please a person of such refined taste.'

She led him to a small gilded couch, and lingered long enough for him to take in the cleavage between her full breasts, and the seductive tones of her perfume. 'Perhaps it would be a good idea to draw the blind and even better to lock the door,' she said, patting Rognon's hand, 'and then there will be no distraction.'

These matters attended to, she went behind the counter and, opening the drawers, lifted out many gauzy and wispy small garments of silk and lace, taffeta and crêpe de Chine. They made a charming collection; pale pastel shades mixed with ivory and cream, with dramatic black contrasts, and scarlet slashes of colour. Vera came to sit close to Rognon's side. 'A wonderful shop,' she confided in his ear.

Arlette lifted the garments one by one. Each was a minor masterpiece; an individual and enticing piece of underwear which any lady of style would envy. Lidova clapped her hands together in delight, and Rognon breathed excitedly, thinking of her wearing such creations. Arlette, thinking of her percentage, was suddenly inspired.

'But Madame Lidova, Monsieur Rognon has no idea what they look like on. *Attends un moment.*'

She darted behind a screen and came out a few moments later. Rognon was shocked. She seemed to be entirely naked as she strode across the floor and stood before him. 'I shall model for you,' she said brightly.

On closer inspection, he found that though she presented a wildly appealing picture, long legs, full high bust and well shaped posterior, in fact the bounds of decency were not totally broken. She wore a G-string of silk over her pubis, and two cunning florets of lace covered her nipples.

Arlette had, in fact, performed this modelling service on many occasions, though it was her clever practice to let her customers think it was a personal favour, done out of kindness. Rognon was in seventh heaven.

She slipped into the first outfit, gliding silk camiknickers up her thighs with practised ease, and paraded about the room, adding little wriggles as she turned, stroking the silk with her finger tips and exclaiming how fine the fabric was. On the second tour, in a slit petticoat of *eau de nil* crêpe, she invited the art dealer to slide a palm down her thigh. 'So supple, and intoxicating, *non*?' she laughed. By the third promenade, this time revealing a transparent *peignoir* of pale blue chiffon, trimmed with maribou, Rognon's disturbed organ visibly throbbed against his suit.

'I'll take the lot,' he cried. 'Vera, you will look divine in them.' He turned to Arlette, 'Thank you madame, it has been a privilege. Please send everything to Madame Lidova at the Hotel de Paris, and post the bill to me at the Gallerie Rognon.' Vera hugged him. 'What a kind darling. I adore you.' She smothered his face with a dozen kisses and discreetly pinched his behind. 'Come with me to hotel, I must take bath before photographer comes.

Rognon staggered to his feet. He was exhausted already from the giddy round of pleasure, and of course he had no idea what a dance Vera was going to lead him later. The art dealer could not remember when he was last in such a sexual turmoil. He had to trot almost to keep up with the ballerina. Her swaying hips went ahead, tantalising him with the athletic buttocks he wished to get his hands on. All the excitement of the day, the constant stimulation, had conspired to make his private parts so relentlessly aggravated and distended, that he felt he would explode unless she granted him the opportunity of another flow of semen.

She burst through the revolving doors of the Hotel de Paris and was accosted immediately by the irate under-manager, Monsieur Vouvray, who had been lying in wait for her. Waving a large sheaf of bills under her nose he quite rudely said, 'Madame Lidova, the management of the hotel has been very forbearing, very forbearing indeed. However I must tell you that unless you pay your account forthwith, you will be required to pack your bags and leave.'

She laughed brazenly. 'What nonsense, how ridiculous! I, the great ballerina, Vera Lidova, international star, will not be told by idiot of office who cannot add two and two. Send for my friend Monsieur Pamplemousse right away. Vera Lidova only speak to top dog.'

This was refused of course. Pamplemousse had a weakness for artistes. If he had had his way the actors, concert pianists and opera singers who ran up huge bills in the establishment and then found they could not pay, would have bankrupted the hotel years ago. So Vouvray was put in special charge and was notorious for instant expulsions.

Vera started to cry. 'But season not started. No proper money yet, darling,' she wailed. 'No money, no pay.'

Rognon was aghast at this treatment of his beloved. 'How dare you, you little upstart,' he yelled. 'This lady, who is my protégée, has the world at her feet. Apologise instantly. Give me the bill, you shall have your filthy cash at once.' Opening his wallet he threw thousands of francs into the air. 'Grovel for it,' Rognon screamed, 'and don't forget the change.'

The gibbering under-manager fell to his knees to gather up the bills. Placed where he was, at Lidova's feet, it looked like an act of homage, which pleased her enormously.

'Come darling,' she laughed light-heartedly. 'I love man who is knowing how to deal with peasants.' They marched arm in arm to the lift. She was elated to have been bought further time, and he thought that his time had come.

In her suite she threw off her clothes and ran a bath, singing gaily.

'You scrubbing back,' she giggled,' and then toes, *non*?'

The sight of her taut body and marble white skin sent Rognon into further ecstasies. As he dabbled with the sponge and the highly scented soap, lascivious thoughts teemed in his brain. When she stood up in the foaming water and offered him her breasts, he stood for a moment in silent adoration before he commenced the cleansing of the lovely mounds. Vera closed her eyes, acting out the part, swaying slightly in time to his massage.

'So good,' she said dreamily, and then pushed his hand down towards her private parts, taking care to open her legs just wide enough to allow the sponge in between them.

The effect on Rognon was devastating. His other hand went to his flies in order to release his pounding organ from the constriction of his trousers. Vera, however, noticed, and took hold of the hand, slid it around her buttocks and let it play for a while in the cleavage between them. By now he was in his sixth heaven, and desperate to be in his seventh.

'My God,' she exclaimed, seizing a towel and leaping from the bath, 'it is so late. Newspaper photographer will be crazy with me. Come darling, and thank you so much for helping.'

In a trice she was dressed. After years of quick changes in the theatre she was an expert, of course, and before Rognon had got his breath back, they were in the lift on their way back to the lobby.

'Very worried about what to wear,' she moaned, and explained that important international newspapers would be represented at the photo-call. 'Must be looking good, like star,' she said, twinkling.

Vouvray came forward, humbly, and bowed low, to hand Rognon the change from the bill. '*A votre service, monsieur, et milles pardons.*'

Rognon gave him an icy stare. When he turned, Lidova was

gone from his side. He found her at the counter of the hotel's boutique, gazing with unalloyed joy at the rich display of jewellery.

'Is perfect,' she murmured, as she stole a hand round his waist in the manner of a practised lover. 'Is just what Vera needs to be glamorous star.'

She was staring transfixed at a set of rubies; a necklace, earrings, and bracelet. They were indeed beautiful. Rognon was moved by the lustrous appeal of her pleading eyes and the pressure of her fingertips which were digging into his flesh.

'You shall have them,' he declared. 'Nothing but the best for my little treasure. Mademoiselle, wrap them up immediately.'

Lidova kissed him fervently on the mouth and on his neck, and made small intimate gushing sounds in his ear. One of her hands even stole down to stroke his hard protuberance for an indiscreet moment. The *vendeuse* was unimpressed by this lewd behaviour. She had seen it all before.

Their whirlwind progress took them, after Rognon surrendered the last contents of his wallet and a further vast amount by way of a cheque, to the theatre. He was denied entrance to her dressing room, and waited feverishly for her return.

On the stage, a simple rostrum had been set up and all the lights switched on. A crowd of journalists and photographers awaited the star. Her entrance was stunning. She had chosen to wear the tutu she used in the celebrated *Don Quixote pas de deux*; a brilliant scarlet affair decorated with thousands of gleaming sequins. At her throat she wore the new necklace; the wide bracelet sparkled at her wrist, and the pendant earrings completed the entrancing costume.

Rognon's heart felt fit to burst with pride and lust when the assembled crowd burst into spontaneous applause. On an impulse, he planted a kiss on her cheek. She turned on him with an icy stare.

'Please not to spoil make-up,' she glared.

Rognon retreated to the side of the stage to watch the photocall. The short rebuff did nothing to cool his ardour. He could only think that soon the divine creature would be his.

The cameras flashed and popped. Lidova was truly magnificent, every inch a star and a glamour queen. Soon her picture would be on news stands all over the globe.

A reporter from the *New York Times* kissed her hand reverentially. 'Madame Lidova, my compliments, and best wishes for the season. It has been an honour to meet you. I think you will like our banner headline when it appears . . . "Prima Ballerina of the Twentieth Century".'

After the photographers had all left Rognon and Vera found themselves alone on the darkened stage.

'I am so proud of you,' he said. 'I worship you. I adore you.'

Then, almost in a grovelling manner, 'Please may we go back to the hotel. We have a lot of catching up to do.'

'What do you mean?' she asked, with a cool look.

'I am desperate,' he whimpered.

'What for?' Vera asked casually, as if they were strangers.

'Your body,' Rognon pleaded.

'Nonsense, my friend. Dancer's body is sacred. Only for performance,' she said, with the utmost coldness.

'But I love you,' Rognon gasped, almost in tears.

'Love is what makes go the world round, darling,' she laughed lightly. 'Oh, go round, yes. I must practise my *fouettes*. Please to stand aside.'

Rognon stood in the shaded space of the wings and watched as she placed her feet in the fifth position, and after the correct preparation, whirled into a perfect set of the thirty two spins that is the greatest test, to this day, for a classical dancer. And as she turned at breathtaking speed, the rubies glittered and flashed, as harshly and as cruelly as the pain which burned in Rognon's heart.

Chapter Six

Life at the mansion was sublime. Things had returned to normal quickly after the brouhaha caused by Arthur's tactless behaviour in giving a lift to Annabelle.

Sophie, on reflection, thought that his impetuous and generous offer to escort the debutante to the Riviera—even as far as Bernadette's doorstep—betrayed a charming naiveté. The ex-officer was even more adorable in her eyes now; especially as he had ravished her so deliciously when she had recovered from her unfortunate fainting fit—three times, actually—twice with his boots on.

'I told you so,' Bernadette said. 'I never doubted his honour for one moment. Arthur is such a divine boy.' By now she had conveniently forgotten her rage on the morning of Arthur's arrival, and even the horrible scene she had made when she suspected Marcel of a dalliance with Vera Lidova in the changing room of his boutique.

Marcel had very nicely explained the state of his unbuttoned trousers on the day she had stalked into the fitting session. The new tailor who had supplied the particular suit had obviously been economising on button thread, or had not insisted on a rigorous enough quality control. Either way, missing buttons had resulted, as he found out when he went to relieve himself in the *cabinet de toilette*. There had been no time to get a seamstress to repair the damage before the great ballerina swept in to try on lingerie. Such a great artiste had to be attended to immediately, regardless of the state of his dress.

Bernadette had to agree. It was this sympathetic and caring attitude, and professional expertise, that endeared Marcel to the breasts of ladies of the Cote d'Azur who could afford his ravishing creations. Moreover, Marcel had been even more zealous in his attentions to the vicomtesse since the unfortunate episode; bringing her amusing little gifts and posies of flowers, in fact behaving like a young, ardent new lover.

How she loved the clockwork monkey which beat on a drum when wound up, and the spangled fairy which turned on the lid of an enchanting musical box; the tune, a Strauss waltz, reminded Bernadette of the night at a grand charity ball when Marcel had proposed. How could one have doubts about the faithfulness of a man who was so divinely sentimental and thoughtful?

Marcel, on his part, breathed a few sighs of relief, and vowed to be a little more discreet in his amorous life. He had too much to lose if she discovered even half of his misdeeds.

Arthur was blissfully happy; no more square-bashing orders to make, no route marches, bivouacs, canteen food, itchy khaki uniforms, and the rest. He contemplated a life of harmonious luxury with the *beau monde*, supported completely by his accommodating new wife, who was totally captivated by his good looks and his generously-sized genitals. All he had to do, besides being charming (and that came naturally), was to keep his physical attributes in good shape. His general appearance and its upkeep presented no difficulties, since he could now afford as many fashionable clothes as he desired, as well as the attentions of the best masseurs, manicurists and hairdressers.

As for the other department, he had been endowed by nature with an organ whose size and capabilities were of truly outstanding quality. The libido necessary to make the giant phallus spring to life had always been abundantly present. In fact, his massive organ seemed to have a life of its own. Indeed, now he was having daily intercourse with his curvaceous bride, the lusty Englishman, at the height of his sexual prime, found that each encounter in the bedroom, or wherever, increased his appetite, rather than diminished it as some may think. Just as some men are compulsive eaters, or even worse, drinkers, Arthur was committed by his glands to a life of persistent love-making.

The only blot on Arthur's landscape, at the moment, was his friend Charles—he worried about him, as did Bernadette. Since her conversation with him in her small *salon*, she had been racking her brains, wondering how she could help resolve his situation.

The foursome discussed the subject over dinner one evening.

'Poor boy, he needs a lover,' Sophie said. She was so happy, she wanted everyone to have a similarly stimulating relationship. 'He is handsome and charming . . .'

'And very sexy,' Arthur interrupted.

'Aren't all men?' questioned Marcel, winking at him.

Bernadette paused for a moment, serving the soufflé. The others watched anxiously, as the confection was in imminent danger of collapse.

'His ardour needs to be tamed by a strong woman,' she opined, thoughtfully. 'It seems to me that he is a greedy boy when it comes to love. He does not care to receive the same treatment he hands out himself—as when the American Amazon devastated him.'

'She nearly killed him,' Arthur laughed, but secretly he began to think that an encounter with Edith might be amusing—and challenging.

'Lady Letitia was once enamoured, or rather, besotted by him last year,' Sophie ventured.

'Ah, that stupid woman is now madly in love with that horrible little Italian gigolo, Paolo,' Bernadette countered. 'One hears that she is quite flagrant about the sordid affair. Even her husband knows about it.'

'He must be relieved,' laughed Marcel, 'she gets crazier every day.'

The vicomtesse remembered the telephone call from Sabine asking for help. She had supplied young Alain as curative therapy, and liberated the lady. She must make a similar inventive gesture to help the young Englishman. 'Excuse me for a moment. I must make a telephone call,' she murmured.

When she came back the soufflé had been demolished. '*N'importe quoi*,' she said matter of factly. 'Marie-Therese has come to the rescue. She will meet Charles. She is intrigued, because she has noticed him already and is, shall we say, somewhat attracted. We have agreed on several points. First, he is not to be told that we four are conspirators. Second, she will report daily to us on her progress. Third, she will be extremely strict, and allow him no favours—he must earn her affection if he wishes to make love to her. Lastly, although she will enjoy the game, she will make every effort to remain calm, and even though she enjoys his attentions, absolutely forbid herself to fall in love. Well, what do you think?'

The other three applauded.

'Capital, capital,' cried Arthur, 'what a jape! I say, it's going to be a giggle.'

'Intriguing,' enthused Sophie.

'You are a genius, darling,' Marcel said, embracing the vicomtesse. 'No-one knows more about the machinations of love. Let's drink a toast to Marie-Therese and Charles, and the sport we're going to have following their adventures.'

'Bravo!' they all cried.

Marie-Therese, although a part-time member of Bernadette's circle, was a mysterious figure. It was thought that she was enormously wealthy, and she was certainly descended from one of France's most distinguished old families, whose members included several important scholars and diplomats. She lived in seclusion in a large rambling converted farmhouse in the hills above Monte Carlo with a single servant; a devoted housekeeper who had been her childhood nurse. There she indulged in her favourite pastimes; she was an enthusiastic student of astronomy and astrology and an expert cellist. In the evenings, she played magic music on the valuable old instrument, elegiac and profound sonatas and cadenzas which echoed eerily through the house. Then, in the highest chamber, she would extend the large telescope which she had installed, through a sliding section of the roof, and gaze with rapture at the firmament of the stars.

Her few appearances on the coast invariably caused interest. Marie-Therese had no interest in the prevailing fashions and wore voluminous skirts and a cloak of unrelieved black, topped by a wide brimmed black velour hat. Her long raven hair was pinned into a classical bun at the nape of her neck, unadorned, and she wore no jewellery save for a large gold ring inscribed with the signs of the zodiac. Her features were of outstanding beauty, and her voice was richly harmonious, with a deep timbre which fascinated every man she addressed. Some said that she had powers of clairvoyancy, others that she was a witch. It was certainly an unnerving experience to have her dark eyes burn into one, and watch the slow seductive smile hover round her mouth. It seemed as if she could read into a man's soul, and there were many who wishes she would. But her discretion was such that no-one knew if she had ever taken a lover and that made her even more intriguing. There was hardly a man who did not want to be the first.

Bernadette's commission had captured her interest and amused her. She thought she would begin by making a few observations, and made for the port of Villefranche where Charles was at work that day. She recognised him immediately, as she had met him twice at the mansion and had been moved, to a certain extent, by his good looks. *Nature has been almost too kind to him*, she thought as she leaned on the railing of the quay, *and he is vain as a result*.

Charles was in the process of showing a yacht to a new client. Marie-Therese noticed that he was thoroughly business-like with the man, but that he seemed to flirt with his wife; he flashed quick little smiles in her direction, took just too much care of her, placed a watchful arm around her waist as he escorted her round the deck, helped her negotiate various ropes and pieces of equipment. *He is selling his charm, not the boat.*

She took a glass of lemonade at a nearby café, and for the rest of the morning studied Charles's behaviour. He was certainly dashing and attentive, but she saw with some disdain that he took out his pocket comb and adjusted his hair at least twice, paused once to check on his appearance when it was reflected in the glass of a cabin window, and tweaked his bristly moustache. *He does not care if people find him vain, either*, she thought.

She got up and strolled a little nearer, and watched closer, screened by the newspaper she held open.

A girl ran up the gangplank. Charles kissed her on the

mouth, and laid a hand on her bottom. The girl wriggled her rump with pleasure and laughed out loud. *He gets too much attention. Girls are bowled over by his handsomeness*, she thought. *Being good looking does not necessarily make a man very nice. On the contrary, it can turn him into a monster. I wonder if I could cure him of his craving to be admired.* Laughing, the pair went of to lunch. Marie-Therese shadowed them at a distance. Various passers by stared at her beauty, but she was unaware of their interest, self-contained in her curiosity. Taking a table in a far corner, she noted that Charles, having picked up the menu, ordered for both of them, and did not ask if the girl had any preference for wine, either. *He does not care what the girl wants. He is trying to impress her with his masculine authority*, Marie-Therese mused, and noted the thought, with the others she had recorded that morning, in her notebook.

After lunch, which she had to admit had been a gay occasion for the pair, she followed them to a nearby beach. Charles, as ever charming and witty, stood chatting with a few friends while the girl struggled with a pair of deck chairs. *He would not get me doing that*, Marie Therese thought grimly. *Why does he not assist her instead of trying to impress the others.*

Later, when the pair had changed into their bathing costumes, she watched as the girl applied sun tan lotion to Charles's back. To her disgust, the kindness was not reciprocated. Charles simply lay down on a towel and went to sleep. When he woke, the girl went off and purchased two ice cream cornets and presented one to him. *If his manners in the bedroom are as bad as they are here*, mon Dieu, *there is much to be done*, she thought with some alarm.

She decided there was no time like the present to embark on the strange adventure the vicomtesse had charged her with, so she strolled on to the beach and shed her cloak and other garments. Underneath, she was already dressed for bathing. She let down her long black tresses and stepped into the rippling waters. Every man on the beach watched her elegant progress and calm, strong swimming. She was at one with the element, strong and leisurely, not like the other chattering, splashing hoydens all around.

Charles was no exception. He had twice before met this enigmatic woman and divined something of her mysterious spell, and was drawn again by her magnetism.

He raced into the swell and caught up with her. 'I say, Marie-Therese, it's good to see you again. Saw you at Bernie's, remember?'

Her first therapy was to deny this, of course. 'I don't remember any such thing, young man,' she said, gazing coldly into his bright blue eyes.

Charles was not put off his stride. He laughed and joked amusingly as they lazed in the water together, and did it so well that eventually she had to admit they had met before. Soon he was asking to take her to dinner, and for her telephone number. She told him she was always busy, preoccupied with her studies, and had no time for trivial pursuits. This stung Charles to the bone because he thought he was far from trivial and that any girl was lucky to have him sniffing around. He pestered her as she dressed and followed her up the steps to the promenade, and along to where she got into her car.

'I must think about it,' she said. 'Why don't you telephone the vicomtesse in a few days. She usually knows where I am,' and she was off, in a cloud of exhaust.

When Marie-Therese reported to base, Bernadette was delighted, even more so when Charles repeatedly telephoned about her, only to be put off with some excuse or other. At night Charles dreamed of the mysterious, unattainable figure, and roamed the streets by day looking for her, but she was in her mountain retreat, and unavailable to him.

Finally she announced to Bernadette that he must be let off the hook, and her number was released to him. When he rang, the rich warm voice electrified Charles, as did her manner when they met at a discreet restaurant at Cap d'Antibes.

Marie-Therese wore a dress of figure-hugging lamé, decorated with brilliants, and the cloak of her choice was covered totally with the plumage of peacocks. Her normally scrubbed face had been subjected to the intricacies of fashionable *mascillage*;

painted a lustrous pearly white, with deep red lipstick and silver eye shadow, highlighted on her cheekbones with the palest rouge, her *visage* took Charles's breath away. He had never in his life desired a woman more, and he trembled as he led her to the table reserved for them. She smiled alluringly at him. It was almost as though Hollywood's greatest star had arrived on the Riviera and singled him out for her special attention.

When the wine waiter arrived, Charles ordered the best vintage champagne, but Marie-Therese interrupted his command and said she preferred Sancerre. When he asked for *foie-gras* she wanted *salade nicoise*, and she changed his order for steak tartare to *saumon feuilleté*.

'Plain wine, salad and fish are much more to my taste,' she said firmly.

Charles was nonplussed. 'I want you to have the best,' he pleaded.

'Whose best?' she asked.

Throughout the meal he pondered his tactics. She certainly was an odd fish, this one; he would have to play his cards right.

To his vast surprise, she took hold of his hand at the end of the meal and said, 'I am ready, take me home,' and directed him up and through the twisting upland tracks to the distant farmhouse.

His hands were on the wheel of her car and so could not travel seductively to her thighs, and she made no attempt, not even a hand laid on his knee, to arouse him.

When they were in the house she took up the cello and played, with a look of rapture on her face. Charles could not conceive how, with his presence there, she could be so preoccupied with her instrument.

'May I kiss you,' he asked when the prelude was over.

'Why?' she responded.

'Because you are so beautiful,' she breathed.

'And your kiss is my reward? For my looks?' she laughed lightly. 'I need no prizes.'

'I want to drown in your beauty,' Charles murmured urgently.

'If you do, I shall not come to your rescue,' Marie Therese replied, again with a mysterious look on her fine features. 'Come,' she said authoritatively, 'I want to show you something.'

She led him upstairs, and he could hardly contain himself, thinking that she intended to lead him to her bedroom. His groin already ached from the pressure caused by the stirrings of the evening, and his part felt like bursting, as he followed her up the staircase. To his surprise they came to an attic which was bare save for a giant telescope.

Having focused, she invited him to look through the lens. 'Look at the vast spaces,' she said, 'and the stars that control our destinies.'

Charles was less interested in the galaxies than in his tumescence. He pulled Marie-Therese towards him with his free arm, and pressed his hardness into her thigh.

'You have something very hard in your pocket,' she protested, and pulled herself away.

'It's the effect you have on me,' he groaned. 'I'm bursting. Come here, won't you?'

'I'm not a child,' she said, 'I do know that men masturbate when they are frustrated. Why don't you?'

'Right here and now, with you watching?'

'It wouldn't worry me, Charles, and it would be better than having you press your organ into my body in such a presumptuous way,' she said calmly. 'I'll help you get started, if you like.'

Such a tactic threw him off balance, as it were, and his erection vanished in a trice; so severe was her rejection, and so matter of fact.

'We should go to bed now,' she announced.

The diminished member shot to full length and solidity again, but alas receded once more when she placed him in a guest room and retreated alone to her own chamber, carefully locking the door.

The next morning, when a chastened Charles had been deposited back in town, Marie-Therese reported to the vicomtesse, who later relayed the details to Sophie, Marcel and Arthur.

'A brilliant start,' Bernadette cried. 'Do let me know how the good work continues.'

A week later, after many anguished phone calls from Charles, Marie-Therese allowed herself to be led to the villa he shared with a couple of friends, who had, of course, been instructed to go out for the evening.

He was charming and jolly, anxious not to offend, and she found herself warming to him so much that she had to remind herself of several promises, principally the one concerning her own involvement. When he kissed her cheek lightly, after supper, she responded warmly, and kissed him similarly.

'That was a nice affectionate thing to do,' she said.

'I want to get a lot more than affectionate,' Charles growled, pushing her torso down on to the divan. He wanted to strip her there and then and sate his lust.

'I am not impressed with this reckless speed,' Marie-Therese complained. 'Why do you think that women are animals, ready and willing to be raped when a male is rampant?'

'I have no wish to rape you,' he replied, hurt to the marrow. 'I want to take you gently.'

'You are lying. Go down to my feet and tickle them, lick them, caress them; show me that you adore even my toes, and then we'll see what can be done,' she said coyly.

Charles did his duty. It was agony, but he knew there would be no progress unless he obeyed her instructions.

'You have not paid nearly enough attention to the right one,' she said, extending her leg towards him. She had to admit that his tongue between her toes gave the most delightful sensations, and when he tickled and sucked at her ankles, tremors of the most delicious kind ran up her thighs.

He detached himself from his enforced labours and made a grab for her skirts, but she pushed him away with instructions to attend to her calves and knees.

'If you want to worship my body, it's alright by me,' Marie-Therese, lying back comfortably on the divan, grinned.

Charles wondered why he had to work so hard. All the other women he had known, apart from Edith who took the initiative, let him get on with it, at his own pace. This paragon wanted things her own way.

'The inside of my thighs are dying for a little massage,' Marie-Therese implored. The inflection was real, for the stimulations had already brought her to simmering point; but dedicated to the cause as she was, she felt that she had to stay the course. She knew that her love juices were beginning to be released and that he would discover the fact if she allowed him too much time in that area. She lowered her dress, pulling it downwards over her breasts, and sought his hands.

Naturally they explored her soft flesh and the points of her aroused nipples, and his mouth centred on each of the protuberances in turn. Once again he lunged at her clothes, trying to pull off her camiknickers, this time, but she clamped her thighs together tightly and frustrated his intentions.

With a sigh, she rolled over on her tummy. 'My neck is sore, please give it a little massage.'

Charles wanted only to give her private parts a massage, but he did as he was bid, cursing the flow of his seminal fluids that prematurely exploded from his throbbing glans inside his trousers and underpants. His sighs and moans alerted her to his condition.

'What a hasty chap you are,' she laughed. 'I hope you can stay the course.'

The rebuff not only took Charles by surprise, it literally deflated him. Without the pounding erection that had plagued him all evening, his lust vanished with her rebuke, and he lay down by her side, seemingly exhausted. Marie-Therese knew that the ultimate test, the telling part of the therapy, was imminent.

'Was that it?' she enquired brightly.

Charles had never before been in the position where his attitude and performance were questioned, with the exception of the insatiable Edith, and she was something apart.

Suddenly Marie-Therese was on her feet. 'If you will go about it like a bull in a pen, what do you expect,' she threw at him.

At that moment the sword of Damocles hung over Charles.

She knew for certain that he could either mend his selfish ways once and for all, or be so broken by her accusations that he could be stricken by that accursed affliction known as impotence.

'You have said that you love me, that you worship me, that you want to possess my body,' she murmured, 'and you have tried to get my clothes off in order to do that. Have you changed your mind? Must I find another lover who will satisfy me?'

The brutal confrontation had its effect. Her sad expression moved him to tears, and he advanced towards her with the utmost tenderness. She accepted his kisses greedily, sinking back to the divan in a submissive attitude. *I will show her that I care*, he thought, and sweetly began a series of tender embraces; caressing all the parts of her body that were exposed. He waited for her to signify when she wanted her clothing removed, and performed the task with gravity and care.

The new experience of tenderness moved him with extraordinary effect, emotionally and physically. He could not believe the strength of his returning erection and the power it expressed when it slid in to her prostrate form. For once he sympathised with a woman's erotic feelings as he probed within her, and was not concerned with his own. It was as if his instrument was a diving rod, measuring her joy at receiving his delicate intrusions. The masterfully swelling organ, now properly tuned, provoked her to the most wonderful acceptance and then an increased cooperation as she pushed her groin upwards and forwards to his.

To his surprise, his instincts told him not to be precipitate, and to withdraw almost, to lessen the completeness of feeling and delay the oncoming of his next ejaculatory thrill. He gazed tenderly into her eyes at this moment, imploring her to sense his new found caring attitude. She responded by drawing him into herself and stroking his shoulders, saying how she loved his member and what he was doing with it, but imploring him to begin again slowly. He responded with firm easy strokes and deep kisses, clutching firmly at her buttocks in a movement that made her think of riding the waves of surf, or rising in the saddle of a thoroughbred.

Passion roared through Charles as he quickened the tempo and drove them both forward to a point of no return when every fibre of their bodies strained towards that mutual satisfaction they both craved. It came in a crashing, exploding moment of thrusting power as his extending throbbing organ, pulsating with lightening-quick muscular thickenings, raced inside her up to the hilt of his shaft; drowning her interior with his grateful liquids, and meeting her wash of fluids head-on.

Marie-Therese was so happy with her new love that she forgot to phone in with the expected progress report, and got a sharp reminder from Bernadette.

'You seem to think the purpose of this exercise is to amuse you,' the vicomtesse chided. 'I thought there was a serious side to its nature.'

'Oh, there is,' Marie-Therese exclaimed, 'but do you know, my pupil is doing so well, he's improving so much with every lesson, I've really quite forgotten what the problem was.'

'I am amazed to hear you, a woman I thought to be intensely serious, sound so facetious, Marie-Therese, but at the same time, you sound *trés gai*. Does this mean that the scoundrel's sexual manners have matured, under your direction, then?' the vicomtesse queried.

'*Oui*, out of all recognition. It is because I insist he does things, not only in the proper order, but with due respect for his materials,' the happy woman replied.

'You mean like a good workman prepares the ground to lay a path; or a painter rubs the wall down well before the first application of paint?'

'Precisely.'

'And what does his horoscope say?' for Bernadette believed in Marie-Therese's supernatural gifts.

'I have consulted the stars and the tarot cards. I have also read his teacup, without him realising. All methods divined a happy and contented future for him.'

'And for you?' Bernadette asked.

'My continuing role as a seer,' Marie-Therese answered, in a serious tone.

'I wish you would arrange a forecast for me, darling,' the vicomtesse pleaded, for the occult held great interest for her.

'I have already done so. You will soon meet an absolutely astounding man, and fall headlong over in love.'

'And what about Marcel?' Bernadette asked.

'You stay in love with him, naturally, and enjoy both.'

'What a delicious prospect. I simply can't wait. Goodbye, dearest, you must come to dinner soon,' and the vicomtesse rang off, thrilled with her anticipation of this new love.

The next morning she told Sophie of Marie-Therese's success with Charles, how she had trained him to control his libido and behave in a more civilised manner.

Sophie was charmed. 'He will be so much happier for understanding how a woman's psycho-sexual functions dictate her response and enjoyment,' she said gravely. 'Thank goodness I have never had problems of this nature with Arthur,' she added, smiling like a cat who had just eaten the cream. Her husband had just finished pleasuring her; once on rising, with his usual morning erection desperate for quick satisfaction; and again at a more leisurely pace which was utterly satisfying except for the little subterfuge they had to make, diving under the sheets, when Mariette brought in the coffee without first knocking on the door.

When Arthur was told the good news he rang his chum.

'Charles, old boy, I hear you're hot on the cello these days, must meet so you can tell me all about it. How about a drink and a little chin wag this evening about six?'

'She's heaven, old sport, and just you keep out of it. I don't want a dirty old ram like you coming sniffing around her. She's mine you know, for keeps,' Charles answered, sounding on the top of his form.

He should have been elated. Marie-Therese had decided to reward him for the patience and consideration he had displayed throughout a long night of love. As Charles spoke on the telephone with his friend, she had both of her hands clamped firmly around his stem, and her mouth, opened to its widest extent, devouring the bulbous, deeply satisfied, pink glans.

Chapter Seven

Word about M. Rognon's debacle with Vera Lidova raced around the Riviera as fast as the bush fires which sometimes devastate the foothills behind the coast. Fanshawe found him in tears literally. He had been reduced to selling part of his private collection of fine art; items he had carefully purchased over a lifetime of dedicated scholarship. The Utrillo had had to go, then a Pissaro, and last, causing the most grief, a pair of exquisite drawings by Degas; ironically studies of dancers at practice.

'Another case of a man losing his head over a bit of twat,' the novelist said gloomily.

'The rotten thing is, I didn't get any,' Rognon moaned, 'just a bit of a grope, that's all.'

'The woman's a bitch, a whore,' Fanshawe swore. 'A Russian tart. She should be sent to Siberia.'

'That's where *I'll* finish up if I don't clear my debts,' the impoverished art dealer whimpered.

They were joined at their table by Gavroche and Josette.

'You're paying for the drinks,' Fanshawe said grimly. 'This old fart hasn't got a franc to his name, and I seem to remember doing the buying for you guys that time you got me story telling in the café.' He remembered, rather bitterly, having spent the whole of Letitia's gift on lunch for the crowd at the Bistro Latouche. He knew also that Gavroche had done rather well out of it, as the sexy paintings which he had drawn, inspired by the lurid rural tale, were selling well at Rognon's gallery.

'Have you any more canvasses ready?' the art dealer asked Gavroche. 'Everything you have brought to me is already sold.'

'No wonder, when the model is a gorgeous woman like me,' Josette purred, snuggling up to her lover.

'Got a couple drying off right now,' Gavroche replied. 'You shall have them tomorrow.'

Rognon sighed a little with relief; anything would help to get him out of his financial predicament.

'How's the wife?' Josette asked Fanshawe.

'She's pissed off with that little Italian scumbag of a pimp, and good riddance, sweetheart,' the failed author drawled. 'You know, the dirty bit of macaroni is so young, who knows, she might get arrested for paedophilia.'

'I'll have to get you fixed up, cheri,' Josette winked. 'Good looking stud like you going to waste.'

'Don't bother, honey. The spirit's willing, but the flesh is weak,' Fanshawe smiled wanly. He was glad the fires of his old volcano had long since ceased to erupt. Booze and blessed tranquillity were the only things he wanted in life now.

Gavroche broke into Fanshawe's reverie. 'What happened to those two country lads when they went back to see the old girl, then?' he asked.

Rognon could not imagine what the painter was rambling on about, as he had not been present when Frederick delivered his impromptu novelette.

'Oh, they had a lot of fun,' Fanshawe replied.

Josette explained to the art dealer: 'He told us this marvellous yarn, you see. Two country bumpkins with big pricks come across these two virgins out on a walk and ravish them. The next day they swap over and have the other one, then the aunt comes into the barn and whacks them with her whip.'

'I like the bit where she squeezes their pricks and they shoot all over her skirt,' Gavroche leered.

Fanshawe sighed. What use was it, he pondered, drumming up out such lyrical prose about the meadow flowers, the owls, the sunset, if barbarians like these reduced his stories to common pornography. What of his description of the girls, pale and pastel shaded like anemones—and the bunches of sweet herbs they had used to dry their legs after splashing in the stream; the smell of the rabbit's fur on the boy's hands; my God, D. H. Lawrence couldn't do better.

'Get me a drink, you dauber,' he demanded of Gavroche, 'and make it a bottle while you're at it.'

At that moment Charles and Arthur strolled in to the café. They had met on the corner for the drink they had promised.

'Hi,' said Fanshawe. 'You know Rognon, don't you? And this is Gavroche and his painter's moll, Josette.'

'*Enchanté*,' the Englishmen exclaimed together, thrilled with Josette's mountainous breasts.

Charles could not resist a sly dig. 'Hear you've been selling off a few things, old boy,' he sympathised with Rognon. 'Been having a bit of trouble, eh?'

Rognon's eyes blazed as fiercely as the rubies with which he had endowed the treacherous ballerina. 'I am done with women. I have learned my lesson, gentlemen,' he said furiously but then regained his composure. 'Please join us, Fanshawe is about to tell us one of his erotic tales.'

After he had helped himself to half a tumbler of Pernod, Frederick began. 'You remember, those of you who heard the first part, that Aunt Berthe, the tough old owner of the Chateau de Brazande, fancied those two rascals she caught at her nieces' parts in the barn. ' "I could use a couple of strong lads like you," she said, eyeing the bulges in their crotches after they'd stuffed their parts back in their corduroys. She told them to come back the next week after the girls had gone back to Paris. So they did, trembling nervously because she had regarded them with such lust.

' "We can't come to any harm," Guillaume tried to reassure his friend Pierre. "She's too old and posh to try anything on with us."

'He was wrong. When they arrived she set them to work in the vegetable garden and watched them slaving in the hot sun of the *midi*. Sweat poured off their foreheads and she suggested they take off their shirts.'

'Dirty old bag, I know what's coming,' Josette exclaimed, clapping her hands together with glee.

'I expect those randy boys did, too,' added Gavroche.

'She went and lay in a hammock and pretended to go to sleep,' Fanshawe continued, 'but those hooded eyelids of hers, like a toad's were not quite closed. How she loved their rippling muscles as they hoed and raked out the weeds, and their outstanding biceps when they pushed the heavy barrow across the patch. She had told them to dig a trench for planting celery. Very manly they looked as they attacked the ground with spades, throwing the earth to one side as they got deeper into the hole. The old girl's lust was stirred by now. Under cover of her apron she touched the part that had been neglected for years. Memories of Bouchon, her long departed husband, returned at the moment her finger alighted on her most sensitive spot.'

'How old was she?' Rognon asked.

'About forty five,' Fanshawe replied.

'That's not old.' Rognon protested. 'And anyway, you said she was a bit of a harridan.'

'To these country lads she was as old as Methuselah. Remember they had just ravished those naive beautiful girls, her nieces. The contrast must have been shocking. Think of her sunburnt, raddled face, wrinkled like a dried-up apple,' Fanshawe replied. 'Anyway,' he continued, 'she got out of the hammock and went over to them.

' "You have worked very well," she said. "Now you must come in to the farmhouse for some refreshing cool drinks."

'On the way across the yard she had a sudden inspiration. She pumped at the handle of the old well and brought up some water into a large tin bowl. "This will cool you off," she said, playfully flicking few drops at their heaving chests.

'They cooled themselves with the water, splashing gratefully, cleansing their chests and hairy armpits, all of which ravished her senses. She watched fascinated as a stream of water travelled down Pierre's matted chest and abdomen and ran between the waistband of his trousers and the pointed area of hair that finished at his navel. She wondered if it ran as far as his pubic hair, and shivered at the thought.

'Guillaume stooped and dipped his dark head into what remained of the water in the bowl. He shook his black hair like a dog shakes when it emerges from a pond, and wiped his mouth and nose with the back of his hand—a gesture which enthralled Berthe.

' "Come," she said, and led the way into the interior.

'It was richly perfumed with the smell of smoked hams and sausages hanging from the ancient beams, and a slow log fire burned at the hearth, over which she had suspended a delicious *blanquette de veau* in a stew pot to simmer away for their lunch.'

'For the Lord's sake, cut the arty stuff and get to the action,' cried Charles.

Fanshawe was deeply offended by this intervention. He thought the food-stuffs added a nice touch to the scene and were perfectly allowable. 'I always thought the English were Philistines,' he said. 'Now I know they are. However, to continue, Berthe went to the armoire and brought out a bottle of her own marc, that fierce brandy which can bring a fellow to his knees after a couple of shots. She poured large draughts of the fiery liquid for the strapping lads and watched them sip it.

' "Oh, come on now," she urged, tilting Guillaume's glass as it was poised at his lips, causing the drink to flow down his throat, "you don't have to be cautious here. I like a bloke who likes a drink."

'She moved over to Pierre who was sitting uncomfortably on a hard high wooden chair, and pressed her heaving bosom into his shoulder. "Drink up, lad. There's more where that came from."

'She went to the fire and placed another log on the flames. "Your dinner will be ready soon," she said, giving them a tender glance. The boys began to relax and stretch their legs. Her eyes were drawn again to their buttoned flies and the lumpy containments they covered. "Saucy, weren't you, getting at my girls? But I don't blame you. They're so pretty," she murmured. "I expect you properly got the hots, eh?"

'The memory of their attack on her nieces' parts stirred in the pair, and encouraged by the effect of the marc, they relaxed enough to experience the mildest swelling of their organs inside their hot breeches.

'Berthe stooped to pat Pierre on the knee. "You're good lads," she cooed, "strong and healthy. I expect you gave those minxes what for, eh?"

'Her hand strayed a little on his thigh and he uttered a low groan. "You were very angry with us that day,' he said. "You took your whip to us."

' "I know, I'm sorry," she whispered hoarsely. "I hope I didn't hurt your back when I lashed you."

'The natural progression of her tactics led her to run a sympathetic hand over Pierre's shoulders and down his back, and give a little pat on his rosy cheek. Then she turned to Guillaume, who had helped himself to another glass of the fortifying liquor; but instead of ministering to him from the rear, as she had done with Pierre, she pulled his head towards her ample bosom and stroked his back with both hands from that position.

'Her breasts, under her apron smelled of good things like breadmaking and jam; comfortable and warming scents which reminded him of childhood. He nuzzled appreciatively in the softness, relaxed from her gentle massage, and she lightly brushed his curls with a gentle kiss.

' "You're a bad lad," she teased. "I know what I would do with you if I were younger." One of her hands roved down his bare chest, lingering on his nipples and then down to the fur on his belly. Pierre watched, with a growing hardness in his groin, his breath coming in surprisingly short gasps.

Guillaume winked slyly at his friend. The drink and the novelty of the situation, plus the warmth from the fire, created a drowsy sort of lustfulness in both boys. Pierre rose to re-fill his glass and watched Berthe nuzzle Guillaume's head deeper into her cleavage.

'He ambled nearer. "It's not fair," he said, "he's getting all the cuddles. Don't you think I'm worth giving any to?"

'At that moment he was lightly pressed into her bottom, swaying gently, with his aroused member directly between the cheeks of her buttocks. She tensed her strong thighs and pressed against his hardness.

' "Cheeky monkey," she said, "you're trying on me what you did to my girls. Do you know," she said to Guillaume, "your friend's got a hard on. I wonder if you have too.

' "Better see," he murmured and opened the top button of his trousers.

' "You're drunk," she said. "Let me do it."'

One by one the buttons were opened to reveal first, the gorged head of his stamen and then, its full length. Pierre, still behind Berthe, slipped his hands under her apron and sought her breasts which he kneaded with some vigour.

' "My, my" she said. "Two whoppers. One in front and one behind. It's enough to make me feel quite giddy," she laughed, grasping Gillaume's tool with a hand, and searching round behind her for Pierre's, which the lusty lad had extricated in readiness.

'She gloated at the hardness of the two well-matched objects, almost swooning at the thought of the use she would put them to. In her near delirium, she did not resist when Guillaume, taking hold of her neck, brought her mouth down over his throbbing member.

'Pierre lifted her skirts and, to his surprise, found no underwear. He grinned wolfishly. She did not want to waste time, he thought.'

'Stop, I can't bear it,' Arthur groaned. His own enormous phallus was bursting at Fanshawe's outrageous and stimulating narrative.

'No, go on,' cried Rognon and Josette together.

'What happened next,' breathed Charles, with his hand on Josette's thigh without, of course, Gavroche knowing.

'The dirty Pierre slid it in,' Fanshawe continued, 'from behind, while the old dame sucked on Guillaume's cock. She'd never had it so good in years. Naturally, when they had all spent, etiquette demanded that the boys reversed positions, and so she got it all over again.'

'I bet the stew got burnt,' Gavroche threw in, for he was feeling hungry.

'Nonsense! She took it off the boil while they went upstairs to the massive old bedroom.' Fanshawe invented spontaneously. 'They laid about her for hours. Each one took a leg and parted her thighs and played on her lubricated parts gleefully, giving her her money's worth.'

'Oh, they got paid?' asked Arthur, whose flowing seminal fluids had quite dampened his underwear.

'Oh, yeah,' Fanshawe rambled on with instant invention.

'Each time they took her they got what they wanted; a bottle of marc, a crate of wine, a turkey, a sack of potatoes, a jar of preserved peaches, a smoked ham. Yeah, they got a whole load of goodies. And oh, I forgot. They went off with old Bouchon's fob watch and chain, and a silver hip flask Berthe gave him on their wedding day.'

'What did they do with all these things?' Josette asked.

'Oh, they and their families ate the food and drank the booze, then they sold the watch and the flask, and split the money between them. They're coming here tonight to celebrate. A little dinner, you know.' He laughed uproariously that the company turned to the window and looked out, expecting his imaginary characters to actually turn up and come in the Cafe Latouche. 'Fooled yer,' Fanshawe gloated.

The little gathering applauded generously, appreciating both his joke and the vividness of his story, and called for further drinks, as Fanshawe had emptied the bottle.

'My, your tale packed a punch,' Arthur ventured. 'You've got me going rather.'

'Quite,' said Charles, whose genitals had been more than a little troubled by the narrative.

Gavroche thanked Fanshawe effusively. 'You've given me new inspiration,' he cried, leading Josette towards the door. 'I've much work to do. Goodbye.'

Rognon rubbed his hands. He knew that several large erotic canvasses would be delivered soon to the Gallerie Rognon in Place Napoleon.

'Well, what did you think?' Fanshawe asked. 'Not bad, eh?'

'The story?' Rognon asked. 'Yes, it was very moving, but there were just a couple of things, First, in the kitchen things came to rather an abrupt end, and the same upstairs. You didn't finish it off properly.'

'Well,' Fanshawe drawled, 'I got bored with it, to tell the truth. Sex is pretty much the same, the whole world over, isn't it? Boring, boring, boring,' and as his voice trailed away his head dropped on to the table and he fell into a deep slumber.

'That's odd, isn't it? Telling an extremely titillating story and then saying that, well, you know, having a bash is boring,' Charles reflected.

'Quite, quite,' Arthur twinkled at his chum. 'I mean, you're the expert in that department, so I hear. And tell me, is it true that Marie-Therese has given up the cello?' Here he paused for a moment and then, as only close men friends are allowed to do, gave Charles a cheeky affectionate squeeze of his private parts. 'I gather,' he smiled, 'that's she's taken up a new instrument.'

Gavroche was elated. For the first time ever he had enough cash to buy canvasses, pigments and oils in sufficient quantities to match his artistic drive.

He came back to his rooms ladened with new materials, and Josette soon arrived with celebratory food and wine purchased from the nearby market. They opened a bottle of Provencale *vin rosé* and toasted each other.

'It's wonderful, isn't it, darling,' he said, 'having a bit of success.'

'A bit? I should say more than that. You're a big hit, sweetheart,' Josette cried, giving him a big sloppy kiss on the mouth.

'I'm getting a bit stymied, though, without the right models,' he complained.

'Ha, *mon Dieu*, what are you telling me? *Zut alors, sacré bleu*,' she yelled. 'I slave for you all day, and you ravage my body all night. What do you mean, the right bloody models!' she raged.

'You're the very best woman in the world for me. You inspire me. But I also need male models for my pictures. Any artist would.'

'Aaaaah, I understand, my little cabbage,' she sighed. 'I am so sorry I shouted. We must find you one.'

'Two, I need two, *ma petite*, for my next series,' she said thoughtfully. Footsteps could be heard on the stairs. 'I have a good idea,' Gavroche exclaimed, rushing to the door. 'Ah, *bon jour*, Vladimir,' he said shaking the Mongolian's hand. 'I want you to model for me. I will pay of course. When can you start.'

The *corps de ballet* boy understood not a word, so Josette fetched Angelique and explained the idea. The young mother thought it an excellent idea, a good boost for their income, and promised to bring along another of the dancers, a friend of Vladimir's who would similarly like a little extra income.

'Leave it to me,' Angelique smiled, and squeezed her boyfriend's hand.

There was a jolly dinner that evening. All four pooled their resources and ate far better than they had in ages. It was a celebration of their love and happiness and the *vie bohême*.

Next day, after morning practice, Vladimir and his colleague Ivan presented themselves at Gavroche's rooms.

Josette was already in place, in a startling sensuous pose. Her head was tossed back over a pillow. One of her hands was placed on a breast, and the other covered some, but not all of her private area. Her face expressed the most avid sexuality, with her dark eyes directed straight, provocatively, towards the artist.

'*Bon jour*,' Gavroche beamed, laying down his brushes for a moment. 'Please undress, we'll start immediately.' Neither understood, so he mimed taking off his pants. The boys laughed uproariously and stripped in a few seconds. Gavroche appraised them with a professional eye. 'Marvellous, darling, they're bloody marvellous,' he cried, contemplating both their finely tuned athlete's bodies which were beautifully muscular in a sinewy fashion and without a trace of excess fat anywhere.

Josette peered round to take a look.

'Don't move, please,' Gavroche yelled. 'The pose is absolutely right, it will take ages to do it again if you shift. 'Now, let me see,' he pondered, and paced all about Josette, looking at her from all angles, shifting small pieces of furniture, and strewing pieces of cloth on the floor for the sake of the composition. 'Come,' he said, taking Vladimir by the arm. He demonstrated how he wanted him to pose.

The Mongolian watched while Gavroche tried different positions in close proximity to Josette. Soon he chose, and clapped his hands together to indicate that Vladimir should copy him, which as he did. Gavroche made a few final adjustments to the disposition of the dancer's limbs and the tilt of his head, and stood back to view the result. The juxtaposition of the two naked bodies was superb. Vladimir's mouth seemed to be poised a centimetre from the nipple of Josette's uncovered breast. Lying by her side, with his groin close to her hip bone, and taking some of his weight on an elbow, one of his hands was placed at her navel, and one of his legs was draped over her nearest thigh, his knee touching the other.

'Don't move,' Gavroche implored, miming as well. Vladimir did not wish to move. The sensation of the close contact with the model's ample flesh was interesting enough.

'Now for Ivan,' the painter said, bringing him forward. Gavroche's placing of his second male model showed a touch of genius. He placed the boy on Josette's other side, but with his head facing away from her. One hand cradled one of Josette's slightly bent knees and the other seemed to toy with the inner side of her nearest thigh. His head was tilted sideways. He seemed to be staring up the length of her leg towards the partly covered mound of Venus. Gavroche paced around the full composition, delighted with the results of his work so far.

Josette seemed to be a venus, attended by two amorous swains. The dancers' perfectly developed strong young bodies added a touch of hardness, or even danger to the grouping. They replaced that usual soft, sentimental atmosphere, which one detects in most nude artwork, with an animal vigour which Gavroche realised would explode from the canvas if his intuitions were correct. He set furiously to work, wielding paints and brushes with practised dexterity and speed, and worked like a man possessed.

The morning wore on. Once Angelique stole in silently, watched for a few moments and then returned to her baby.

Josette was aware of the blood pulses of the pair of models. Their hands and fingertips transmitted their beat, and her hip on one side, and her thigh on the other, picked up the small throb of the boys' organs. If only I did not have to lie so still, she thought, I could reach down and touch their nice bits and pieces.

And the boys thought the same, that in a normal situation, their hands would, naturally, have strayed.

His mouth is so near to my nipple, she thought, the pretty one with the slanted eyes, and if I dared to lift my body a few centimetres, it would be at his lips.

Vladimir stared intently at the same nipple. It was large and outstanding, circled by a darker rose colour. He held the pose beautifully but could think of nothing other than what joy it would be to enclose the nipple in his mouth.

Ivan lay completely still, praying that an erection would not spoil the day. Unlike Vladimir, he did not have a regular partner for love. The sunbathing and games on the beach, the larks in the Hotel de la Poste, and the general state of well-being that is invariably aroused by the Riviera, had conspired to make him feel strong and healthy; he was like a coiled spring, waiting to be loosed. The position in which he had been arranged afforded an intimate view of Josette's pubic area and the delicate flesh underneath. His right hand, which clutched the inside of her thigh seemed to wish to travel up there, as if it had a will of its own, but he resisted gallantly for the sake of art.

Gavroche was unaware of any of the libidinous thoughts which prowled through his studio that morning. To him, the naked bodies were just so much mass, to be broken up by his pigments into so many areas of light and shade, textures and skintones. He typified the artist at work, slavish to his craft and dedicated to the final result.

Josette felt a little alarmed, and more than a little interested when she noticed an intrusive hardness near both of her hip bones. As she concentrated on the sensation, she detected a similar small ticking throb from the slightly swollen stamens on either side. She gave the faintest wriggle, so small that Gavroche could not possibly notice, and then another, more noticeable to the prostrate boys, who were now sweating, not so much from the heat of the room, but from the stimulating close contact.

Her morse code message was received, and returned by a more pronounced signal from both the adjacent roused members. Her part quivered, and internal flutterings caused her to sigh. It was an involuntary noise, and she drew in her breath sharply, afraid that Gavroche would attach some significance to it, but it was alright.

'Oh, I'm so sorry,' he apologised. 'You've all been working a long time, let's break for ten minutes.' With that he put his brushes down.

Josette stirred languidly. '*Eh bien*, why don't you go for a beer and have a little rest in the bar downstairs. I'll get us a drink here. It will save time dressing and undressing again.'

'*Bon idée*,' Gavroche said, picking up his jacket and making for the door. The boys were grateful that he went straightaway and they were not obliged to stand up and reveal their burgeoning flagpoles.

'*Mon Dieu*,' she gasped when Gavroche was gone. 'Oh boys, I'm so randy.' she rolled Vladimir over and found his monstrous erection, and then to her delight, the same swelling in Ivan. 'Feel here,' she moaned, pressing a hand of both of the boys to her moistened parts. The boys leapt to full erection at the lubricity she revealed to their finger tips. She took hold of both parts. 'Come on, or he'll be back,' she cried, spreading her legs for the first.

She neither knew or cared which one it was, and pumped joyously at the shaft which immediately entered and fairly soon spilled massively into her. With hardly a pause after the still inflated organ had been reluctantly withdrawn, for it still had much more to offer, his comrade took over, thrusting like a piston and bringing her to fruition with a hasty, frantic action.

It was quick, but absolutely thrilling. Vladimir and Ivan were ecstatic that as well as getting paid for the job, there were fringe benefits. They had just enough time to wash and compose themselves before Gavroche's return, and the boys splashed lots of cold water on their pricks to help the necessary detumescence.

They were sitting at the table like church mice at a tea party when he returned. His eyes blazed with the fervour of the inspired artist.

'Come on then, let's start again, darlings. Oh, isn't it wonderful. I know we're all going to get on like a house on fire.'

Chapter Eight

The vicomtesse and Sophie decided, as it was a gorgeous day, that a swim was in order, and repaired to the heavenly pool in the gardens of the mansion. Lying on their backs in the water with the hot sun playing on their naked breasts, they gossiped and exchanged views about the Season so far. It had not been particularly exciting to date, but it was early in the day as it were, more interesting people were turning up by the minute.

'Perhaps the wonderful man that Marie-Therese forecast will come into your life, darling cousin, is on the *Train Bleu* at this very moment,' Sophie teased.

Bernadette was puzzled why the amateur astrologer's prediction had excited her curiosity to such a degree. Her life with Marcel was romantic and comfortable, now that they had recovered from the incident involving Vera Lidova; she was surrounded by all the creature comforts that anyone could desire, and she had the widest circle of amusing friends. What more could anybody wish?

Sophie divined her cousin's discontent. 'You are a victim of our present society and the era we live in,' she announced after much pondering. These concentrated thoughts were necessary. No-one with any judgement would ever have dreamed of calling her an intellectual. Quick decisions about a new handbag, invitations to a cocktail party, or a choice between the dishes in a restaurant, she could solve at a moment's notice; anything more profound took a great deal more concentration. 'It's the time we live in,' she repeated, 'the Jazz Age, the Roaring Twenties, call it what you will. It's a very unsettling period. Every day something new. The world is going mad, seeking a new novelty at every turn. The old values are gone.'

'Listen to who's talking,' Bernadette retorted. 'Why, you are one of the worst. New dresses, new hair styles, and until dear Arthur, new men friends, one after the other. You're in a constant whirl of change. Nothing pleases you for more than a minute.'

'Yes it does, darling, one thing in my life stays constant, and that is my love for you,' Sophie said simply, touching her cousin deeply.

'That is a lovely compliment, Sophie. You are my most treasured companion and friend,' the vicomtesse replied.

They lazed happily in the water and afterwards took drinks at the poolside cocktail bar.

'What I am trying to say,' Sophie said carefully, attempting to compose her thoughts and express them with some clarity, 'is that, while the present decade is outwardly *très gai* and *ravissant* in every way, maybe there lurks behind our pursuit of pleasure a deep *malaise*.' Bernadette was thunderstruck to hear sentiments of such gravity come from her cousin, who to say the least, was not noted for her seriousness. She wondered if she was suffering from a mild sunstroke or the effect of the White Lady she had composed for their aperitif. 'My dear, it is relentless,' Sophie continued, 'like the rhythms of hot jazz. We rush from one event to another, the opening of an exhibition, a fashion show, a gala, or a charity ball. The noise and the chatter is interminable.'

'Quite,' Bernadette nodded. Sophie was certainly doing enough chattering at the moment.

'It is the Age of Anxiety,' Sophie pronounced. 'Just listen to the discordances of the new music. Monsieur Stravinsky is the worst. I am simply dreading the new ballet at the Opera House. I shall sit with plugs in my ears. What is wrong with Delibes and Tchaikovsky, anyway?'

'I rather think it is the Age of Arousal,' Bernadette countered. 'For far too long society had been cocooned in boring sets of rules. Puritanism, hypocrisy, conformity, and repression of the sexual phsyche, have been the norms. Why now, even a *midinette* is liberated. We should give thanks for the New Thinking.'

Such philosophical discussion did not occupy the ladies for long. A luncheon party had to be arranged. It was to celebrate Marcel's birthday. They pondered a possible guest list.

'How can I ask the dreaded Lady Letitia to come without her awful little Italian gigolo?' asked Bernadette.

'Be very firm, darling. Just say it's for close friends of the family, and have done with it,' Sophie replied peremptorily.

'And I certainly will not be inviting her alcoholic husband, either. The last time he came here, he fell dead drunk down the staircase and demolished the Capo di Monte jardinière at the foot of the banister,' the vicomtesse affirmed.

'The young Scottish pair?' Sophie asked.

'Ah, the relatives of Letitia. Of course. They are charming,' her cousin agreed.

'By the way, we have let them slip through our fingers, as it were, since the day of their arrival, although they were so adorable in the shower. You remember the enchanting episode? Their flame coloured public hair?'

'Like highland cats,' Sophie interrupted.

'I wonder why we have not given ourselves the opportunity of observing their youthful loveplay again. Let us remind ourselves to enter the secret room once again and see how they are getting on,' the vicomtesse urged. 'And we must have Marie-Therese and Charles.'

'We must ask her to bring the tarot cards so she can give me a reading,' added Sophie, for secretly she was envious of the prediction that her cousin was to meet a new hero. Life with Arthur was heaven, but as the reader will know, hardly a woman goes through life without the occasional romantic yearning for a sexual adventure.

So the morning wore on in amiable discussion. The list was finally agreed and drawn up, and the chef M. Ratatouille was informed and asked to consult with M. Moutarde, the butler, and arrange a suitable menu.

There was a telephone call from Borzdoff, the manager of the Ballets Russes. He was having great difficulty in raising enough cash to pay for the season. Even with highly inflated seat prices, the proceeds from a Gala, and souvenir brochures, it was unlikely that he would break even. If he could not pay the dancers' salaries, he was truly afraid that the lunatic Dhokouminksy would kill him. 'Last year Lidova got us a lot of support and hard cash from the Greek millionaire,' she complained. 'This year he is uninterested in her. What can I do?'

'Get her to sell those jewels she cheated from poor Monsieur Rognon,' the vicomtesse responded icily. 'It is a vulgar monstrosity to prostitute art in such a way. I feel *desolé* for the sorry old fool.'

'I am distraught,' the *regisseur* groaned. 'I shall be bankrupt, and disgraced, and my company will be broken up after all these years of slaving.' His Russian passion, that mixture of melancholy and fire that marks the true manic-depressive muscovite, came to his rescue. He burst into tears and sobbed uncontrollably.

Sophie and Bernadette listened to his anguished howls on the other end of the line.

'It sounds like the cries of a Siberian wolf, hungry and alone in the silence of the great Steppes,' said Sophie, with some poetic invention.

'*Calmez-vous*,' Bernadette implored, for even though she knew Borzdoff was a liar and a cheat, she had the proverbial soft spot for him. 'Tell us what we can do.'

The wily manager dried his tears. He asked them for the favour of coming to a little lunch at Juan les Pins the following day. He wanted all the advice they could give him, maybe the names of a few potential sponsors. 'After all,' he flattered, 'you two divine ladies are the toast of the Riviera; the most admired hostesses and leaders of society. If I have your support, others will follow.'

His oily and ingratiating remark was magic to their ears, therefore they graciously accepted the invitation and duly arrived. They were the picture of health, wealth, fashion and distinction; with that unmistakeable air that belongs only to the *haut monde*.

'This is Paquin, my new soloist,' Borzdoff said proudly. 'He comes direct from starring at the Paris Opera.' The tall aquiline dancer was pushed forward to greet the ladies. He was incredibly suave and handsome, tall, narrow-hipped, and exuded a smouldering sexuality that made their knees go weak. 'And this is Anton who is English, and my latest acquisition,' Borzdoff continued. 'He is my new secret weapon, he will be outstanding in the new repertoire.'

'I adore the English,' Sophie gushed, 'but why are you called Anton?'

'It's tradition, madam. The public expect dancers to be Russian, you know, so we must appear with a Russian name. I hope you don't mind the little deception,' Anton smiled, kissing Sophie's hand with an interesting intensity; it had the same effect, he noticed, as Paquin's studied greeting to Bernadette.

The vicomtesse trembled at the contact with the Parisian star. Could this be the handsome dark stranger promised by Marie-Therese, whose extra sensory powers had warned of a fateful meeting? Borzdoff grinned amiably and called for champagne. What strategy, he thought, what business acumen, and what an understanding of that condition in the female make-up that decrees the heart rules the head.

Sophie looked demurely at the gravely beautiful Anton, a fair-haired Adonis with wide eyes of emerald green. He was in exactly the Anglo-Saxon mould which she had come to love. Could this be the hero she longed for, to keep up with the adventures her cousin was promised by Marie-Therese? A session with the tarot cards would soon find out.

Anton got to work instantly. Both men had been properly primed by Borzdoff. He told them that without extra funding the company would close. The brutal truth was that the scenery and costumes would have to be sold, and there would be no money for rail fares. Everybody would be stranded on the ridiculously expensive riviera. Taking Sophie's hand lightly after they were seated in the restaurant, he stroked it gently. 'What wonderful taste you have,' he murmured, gazing at her enormous and valuable emerald ring. 'I love the colour, it's so deep, and of great beauty.' Sophie was intensely flattered. It was one thing to be rich, she thought with satisfaction, and another to know a tasteful object from a cheap looking tawdry one. 'Thank you,' she murmured, making a mental note in advance, thinking that a pair of cufflinks set with the same gems would make a suitable present if a liaison between them happened to occur.

Anton favoured her with flattering glances as he reminded himself further of what the manager had revealed, namely that, even if the season were saved, the first things to be cancelled would be the modern works that he had been brought into the company to perform. 'Out with all the modern rubbish,' Borzdoff had cried, 'Picasso designs like sardine tins, Stravinsky music like screeching of tomcats, public only wants *Swan Lake, Coppelia, Les Sylphides*. Then you have no work, you go, yes?'

The manager had tried a different tactic with Paquin. He assured him that if he managed to use his charms well enough to raise some cash, Vera Lidova would be deposed from her position as prima ballerina, and Paquin's lover in Paris, Rose de la Touche, substituted as lead of the company. Consequently Paquin's dark fiery eyes burned on Bernadette with an intensity which completely captivated her. He must be the one, she thought, and vowed to live her life from that moment on according to Marie-Therese's dictates. She had supernatural powers, after all, which must be obeyed.

Borzdoff watched his boys in action. He was proud of them. What artistes, what astute business men, he thought, calling for the wine waiter to top their glasses.

The lunch was gay and lighthearted. The ladies felt privileged to join in an interesting discussion about company policy, and were enthraled by the manager's greatly exaggerated account of the South American tour, and the brilliant reviews for the seasons in London, Paris and New York. 'Why don't you write a scenario for me,' he suddenly asked the vicomtesse. 'Something very amusing, a ballet set on the beach, for instance, or concerned with the *couture*. No-one understands the Jazz Age and its glamour more than you.'

Bernadette was bowled over. The suggestion, coming so soon after the philosophical conversation with Sophie the day before, seemed to be further evidence that mysterious forces were at work.

Paquin and Anton were wild with enthusiasm. Such a venture would be chic and modern, they assured the vicomtesse, and need not cost a fortune. They would help her, themselves, and perhaps Madame Sophie would collaborate as well.

Sophie clapped her hands with glee. She could think of nothing better than collaborating with two such adorable hunks of masculinity. Prospects of enchanting afternoons at the poolside, and intimate dinners for four—or even better, for two—concentrated in her mind.

It was all made easier because, by now, Anton had changed places for the pudding course and was ensconced by her side, talking confidently and with great charm into her ear, as easily as if they were already lovers. Likewise Paquin had moved in on Bernadette who was completely possessed by his presence. Stirrings and vibrations of all kinds coursed through her mind and body, and with the added effect of the champagne which kept coming as if by magic to the table, reduced her to a state of passivity. Paquin's smouldering handsomeness, his cologne and brilliantine, his flashing white teeth, and exquisite manners were the ingredients of the trap. She felt irresistibly drawn, as a bee is to pollen, or a fly to a spider's web. *I am drowning*, she thought, but the sensation was good. *He is so ravishing I may fall in love, or at least be infatuated, and his attentions are so flattering and amusing there can be no harm, only pleasure.*

Such persuasive sentiments surged through Sophie's breast as well. Just as she had enjoyed her food and the delicious wine, it occurred to her, so she should enjoy this refined flirtation which Anton lavished on her; gazing with awe at her cleavage, and with a hand lightly resting on her silk-clad knee. Frissons of pleasure made her tremble. It was a hedonistic experience of the purest kind, and she was more than a willing participant. *I am falling into a vortex*, she sighed, inwardly, returning Anton's pressure on her thigh. The strong muscles of the dancer's legs clenched at her touch, causing an even greater tremor to pass through her frame.

Borzdoff watched with a beady eye as Paquin took up a large ripe strawberry and dipped it in the sugar and cream, and approved of the delicacy of the moment when he popped it into Bernadette's mouth. *Such simple things never fail*, he mused, with a satisfied grin. Anton scored a similar success with the cube of sugar he immersed for half a second, first in black coffee, and then in chartreuse, before offering it to Sophie. There was contentment all round. The manager was pleased with his boys, and their expert powers of dalliance. He was even more pleased when Bernadette insisted on taking up the bill.

'Excuse me, Monsieur Borzdoff, but you are hard pressed enough. Sophie and I are delighted to have you as our guests, it has been an enchanting afternoon.'

The two ladies excused themselves to the powder room. The ecstatic languor of their behaviour at the luncheon table turned immediately to an excited girlish fever of exchanging notes, making comparisons, listing their respective beaux' seductive charms.

'Isn't it delicious,' Sophie exclaimed. 'I feel like a sixteen year old, at her first romantic meeting.'

'*Naturallement, cherie*,' the vicomtesse laughed, as she too was light headed enough to want to dance and sing her happiness, 'but I am sure that, like me, perhaps you may be planning further meetings of a more, er, shall we say, mature kind?'

'It is fate,' Sophie declared, 'we must abandon ourselves to it.'

'Darling,' the vicomtesse replied, 'I already have.'

Feelings of abandonment were their principal sensations over the next few days, hardly ever confused by any feelings of guilt that, with any luck, they would soon be unfaithful to their husbands. They checked through their wardrobes with the enthusiasm that young brides inspect their trousseaux, and spent hours at the *coiffeur* experimenting with the latest cuts and tints.

'The waiting is delightful,' Sophie exclaimed, expressing exactly the mood, 'when one knows something is going to happen. An inevitability, as it were, like a birthday present, for instance. One can hardly contain oneself.

'Agreed,' said Bernadette who was getting just a little tired of Sophie's new-found verbosity, 'we shall just have to wait and see.'

They were in the small *salon*, wondering if it was the right day to pay attention to Cynthia and Ian from the confines of the secret garden room, when Yves, the bootboy, arrived with a small, beautifully wrapped gift box. They tore it open with undisguised haste. Inside lay a white gardenia, tied with a white ribbon, addressed to Bernadette. By its side there was a pink camelia, tied with a pink ribbon, with an inscribed card for Sophie.

'How absolutely charming, how adorable, how utterly romantic,' they cried, pressing the blooms to their respective breasts.

'I knew those darling boys would get in contact soon, but I had no idea it would be such an imaginative expression of their ardour,' Sophie whimpered, almost moved to tears.

'What does the note say,' asked the more practical vicomtesse, tearing open the envelope. She read out the following. *'Dear ladies, what an honour and a pleasure it was to meet two such enchanting creatures at lunch the other day. Borzdoff goes up in our estimation! What a rogue! He has kept you to himself for too long! May we meet again? On Saturday we have a free day. No rehearsals! We have hired a yacht for an outing, a little sea trip to get some fresh air in our lungs. Please will you accompany us. There will be a picnic, naturally, and we promise to give you a lovely time. Please answer to the stage door as soon as you can. We die to get your reply. Signed Anton, Ivan, who will die if you say no.*

Sophie leapt about the room with glee, her full breasts bouncing underneath her transparent négligé. 'I told you, I told you. They are mad for us. Isn't it thrilling! They are so young and sweet. It's amazing they have fallen for women of our age.'

'Speak for yourself, *cherie*,' Bernadette warned. She was feeling particularly youthful at that moment. Visions of riding the waves across a blue sea, with little scudding clouds racing across the sky, came into her mind. Paquin at the tiller, wind-blown and heroic, utterly divine, and she, with a trailing scarf in the manner of Isadora Duncan at his side, in a close and intimate embrace. She wondered how it would be as, lying on the heaving deck with the handsome captain naked over her prostrate form, the movement of the swell coincided with his amorous attentions.

Sophie had a more exotic vision of a desert island off the coast of Africa, with swaying palm trees. Arthur and she were wearing djellebahs and smoking together from a pipe containing aphrodisiacal substances. The scene was prompted by a similarly erotic moment in a film she had seen recently which starred Ramon Navarra.

It was with these feelings of heightened expectations and lustful desire that they stole into the secret garden room to satisfy their curiosity concerning the Scottish newly weds. As they drew aside the covering brocade curtain from the magic mirror, Ian came into view, returning from the shower. His freckled dead-white skin had turned a lobster pink in the sun which burned on the Cote d'Azur. Even his member was tinted the same colour, they noticed with satisfaction. The pair must have been indulging in some nude sunbathing, the ladies surmised. This was borne out when Cynthia appeared. She, likewise had gone a peculiar colour, but in her case, Bernadette and Sophie were reminded more of ripe tomatoes, especially by Cynthia's plump buttocks.

'It is bizarre,' Sophie whispered, 'and his equipment must have been so painful when it got so sunburned.'

'I do not suppose the poor things have had much fun, *alors*,' Bernadette sympathised for the pair, who of course had no idea that they were under observation.

'Also her breasts. See how they are peeling. The skin is quite damaged,' her cousin breathed. 'I do not think she would wish to accept his weight on her front in that condition.'

'The British can be so stupid,' Bernadette complained, but hurriedly added, 'except for Arthur, of course, darling, who is extremely intelligent.'

'I quite agree. But in their defence, I suppose, living as they do in a permanent fog, temperatures way below freezing, the poor creatures cannot be blamed for running amok when they arrive in a paradise such as we have here,' Sophie mused.

Cynthia approached her beloved with a large bottle in her hands. She shook it violently and then removed the cap. Ian laid himself down on the bed, with his legs wide apart. He seemed to groan as he did so. Cynthia plopped a handful of a thick pink liquid over Ian's inflamed parts. The poor boy howled with pain and jumped from the bed, hopping and jumping in a strange version of a Scottish reel.

'It is calamine lotion,'' Bernadette guessed. 'That should do the trick.'

'Oh, oh, oh,' they heard the boy shout. His painfully blistered organ bounced up and down as he ran, and Cynthia chased him, slapping more of the unguent on his backside. 'I can't stand it,' he yelled and went to dive once more under the cold shower.

Cynthia then cried as she applied some to her sore breasts and implored her husband to come out and attend to her rump, but he remained under the cold jet, singing 'Scotland the Brave', with much gusto and that fortitude for which the Highland race is famed.

'Come, Sophie,' Bernadette said wearily, 'this is tedious. There will be no fun here today,' and the pair of them stole away to prepare for their forthcoming maritime adventure.

The principle preoccupation was what to wear. Sophie brushed aside Bernadette's idea of chiffon draperies and scarves à la Duncan. 'Think what happened to the poor creature,' she sighed, 'when the terrible accident occurred, and the scarves were caught in the wheels of the automobile. Death at sea would be even worse.'

They settled eventually on something with a nautical theme; white drill shorts, just above the knee, short sleeved shirts with sailor collars, and navy blue caps at a saucy angle. With great daring, the vicomtesse ordered the outfits to be made up at Marcel's workrooms.

'Where are you going that you need these extraordinary garments?' the couturier asked.

'We are going out for a day's sailing with the Ballets Russes,' his wife truthfully answered, omitting to mention though that there would only be two members of the company present on the escapade. 'Ah, Letitia, how lovely to see you,' she lied, as the English aristocrat entered the *salon*, accompanied by the suave Paolo. There were many of those exchanged kisses that occur when a number of folk meet in France. The permutations of the number deemed necessary between a group of, in this case, five, or six if one includes Arlette the *vendeuse*, are endless. When it was all over Bernadette, with a level gaze, faced Letitia. 'I hear you have left your husband, in favour of this young man,' she said coolly.

'Yes, it's true I have,' Letitia answered as demurely as she could muster. 'But do you not think that, at our age, youth and beauty in the opposite sex begin to have an amazingly unnerving effect?' Then she turned to Marcel with an artful smile, the cunning barely disguised. 'You must watch out, *cher* Marcel, Bernadette may be deceiving you.' As she turned on her heel to walk towards the fitting room, shadowed by the polished Italian, she added, over her shoulder, 'and in my view she would be entitled to, if it's true what I hear, that you have been cheating on her with another woman.'

'She is appalling,' Sophie exclaimed. 'A slanderer,' as Letitia slammed the door behind her.

'She is a child stealer and a decadent,' said Bernadette, and whispering in her cousin's ear added, 'that terrible Vera Lidova must have been gossiping. I must think how to deal with her.' Then, loudly, 'Come, darling, we have much to do. Goodbye Arlette,' and the two ladies swept out onto the crowded boulevard.

The day of the excursion at sea arrived. Heady with excitement Bernadette and Sophie were driven by Jean-Paul to the harbour for embarkation. It was, as always, a peerless day, and their spirits were soaring. Gulls and terns flying overhead seemed to express the same freedom the pair felt in their hearts. The sight of so many pleasure craft gently bobbing up and down in the water, waiting for their owners, made a pretty picture, with sunlight bouncing against the brightly coloured paintwork. Young things strolled everywhere, assembling tackle and picnic baskets. The holiday mood was infectious. Suddenly they spotted Anton and Paquin and waved gaily. The boys ran over to them, whooping and leaping. '*Ravissante*,' said one, and '*Adorable*,' the other, as they contemplated the ladies in their sporty costumes. They all kissed on the cheek, lingering more than is the custom, and boarded with alacrity, anxious to be away.

It was carefree and idyllic as the boys negotiated the way through the harbour, and past the wall into open sea. Anton was expert, having sailed a lot back home in England, and Paquin learned the ropes quickly. The ladies lay back on the deck admiring their skill and seamanship. They looked so rugged and virile, stripped already to the waist, with their bare torsos gleaming bronze in the sunlight.

'Are you happy?' Paquin called out, ducking in the spray.

'It's wonderful,' they answered, '*magnifique*!'

And so they sailed for the whole morning, the craft rising and falling gently, curving and wheeling until the ladies were in a delirium of bliss. Paquin opened champagne. It was a heady day. Anton came to lie beside Sophie, and a moment later Paquin anchored and came to sprawl by Bernadette. They all drank more champagne, each couple getting closer, exclaiming how perfect it all was. One of the boys, and then the other, stood up and divested himself of his cotton trousers. They lay back in the hot sun, with their heads cradled on the ladies' laps, looking completely relaxed. Their eyes were closed, and they seemed almost to be going to sleep, it was so peaceful.

Sophie looked across at Bernadette and then indicated with a little tilt of her head the satisfactory shapes she had observed in the boys' bathing drawers. 'Dreamy, isn't it,' she said, as she laid a light hand on Anton's chest.

He opened his eyes and looked up. 'You are the perfect companion,' he breathed.

'I could stay here forever,' Paquin murmured, turning his smouldering dark eyes to Bernadette, 'especially with you.'

'You dear boy,' she gushed, and ruffled his hair in a most playful manner.

'Lunch,' Anton announced, 'how do you say we have lunch?'

'I'm starving,' Sophie answered.

'That's where we're going,' Anton shouted from the bows, 'over there, that little island.' He indicated a small rocky outcrop, one of the many that are dotted about the coast, 'It's the perfect spot.'

Soon they were tying up at a convenient post and the boys set to, unloading the hamper and various gear they needed. Naturally they had provided rugs and towels to lie on, an ice container, and all the appropriate suntan oils and lotions. There was a favoured spot on the seaward lee, a small patch of sand in a dove which gave complete seclusion. When the ladies were settled and had been supplied with fresh drinks, the boys tore off their drawers and dived into the water from a high rock.

Their slim, lithe legs and tight buttocks flashed in the sunlight as they flew in perfect arcs into the waves and disappeared. They were gone from sight so long the ladies jumped to their feet, fearful for their safety, and to their relief, they surfaced a hundred metres away, waving and gesticulating wildly.

'They mean business,' said Bernadette.

'I am afraid so,' agreed Sophie.

'And you?' Bernadette asked.

'I shall have no power to resist,' her cousin answered.

'Me neither,' Bernadette smiled.

By the time the two dancers returned, the ladies had removed their nautical costumes and were partially immersed in a small rock pool.

'It's so warm in here,' Sophie enthused, 'I suppose the sun has been on the water all morning. It's like a warm bath.'

'Then we must join you,' Paquin grinned.

They advanced towards the pool, sea water sparkling on their bodies, and caught in the denseness of their pubic hair.

'What a pretty picture,' Bernadette laughed, holding out her arms wide to receive the Parisian paragon. She kissed him cheerfully on the mouth. 'You taste of salt water,' she complained, twinkling.

'*Naturellement*,' he replied, taking her firmly in his arms and rolling her over with him in the shallow pool.

Anton stood over Sophie, with water dripping down from his body on to her breast. She looked up at his weapon and knew soon it would impale her. 'Come here, you naughty thing,' she said, 'how dare you strip off in front of a lady?'

'You don't look very shocked to me,' the young buck retorted with a wink. 'I bet you've seen plenty of these things before.' The cheeky lad took hold of his implement with two fingers and shook it amusingly, flicking a few drops of sea water over her.

'I swear it's getting bigger by the second,' she murmured in a husky voice as he stretched out beside her. They both looked down. It did indeed grow in the warmth to an interesting shape.

'That's the effect you have on me darling,' Anton laughed. He turned towards her and planted a kiss on her expectant mouth.

Sophie melted at his lips and tongue. He burrowed deep, exploring, and tenderly squeezed one of her full breasts. She gave herself to the sun and his exquisite attentions, sighing when he left her mouth for a moment to close his lips on her growing nipple. 'You don't waste any time,' she said, in a low voice, passing a hand between them searching to hold his member.

'I'm afire,' he said, guiding her hand towards his now-throbbing stamen.

'Kiss me again, I adore it, you are such a divine boy,' she groaned, and as he did she felt his hot sperms shoot into her hand, in a gushing amount that spoke volumes of his sexual capacity. She was thrilled.

Paquin was straddled over Bernadette, one thigh over her hips, and with a hand underneath it, searching out her agitated part. He gently prised open the lips that covered her lubricating channel. She throbbed at his touch and her muscles sent an inviting message, whereon he re-arranged his legs and took her from behind in one gliding silky action, thrusting his stem inside to the very hilt, in the lukewarm waters of the pool. Bernadette gasped in her pleasure and squeezed down on the enclosed member, dragging deliciously on it as he disgorged inside her with a wave of intensity that made her call out.

'But you're so spontaneous,' Sophie told Anton, massaging his still swollen tumescence, 'I love such impetuosity.'

'You'll love this more,' he said gruffly, taking hold of her and hoisting her from the pool. He laid her on the towels and clambered between her plump knees. Taking hold of them he spread them apart, with no resistance from her, and placed the tip of his organ at the opening of her front. With a hand clasped around the stiffened stem, he played at the entrance, smoothing soft juices over it until he felt obliged to enter and play inside. Sophie gasped as he pushed with inordinate strength, tilting his pelvis the better to gain a deeper penetration.

'*Mon Dieu*, you are an expert,' she managed to hiss in his ear, 'and you fill me enough to make me burst.'

Anton took hold of her underneath her armpits and heaved, leaning backwards and pulling her on to him until, without releasing the heavenly grip of his mightily expanded phallus from her love-chamber, she lay heaving on top of him. He pushed his hips skywards, in a convex stretch that threw her into ecstasy, and held the position while she pumped her hips at him and exploded in orgasmic intensity, gasping her love for the boy and his wonderfully inventive arousals. When she recovered somewhat, Sophie glanced briefly, for the sake of discretion, at her cousin and Paquin.

At that moment Bernadette was lying on her back on a rug. Paquin had hold of her calves and had pushed her legs behind her head. His back was arched and he was quite obviously thrust into her interior space as deeply as could be managed. The pose was static and beautiful. Both had just completed a ravishing anointment, and were in the throes of the most delicious post-coital tenderness.

Anton looked towards Paquin, grinning sheepishly. The other returned his smile and detached himself from his partner. Anton did the same. Their organs were still proud and erect, pulsating with life. The boys winked at each other and gave a secret mocking tug at their parts, but the ladies missed the gesture because they were both still overwhelmed, and when they had roused themselves, their lovers were again in the water, swimming in slow circles on their backs, with their proud possessions sticking upwards towards the sun. Such faun-like insouciance provoked Sophie and Bernadette to further lust.

'Come back at once, I haven't finished with you yet,' Bernadette implored.

Sophie fell on her knees, clutching at her head, in a mock pantomime. 'Help,' she cried, 'I am marooned on a desert island. Is there a strong man anywhere who can help?'

The afternoon passed in play and erotic games, each one a further provocation, until all four were deeply satisfied and exhausted.

Each one of the foursome was consumed with fulfilment and joy as the yacht brought them back to port. They sipped from the last bottle and kissed each other fond farewells. In truth, Sophie and Bernadette were almost in tears as they both realised that it would not be prudent to carry on with these *liaisons dangereuses*.

Borzdoff was delighted when he received a large cheque. He called Anton and Paquin to his office. 'Bravo, my boys, I'm proud of you. You are good ambassadors. Your little friends send plenty money. The company is saved. Is good, yes?' He offered them cigarettes and bent low to their ears. 'You must be very good, is nice cheque.' The pair smiled at the compliment. 'I have something here for you,' he said, opening a drawer in his desk. He pulled out two bundles of notes, 'ten per cent, bravo.'

The boys could hardly believe their eyes and thanked him profusely, but they were no fools. Over a celebratory beer in the bar of the Hotel de Paris, they worked out on the back of a tariff card, that the thieving manager could only have given them, at the most, a half of one per cent of the ladies' likely donation.

'The bastard,' Anton laughed, 'but who's complaining, getting paid for such nice work?'

Chapter Nine

Letitia began to realise that she had gone too far. Marcel used less than his usual charm and tact when he supervised the fitting of her new ball gown. He was coldly furious that she had nearly let the cat out of the bag concerning his infatuation with Vera Lidova. She had been dying to do this of course, and it was only the prospect of an immediate stupendous quarrel that had prevented her revelation. In any case, it was more in her nature to insinuate rather than openly accuse. Where men were concerned Letitia could be charming, but as Sophie and Bernadette found out, with her women friends, she could be vituperous.

When she asked Marcel if the line of the dress suited her, or if the basic colour flattered her complexion, he merely shrugged and stuck more pins in his mouth, making himself unavailable for questioning, and when she stood completely undressed, save for the sheerest silk petticoat, he averted his eyes.

Marcel later told Arlette to double the bill for his creation, hoping to drive Letitia's custom away. 'I am a success,' he said, 'and an artiste. Why should I put up with this nosey interfering madwoman.' None of the usual aperitifs were served, either, and Letitia left under a cloud, ruing her indiscretion. When she came across the prima ballerina at the hairdresser's, she discovered that she too was somewhat miffed.

'I am worried about Vossoudossoulos,' Vera complained. 'He neglects me dreadful. Do you know, Letitia, if he is seeing other woman?'

Letitia had not seen the Greek millionaire at all this Season and presumed he was away on his interminable business. It had been rumoured that he was connected with certain groups of Corsican and American villains involved in the sale of illicit alcohol in the United States. 'Don't worry, darling, other men will soon come,' Vera said, but in fact she was deeply disturbed. Last year Vossoudossoulos had kept her in style at the Hotel de Paris, and also kept her extremely happy in bed, being the possessor of a magnificent sexual organ whose size and capabilities were of legendary stuff. The rubies she had cheated from M. Rognon were all very nice, she thought, but they would not pay the bills, and even if she sold them, at the rate one got for second hand goods, she would only be covered for about a week at the phenomenal rates the hotel charged. 'How is your pretty Italian boy?' Vera winked.

'I'd thank you to keep your hands off him, darling, and anyway he's got no money,' Letitia replied sharply.

'And not has your husband, Fanshawe, but what you give him,' the ballerina added caustically.

Letitia had made a plan for Frederick. She thought of hiring a villa, complete with bodyguard and locked gates, setting him up there, virtually imprisoned, with a typewriter and some paper, and not letting him out unless he completed a worthwhile manuscript. There would be no drink allowed in the house, no visitors, no distractions of any kind, and she herself would inspect his daily output and refuse him cash for food if he was not up to scratch. That'll fix him, she thought.

Vera asked Letitia about her book. She had read reviews in the international press, and was interested in finding out how such a dim-witted female could have achieved such an enormous success with her very first publication.

'I'll give you a signed copy,' Letitia glowed. 'Do you know darling, it's the rage, even museums and universities are buying the book for research purposes?' She explained how she had received her first inspiration while she dallied with Paolo last year in Florence. His beautiful phallus had given her the idea of a photographic survey of a quorum of fifty males, showing their organs in both a limp and erect state, with an index and a corollary devoted to examples taken from the most important works of Art. The finished work, entitled 'The Penis: Limp and Erect, in Life and Art,' had become a veritable bestseller, and had already been re-printed and even gone into a second edition. Letitia explained that one of the purposes of the book was to discover if there was any truth in the claim that there was no fixed ratio in the growth of the male organ from limp to rigid.

'Ah,' Lidova sighed, for indeed she had often been surprised by the erect totem-pole of a gentleman who seemed not to be very well endowed the moment he dropped his trousers. 'I think I understand,' she added, with a far-off look in her eyes. 'Your book will a revelation be.'

Letitia thought fondly then about her doe-eyed Italian boy. How sweet he was, how statuesque; the living embodiment of a Donatello or a marble by Michaelangelo. Never had he failed her. The ravishing tool with which he pleasured her had always sprung to life the moment she required it, and lasted in its swollen glory until her very last orgasmic rush. What more could a woman want? She hurried back to the hotel in a fever of lust.

'Madame Ormesby-Gore,' the manager breathed, wringing his hands together in panic, 'Monsieur Paolo has left the hotel. He said he would not be coming back, and declined to give a forwarding address.'

Letitia fainted on the sofa in the lobby, and had to be revived with smelling salts. Then she cried violently, beating her breasts with the fury of an abandoned woman. 'How could he! What have I done to deserve this! My darling Paolo, where is he, what shall I do without him.'

After half an hour of this sort of self indulgent behaviour, the manager, who prided himself on keeping a respectable, quiet establishment, stepped forward, offering Letitia a large brandy. 'Maybe, madame, I can help. The young man left in the company of a Greek gentleman, in a very expensive car. Does this mean anything to you?'

'Greek, very tall, exceptionally tall?' she asked.

'*Oui*, madame.'

'Black hair, big nose, camel hair coat?'

'*Oui*, madame.'

'Mr Vossoudossoulos?'

'Monsieur Paolo addressed the gentleman as "Constantine",' the manager replied.

'It is he!' Letitia yelled. 'The Greek millionaire. The lover of Lidova! Where has he taken my darling?' She rushed by taxi to the Hotel de Paris and sought the ballerina.

Lidova was at first simply furious that Vossoudossoulos had returned to the Riviera without thinking to look her up, but then her suspicious mind began to run around in circles. *Why does he wish to take away this boy?* she asked herself. She slipped the bellhop a large note.

'Yes I did see the Greek gentleman with the English lady's friend,' smiled the little knowall, 'last evening in the bar.' The ladies would have saved time if they had handed over a few more francs, as the lad, with his world weary knowledge of the pitfalls of human life, had noticed in the rapport between the Greek and the Italian boy that certain tenderness that signifies the stirrings of 'the love that dare not speak its name'.

Vera and Letitia took tea and discussed the situation. Perhaps it was a joke, or a surprise trip; surely the pair would be back by the evening with a simple explanation.

Borzdoff joined them in the lounge. He had a knowing look on his face as he accepted a cup. Naturally the ladies told him of the perplexing departure. 'I had always had a question about the millionaire,' he grinned. 'For the pretty boy, Letitia, only can you know about him, but last night they would seem to be, how to say, a little loving inclined.'

The brutal truth was out. Neither could speak for the rage in their bosoms. The horror of betrayal for another woman would be ghastly—but this was ghastly beyond belief.

'We shall find them,' Letitia suddenly exclaimed. 'I am sure he has kidnapped my darling Paolo, or has drugged him. Perhaps even now he is struggling to get out of his bondage.' She made calls to the police and the coastguard, telephoned friends, the press and the British Consul, pleading for help. Eventually there was a breakthrough. The ocean going liner owned by Vossoudossoulos had been spotted off the Italian coast past Vingtimilia a few hours ago, and it was steaming in the direction of Genoa.

Lidova and Letitia hurriedly packed a bag each and soon they were hurtling along the coastal road in an open tourer.

'The ship is there to put us off the scent,' Letitia warned.

They checked at all the major hotels along the route, but came up with no clues until they stopped off at the Hotel Garibald: in Genoa. Yes, a middle aged man and his nephew had stayed the night there, but had checked out that morning, and made off for Rapallo.

Letitia bullied the car into top gear and took amazing risks along the serpentine road, dodging trucks and autobuses with the most reckless daring.

Lidova shut her eyes and prayed. It was a hair-raising experience. The ballerina was aware that, by taking time off like this, she was breaking her contract. Borzdoff would be outraged that she was not at rehearsal at a time so close to the Gala opening of the season, but she was so determined to find Vossoudossoulos and his bankroll that she was driven to recklessness. 'Go faster,' she implored, 'We must find them.'

They came to a hairpin bend on a high cliff, the sort of place where vehicles can crash down into the sea, and often do. Way out in the Mediterranean they could see the *Aphrodite*, the millionaire's flagship, riding at anchor, and guessed they were near to finding the errant pair.

'I could that ship own,' Lidova said, weeping copiously into her handkerchief, 'or be the wife of the owner, if he is a normal man. Why is the life so hard?' She thought of the cruises to Egypt, Turkey, the Black Sea, and the Bosphorus; why, perhaps even the Prince of Wales might be her guest, or Hemingway, or Scott and Zelda.

It was nearly midnight by now, so they took rooms at a small *pension* and spent a fitful night dreaming of their missing lovers.

Back in Monte Carlo, Borzdoff, grateful of the opportunity presented by Lidova's absence, called Paquin. 'Call Rosa la Touche,' he commanded. 'Vera has gone away. I hope she does not come back.'

Paquin was delighted to oblige. His Parisian partner and lover was a lot easier to dance with than Lidova, and certainly weighed about three kilos less than the Russian termagent, which was a bonus when it came to lifting her.

Fanshawe was alerted to the search. Like Borzdoff, he hoped the two ladies would get lost somewhere on the Italian coast and never return.

Letitia and Vera were red-eyed by dawn. They scanned the horizon from a one franc telescope on the sea front, hoping to see the *Aphrodite* again, but there was a depressing mist on the water, which hazed the view.

Letitia burst into yet another fit of tears. Vera was getting very bored with this, also there had been no breakfast in the *pension* so she was already a crosspatch.

'Let us to go home, darling,' she pleaded. 'I find another millionaire. I not want this one if he like boys.'

But Letitia was adamant. 'How do I know that the poor boy won't be sold into the slave trade?' she swept. Suddenly, the mist cleared and there was the huge vessel, half a kilometre off the coast. 'They must be here,' she cried and ran along the quayside of the little port, calling her beloved's name.

'They are there,' Lidova yelled, breaking into a series of *jetées* and *bourées* which brought her flying to the jetty. The escaping gentlemen looked startled by this balletic display, and were even more put out when Letitia came running breathless to the scene.

'Stop,' she cried. 'Give him back to me,' and she addressed her paramour, 'Paolo, *carissimo*, come back. We shall go to Florence again. I forgive you.'

But the wretched youth leaped into the waiting motor launch with the waiting Vossoudossoulos and waved her an ironic farewell. He was carrying a single valise and Letitia's only copy of the manual of penises.

The ladies watched the launch tie up to the liner, and the two men climb the ladder. Then the siren sounded and the liner pulled away and made for the horizon, leaving a plume of black smoke behind.

Letitia and Vera slumped on a wooden bench. They looked ten years older than their professed age.

'It is a dark day, to see a fortune like that to go away,' Vera said bleakly, and later, as they were trudging back to the car, 'I not think what Vossoudossoulos to see in your little Italian gigolo.'

'Oh, I don't know,' Letitia wavered, 'if he hasn't found out already, he soon will when he looks at the book.'

Throughout the journey back to the Principality Letitia pondered the situation. Paolo had never given her any reason to doubt his masculinity. On the contrary, he seemed to be the embodiment of male virility, so profoundly had he worshipped at her shrine. Lidova, equally, had been so ravished by the Greek and his dexterous use of his love machine she had never considered the possibility of the millionaire indulging in secret vice.

Still hanging on to a thread of hope, Letitia urged the ballerina to consider the chance that the liaison between her lover and the Greek was of a platonic nature. 'Perhaps it was his beautiful eyes,' she implored, 'or his lovely manners, his grace, and infinite charm?'

'No, darling,' Lidova said adamantly, 'the old dirty man wanted to get into his pants.'

But Letitia would not be moved, and the more she thought about it, the germ of a wonderful new idea was seeded in her brain. She would leave soon for an extended tour of Sicily, North Africa, Apulia, and all the other important areas where, in ancient times, the two great civilisations came together and bloomed; the marriage of two cultures that created history as we know it. She was ecstatic. Yes, her new book would be called 'The Greek meets the Italian' and its subject would be the flowering of the Graeco-Romano world; another bestseller which would put the seal on her growing reputation.

She put her foot down hard, and drove the open tourer with a reckless gaiety that matched the mood of her burgeoning inspiration, and a gleam came into her eye. The one photograph of Paolo she had in her possession was perfect for the front cover of her new tome. It showed him naked, save for a fig leaf at the vital place, on his head he wore a crown of ivy. The curve of his nostrils, the delicacy of his fine bone structure, and the indefinable moving quality of the artless pose, together created an allure that suggested the young Apollo, the god of love.

In spite of hurtling along like a Grand Prix racing driver, when Letitia deposited Vera Lidova at the stage door of the Opera House, it was too late. Rosa la Touche was already rehearsing *The Sleeping Beauty* with her lover Paquin.

The great ballerina was furious and pushed her aside just as she was about to fly across the stage in a soaring 'fish dive'. Instead of landing in the arms of her partner, the newly appointed principal fell into a costume skip.

Vera closed the lid of the wickerwork basket and sat on it, neatly imprisoning her rival. 'Who this monster is?' she screamed. 'And why is she taking my part? I, the great Vera Lidova am insulted. Call for the police and this dreadful woman have arrested.' Borzdoff approached fearfully. Vera slapped him across the face. 'You beast,' she yelled. 'As soon as Vera's back is turned, you making trouble. The role of Princess Aurora is mine, is sacred to Lidova, how dare you give to her?'

The company watched agog as Borzdoff withdrew Vera's contract from his inside pocket and tore it into a myriad of pieces. 'That is what I think of you, darling,' the normally urbane and oily manager riposted. 'You have broken contract, now I am breaking you. Go, leave the theatre, pack your bags and be off, I am finished with you. Bye bye.'

So Vera took the train for Paris, and on to London, where she found immediate work with Mr C. B. Cochran, and an enviable notoriety in society for her daring solos with such names as 'La Cigarette', 'La Petite Midinette', and 'La Jolie Fille de Montmartre'. These erotic dances, wearing the minimum of clothing, but saucily performed *sur les pointes*, brought her to the notice of Hollywood film producers, and soon she was whisked away to a brilliant new life in California. A great success story, it was agreed by all.

Some years later, Vossoudossoulos was sitting in a cinema with his beloved Paolo, and was amazed when a particularly steamy scene featuring the ballerina flashed on to the screen. The siren, bare-legged and provocative, smoking a black Sobranie in a long ivory holder, brazenly aroused the lust of a party of gangsters in a low dance hall, and then was subjected to a number of sexual harassments. The finale of the routine was spectacular. Vera was divested of her flimsy clothing by the ruffians and hoisted aloft spinning on an invisible wire, under the glare of a revolving mirror ball.

The Greek millionaire turned to Paolo, 'And to think that once I was mad for her,' he said. 'But not now, darling. Now I have found the real thing.'

Chapter Ten

It was now the height of summer. Every hotel and villa was bursting at the seams. Bernadette's guests, the young Scottish aristocrats, departed for home. They could no longer stand the relentless sun and heat of the Riviera and longed for the mists and rain of the Highlands. The vicomtesse was spoilt for choice when the time came to decide which further impecunious young persons should be awarded the tenancy of the guest suite.

Sophie introduced a pair of exotic looking Argentineans whom she had discovered at a tango evening in an old fashioned hotel at Eze Sur Mer. 'They perform brilliantly,' she exclaimed.

'But do they do as well in bed, *cherie*?' Bernadette enquired, as the ability to amuse, and satisfy her voyeuristic instincts, when viewed from the secret garden room, was the chief requirement of her guests.

'I've no idea,' Sophie admitted, 'though they look pretty sleek and sexy to me.'

'He is obviously a narcissist, darling. There won't be much fun there,' Bernadette insisted. 'What about those young Swedes we met at the party the other day at the Marquise de Sauvignon-Lafayette house? They are well bred and beautiful, though too well versed in the works of Ibsen and Chekhov, for my taste. However they have exquisite bodies and their long blonde hair makes them look like ancient Vikings—a prince and the bride he has stolen in a rapacious attack on Norway.'

'My darling, does your erotic imagination know no end?' Sophie enthused. 'Of course they are the ones, you are absolutely right. Do invite them at once.'

A luncheon party, the cousins decided, would be the right moment to ask the Danes along to the mansion and introduce them to the guest suite if they accepted the invitation. As the weather was so utterly divine, it would be held under a vast awning in the gardens.

The final guest list included Charles, Marie-Therese, Dhokouminsky, Sabine, M. Rognon, Camille, Arlette, Francois, Igor Polovsky, Galina, Paquin, Anton, The Contessa Lucia di Flagelli, Marcello Cerutti, Erik, Kirsten, Rose la Touche, Carlotta Bombieri, Borzdoff, Gavroche and Josette. At the last minute Letitia had been added also.

An anguished letter of apology had arrived at the mansion, accompanied by a large box of liqueur chocolates.

> *Dearest Bernadette,*
> *I am consumed with self-hate and regret. My world has caved in on me. How could I have been so ghastly to you in dear Marcel's boutique? I insulted you, the person I most admire in the world, and also was beastly to my darling Sophie. When I made that frightful suggestion that Marcel was perhaps being unfaithful, it is clear that I was cruelly motivated by the pure jealousy that I have for your sublime happiness. Such marital joy has always evaded me, as you know.*
>
> *Frederick is now banished to a house of seclusion and will not be released until he is cured of his addiction to alcohol.*
>
> *I have recently suffered another desperate loss. The young man I thought loved me turned out to have been a money grabbing opportunist, and what's more, a sodomist.*
>
> *My life is in tatters, and I am considering putting an end to it.*
>   *In tears,*
>   *Letitia.*

The vicomtesse and Sophie had wept copiously on receiving this pathetic note. 'How that poor woman has suffered,' they cried, and, 'ah, the world is a cruel place', and, 'she shows such remorse that she must be forgiven.'

They were amazed when the lady swept into the mansion looking gay and ravishing with yet another young man in tow.

'Hello, darlings. I knew it was to be a buffet luncheon, so I thought you wouldn't mind if I brought James. This is Professor James Harcourt-Glanville. He's a lecturer in Ancient History at Oxford University.' She explained, in a gushing torrent of adulatory enthusiasm that James was going to assist her with her new book about the Graeco-Romano Empire. The well connected young don, a scion of a great English dynasty whose head was the Earl of—— besides being the heir to vast estates, was an accepted literary genius whose works were now standard reference books.

'I suppose that we must accept also that he is a genius of the boudoir,' Bernadette remarked impishly to her cousin, 'otherwise he would have no interest for Lady Letitia.'

Sophie agreed. The exceedingly tall Englishman, with his aristocratic bearing and exceptional good looks certainly struck a good figure in her eyes. He was shy and reticent, totally unlike all the other hedonists and gregarious revellers who were present that lunchtime. Perhaps, under his owlish spectacles and British tweeds, there lurked a handsome body and a thrilling sexuality. Letitia certainly seemed to have recovered from her minor nervous breakdown, she looked radiant.

Cocktails were served by Mariette, the Corsican, who had her bottom pinched several times by Rognon, Dhokouminsky, Paquin, Marcello Cerruti and the painter Gavroche.

Her lover Yves, the bootboy, who had continued to pleasure her in her attic bedroom with consistent and exhausting ardour, had been deputised to fetch and carry bottles and ash trays. His stocky allure did not go unnoticed by Josette, Gavroche's mistress and model, who adored the enticing bulge in his pants and wondered if there might be an opportunity to investigate it closely at an intimate moment.

Paquin and Anton were charming to Sophie and Bernadette. Keeping a watchful eye on Marcel they managed to divert the ladies' attention for a few minutes and thank them for the blissful picnic and flirtation on the little island. They wondered, politely if such an event could be repeated. Bernadette and Sophie were so inflamed, and the memories of the stimulating afternoon came flooding back with such a powerful insistence and titillating urgency, that they began to reconsider their view not to engage in any more lustful activities with the adorable and well-endowed boys.

'Paquin *cheri*,' murmured Bernadette, 'your attractions and also your divine sexual abilities are already recorded in my intimate journal, and there's a small place for you in my heart. But I love my husband. Why should I be unfaithful to him?'

'Madame,' he replied, kissing her hand with that burning intensity in his dark eyes which so melted her before, 'because I am your slave, and I adore you.'

Anton was much less poetic when he approached Sophie. 'You loved my bit of gristle, didn't you, sweetheart,' he whispered in her ear. 'When can we do it again?'

In truth Sophie would have liked to take him upstairs that very moment, but her duties as a hostess prevented her from such indulgence.

Lucia, the contessa from Verona, was one of those incredibly rich women who flocked to the Riviera each year to buy thrills and participate in the legendary high jinks. Petite and chic, dressed by Schiapparelli, and bejewelled by Cartier, she was the picture of that expensive simple elegance that is the hallmark of wealthy leaders of fashion.

She was accompanied by Marcello Cerruti, an architect of great reputation and a philanderer of awesome notoriety. He had already made a few lewd suggestions to Galina, the *soubrette* of the ballet. In fact she was contemplating seriously whether she should return with him to Rome to indulge in the *dolce vita* to which he so persuasively referred. He painted an attractive picture of money, palaces, lavish parties, and orgies that seemed irresistible, and when he drew her hand down over his crotch, the large soft mass of his organ held the promise of much future enjoyment.

Marie-Therese held on to Charles's arm with grim determination, though she smiled in her mysterious way at everyone. Such a treasure was worth hanging on to, and a recent reading of a tea cup had warned her to beware of rapacious women coming between her and her beloved. She thanked the day Bernadette had consulted her about this errant English philanderer, and commissioned her to reorganise Charles's sexual life. The task had been arduous, but rewarding. His tactics of brute force had changed to more insinuating methods of seduction, with an insistence that his partner's needs came before his own. Now he approached her body with the delicacy of a surgeon preparing an operation, and with the imagination of a poet. She had become his lap-dog, receiving the most relaxing caresses, strokes and cuddles. he held her in his arms and whispered sweet nothings for hours before and after any carnal intensities, stroking and moulding as a sculptor treats his clay. She glowed with satisfaction that by her tutelage he had become so expert. Even now he exuded affection, and seemed to have eyes for no-one else. It was as if they shared a secret which bound them together, an amorous life which surpassed all her expectations. 'I am eternally grateful to you,' she said fervently to the vicomtesse. 'When you asked me to devise a therapy for Charles, I said that I would remain indifferent, but the strange processes that we have been through have not only changed his life, but mine also.'

Her contralto voice, expressing such serious emotions, stirred Bernadette deeply, as if it came from a mystic. 'And what of me, does life hold a similar promise?' she asked.

'Your mission in life is to entertain, and be engaging,' the seer replied. 'I have a vision of you at sea. You are intensely happy, dressed in white, in the arms of a tall young man. You alight on a small deserted island and make wonderful love. Ah, yes, I can see the shining light in his eyes as he declares his passion, mirrored in yours as you abandon yourself to his carnal devotions.'

Bernadette stood rooted to the spot, enthraled with this divination concerning the outing with Paquin. She felt naked under Marie-Therese's scrutiny, and fervently hoped no-one else had heard her speak.

Sophie observed her cousin's rapt expression and excused herself from a conversation with Rognon.

'I need a drink, I am feeling faint,' the vicomtesse said, slightly swaying. Charles obliged with a large gin-fizz.

Marie-Therese continued as if in a trance, speaking directly to Sophie, 'I see you outlined against a red sail. It is morning, misty and hot. Now you are bathing in a rock pool with a handsome blonde gentleman who does not speak your language, but at that moment loves you deeply.'

'Only at that moment?' Sophie asked with a tearful catch in her voice.

'The vision has clouded over,' Marie-Therese concluded, and moved on.

'My goodness, I don't know about that child,' the vicomtesse said to her cousin. 'She's always been a bit strange, playing on her cello halfway up a mountain and gazing at the stars, but I think she's gone a bit off her rocker.'

'It's sex, darling,' Sophie said brightly. 'It does that to people,' and she went off twittering, shaking her little bottom and chattering in her usual gay fashion with anyone wearing trousers.

Borzdoff adored her always. He was glad of an opportunity to chat about Vera Lidova's dramatic departure and the arrival of his new star Rose la Touche. 'That girl friend of Paquin,' he began.

'Oh, he's spoken for, is he?' she asked, concerned for Bernadette who adored Paquin.

'Yes indeed, they are lovers of old,' he replied. 'Anyway, as I was to go saying, she will be stunning, just you see. She is brilliant.'

Sophie could not wait to tell her cousin that the man who had pleasured her so effectively the other day had been unfaithful to Rose la Touche.

Bernadette waved a hand carelessly, 'It is the way of the male of the species,' she exclaimed.

'And also of the female?' her cousin enquired with a twinkle.

'Immorality in men is a curse,' the vicomtesse said airily, 'but in women it is a privilege.'

'I do think we are lucky, darling,' Sophie beamed, 'just take a look at this divine collection of men.' The four cocktails she had consumed had gone to her head with delicious effect. 'The Italian architect is so appealing, and his Latin temperament would ensure he would be a perfect lover. The Swede is ravishing, I wouldn't mind a few hours with him. My Anton is simply stunning, and even old Dhokouminsky still stirs me, though I am happy he has found Sabine. The Englishman, Letitia's friend is so charmingly old-fashioned, and Palovsky is breathtaking. Oh, I am in a delirium.'

'When aren't you?' Bernadette laughed. 'Excuse me, my darling, I must have a word with my husband, and drag him away from that busty lady who models for Gavroche.'

Mariette disengaged herself from M. Rognon's arm which had slid round her waist, and sidled up to Yves who was standing behind the cocktail bar. 'The only thing these posh folk can think about is sex,' she complained to the stocky lad.

'You think you're different?' he grinned, passing a stealthy hand down her thigh.

The gesture was not missed by M. Moutarde, their superior, who had for long envied the bootboy's position, that is to say, the one in the housemaid's bed.

Dhokouminsky had come straight from his morning entanglements with Sabine. The reader will remember that Sabine made great use of Bernadettes' advice to stop pampering her body and to strive for a natural, less sanitised look. After a dalliance with Alain, then a liberating afternoon with George Sombert, she was even prepared to take on the wild Tartar and cope with the relentless demands on her body which were caused by the satyriasis which afflicted him.

Even now, so soon after a series of ejaculations that would render the average man inert for at least the rest of the day, Dhokouminsky had his hands on Josette's ample breasts, and was pressing his hardening part at her pudendum.

Gavroche was so occupied with Rose la Touche that he did not notice this ravishment. Rose was impressed by the painter's attentions and his wish to immortalise her on canvas, especially as he had been so charming in his insistence that, being the possessor of such a wonderful body, she should pose in the nude.

Sabine was in deep conversation with Erik, the tall Swede, who captivated her with his tale about canoeing down the Orinoco in search of a primitive tribe, and how he had recorded on film their strange ceremonies of sexual initiation. She was naturally intrigued when Erik kindly offered to share with her, in the privacy of her apartment, some of the discoveries he had made. But she declined the offer of his tutelage. She had no wish to arouse her splendid lover Dhokouminsky to commit a *crime passionel*.

Erik's partner Kirsten attracted Paquin and Anton like a candle beckons to a moth. Her gown of flowing chiffon was so transparent that it revealed all of her charms in the most ultra modern way. The pair knew, of course, of the Swedes' reputation for sexual liberation; those long twilight hours in the birch woods, nights of midsummer madness inspired by earth worship, and pagan adoration of the *aurora borealise*. Yes, they thought, it would be worth getting to know this little Northerner.

The vicomtesse and Sophie were pleased by the attentions being paid to the Swedes.
'You see how Paquin and Anton are drawn to Kirsten's lure,' Sophie said, 'and those boys are no fools.'
'Quite, and Sabine is lusting for Erik. These blonde children are obviously going to be very entertaining when they are installed in the guest suite, if the sexual attraction they are displaying now is anything to go by.'

'You have not been along to my house, recently, M. Rognon,' the brothel keeper Carlotta Bombieri chided, giving him a lascivious grin, and a small pat on the groin. 'How have you been able to contain yourself so long, my dear?'

'Hello, Lotty,' the art dealer replied, 'You know, I've been busy, but I'll be back soon. Your girls are so lovely. I think about them all the time.' It was a lie, because his every awakened moment was occupied with erotic dreams about Camille, the practitioner of self-induced orgasms, who had aroused such carnal ferocity in him that he had enjoyed an example of that phenomenon himself, the very first since he was a lad of twenty.

Camille was enthralled by Igor Polovsky, the conductor of the ballet. The elegant maestro, dressed in his perfectly fitting suit and reeking of cologne, had driven her so wild with emotion, and she was so flushed from the engaging climax she had suffered, that she had to retreat to the shade of a hibiscus at the end of the terrace.

Igor's partner, Galina, still pondering the delights of Cerutti's Rome, had transferred her interest to Letitia's co-author, James. 'England sound so lovely, so pretty. Maybe I come. Stay with you, eh? I was once rider in circus. You have horses?'

'Oh my goodness, dozens,' the landed gentleman replied, astonished that she seemed to be offering herself up for the price of a pony.

M. Moutarde announced lunch. M. Ratatouille had surpassed himself. The first course was a cold *bouillon*, served with smoked quails eggs and *foie gras*, and was followed by fresh water crayfish in a delicate champagne sauce.

Dhokouminsky surprised no-one with his greed. By now it was common knowledge that he was a glutton. But Ratatouille had been warned by his employer, and with great aplomb, brought along another dish of the tasty morsels.

The main fish course, poached fillets of red mullet, was superb, as was the accompanying white wine, a delicious Chateau Périgord of clarity and distinction.

Dhokouminsky knocked it back as if it were lemonade.

'This is the piss of cats,' he pronounced, and demanded vodka.

Marcel was charming to Letitia. After all, she had apologised, and her custom at the *salon* was useful. 'Come see me tomorrow,' he breathed. 'I have had a veritable inspiration for your dress for the Gala opening of the ballet. It will make you the star of the evening.'

Ratatouille's desserts were incomparable. Souflées, meringues, chocolate mousses, crême caramels and bombes glacées followed in quick succession, to be devoured at once by the ensemble who were by now well into the drink.

The talk grew careless, postures became more relaxed, and by the time coffee was served, most of the company had changed places. It was rather like a chess game. Some of the pieces retired, defeated, others ploughed on to the bitter end. Some flaked out in deck chairs, or fell asleep under the trees.

James, the historian found the changing pavilion at the side of the pool and while Letitia dozed in the rose garden, found joy in Galina, riding her as well as she had ridden her circus animals.

Cerruti discovered an arbour covered with honeysuckle and spent an agreeable hour there with the model Josette. They did not talk about either architecture or painting.

Anton took Kirsten for a stroll on the small island in the middle of the lagoon, and fell on her in the shade of the enormous willow that grew there. His own willow, as hard as a cricket bat, scored a century several times over.

The Contessa Lucia di Flagelli was escorted to a guest room in the mansion by Dhokouminsky who slipped Mariette a few francs.

Sabine was unconcerned, because she, in the arms of Erik, the Swedish anthropologist, was almost dying of ecstasy in the waters of the pool.

Marcel and Bernadette waited until the guests had departed before they retired for post-prandial exercise.

Sophie, after going to the kitchens to thank Ratatouille for his commendable efforts, collapsed in bed with Arthur, grateful for the ever willing attitude of his outstanding part.

The room was shuttered and cool, inviting and heavily perfumed. Arthur needed no encouragement, the day had been provocative enough. As he drove at Sophie's parts, in his imagination he recalled the sensuous looks of Rose la Touche, and Sabine's amatory glances. In other words, besides enjoying his beloved, there was the double bonus of the stimulation the thought of those ladies provoked.

Sophie, warm and intoxicated, abandoned herself to Arthur's ram-rod thrusts, dreaming of the afternoon on the rocks with Anton, and the silly imploring glances with which he had favoured her as the luncheon progressed from sobriety to lustful and self-indulgent salaciousness. 'What a blissful day', she moaned when Arthur paused briefly, 'and what a delicious way to celebrate it coming to an end.'

'Yes, yes,' Arthur agreed with some urgency, as he was coming close to his climax.

'Ah, my love,' she cried, as he brought her with lightening strokes nearer to completion, 'you have a glorious service.' Seconds later, as they both roared into carnal fulfilment, with Arthur thrust deeper than she had ever experienced before, she called out, each separate syllable matched by an orgasmic pulse of the most thrilling kind, 'Bra . . . vo . . . game . . . set . . . and . . . match . . . to . . . you.'

In the adjoining principal suite of rooms, the mistress of the house was engaged in a similar exercise with the master.

Marcel had been intensely stimulated by the presence of so many gorgeous women at the luncheon party. Kirsten, the blonde seductress from Sweden had particularly distracted him with her loosed limbed swaying gait and the transparency of her daring dress. She had entranced him with her tales of reckless profligacy in the forests of her motherland, boating parties on the innumerable secret lakes of the vast interior, idyllic outdoor feasts and romps in the birchwoods. Such a natural outdoor life appealed to the couturier, who spent his life in stuffy fitting rooms, albeit attending to attractive ladies. The thought of so much naked flesh, so wantonly displayed, had disturbed the composure of his genitals all afternoon to such a pitch that he was desperate for some relief.

Bernadette had also suffered various erotic arousals. Throughout the day she had been aware of the brooding presence of Paquin, and the few moments she had allowed them to converse with any intimacy had affected her immensely. Even now she was thinking of him with a deep longing, stroking her thighs with relish. The next meeting, she promised herself, would be a more private affair than a shared foursome, in a setting more conducive to prolonged foreplay, with a more leisurely approach that would allow Paquin to reveal the full extent of his sexual techniques. Other elements crept into her erotic fantasies. Erik's muscular frame stood out in her imagination, inviting her to contemplate his rippling muscles, and she had a vision of the elegant Polovsky dressed in white tie and tails conducting a large symphony orchestra with manic drive and superb musicianship.

Marcel was making his music on her private parts, kisses and nudging little presses with his tongue that further aroused her. 'I adore you.' Marcel whispered between mouthfuls, now squeezing at her breasts.

'You are the only man I have ever loved, apart from my late husband,' the vicomtesse lied. 'For me other men have no interest at all.'

'It's the same thing with me, darling,' Marcel murmured, dreaming of a wild afternoon in the woods with Kirsten.

Bernadette gently led his fingers towards her treasure trove and insinuated one of them in her moist tunnel. It reminded her of the sensation she received from Paquin in the rock pool, and for Marcel it was the delirious-making start of a randy attack on the Swedish girl.

'Oh, Paquin,' Bernadette groaned, 'it's marvellous.'

'What's that?' Marcel cried.

'Oh, I'm sorry darling,' she said hastily, and with great invention, 'I was just thinking how lovely it is for him to be reunited with Rose la Touche.'

'Of course, my sweet one, lovers should never be apart,' Marcel crooned in her ear, wishing that his separation from the object of his desire, the lovely Kirsten, would not last too long.

'Take me now,' she urged.

'Of course, Kirsten,' Marcel gasped.

'What's that?' cried Bernadette.

'I said of course Kirsten. I was thrilled you had offered them the little apartment,' was her husband's quick response.

'It will be marvellous having them, won't it,' Bernadette breathed, thinking of the great pleasures to come for her and her cousin in the secret garden room, observing the Northern pair at play. Memories of carnal scenes she had witnessed through the two-way mirror and the hidden peep-hole came flooding back as Marcel inserted his priapus, and slid in to the hilt of that handsome weapon. A procession of former tenants of the guest wing passed before her eyes, and she enjoyed every one.

Marcel, thrusting manfully as he induced these visions for Bernadette, first took Camille, the sensual, leonine paragon. Then, pausing with the tip of his palpitating organ poised at the surface of the outer labia of his expectant wife, drove into Sabine, whose sexuality had long intrigued him. He savoured her delights for a long while, without agitating his pelvis, and throbbed the muscles of his member to electric effect, reminding Bernadette of yet another of Paquin's Parisian tricks. As the vicomtesse responded, with an amazing series of vaginal contractions which almost resulted in a premature extraction of his seminal fluids, Marcel imagined himself locked in the same delicious grip with the unattainable Marie-Therese. The thought inspired him to recommence his missionary devotions. Each push and withdrawal brought fresh pictures into both of their minds' eye, in a banquet of sensations as lavish as the foregoing luncheon, until the blinding light which attacks frenzied lovers streamed into their consciousness and they exploded in miraculous and deliciously deceitful paroxysms of joyful orgasm.

Over their heads in the hot attics where the servants were accommodated, Yves and Mariette had only just started to get undressed. They had much clearing up to do after the guests had left; sweeping, tidying, cleaning the kitchen, and removing the large number of empty wine bottles, had kept them busy for several more hours. Their exhaustion was made the worse on account of their early rise that morning to prepare for the feast.

Yves managed to clean his teeth and then promptly fell asleep in his narrow bed, snoring and twitching in a slumber so profound that Mariette crept out and retired to bed in her own room next door. It was hot and sultry. She was too tired now to sleep and tossed and turned, with the sheets turned back, in a lather of heat and exhaustion.

The fading photograph of her bandit lover from Corsica, now on the run with the Foreign Legion in the Sahara, stood on the small bedside table. Mariette gazed at it with lust. It was while she was manipulating herself with a forefinger, stimulated by carnal memories of the dark-haired peasant, that Yves had insinuated himself stealthily into her room, his bursting member also the subject of self-abuse. How they had laughed and giggled at the ridiculous situation and decided that love for two was better than solitary, self-controlled affairs. The shameful moment when they discovered each other resorting to such wasteful practices was soon forgotten the minute Yves displayed is handsome organ to the fevered woman. He quickly showed her how the real thing was better than the imagined object of her frustrated desire.

Such recollections came flooding back to the busty maid and aroused her lust, causing her to reach for the sepia photograph in its wooden frame. But there was no relief in it for her that hot night. The magic had worn off, and all she could think of was the fat, juicy stamen that Yves was no doubt cradling in his sleep next door. It was dawn before she slept, and then only fitfully. Outside, the morning chorus of the birds started up, and distant sounds of traffic on the boulevard disturbed her even more.

Mariette rose from her crumpled bed and paced the floor. She then washed every part of her body at the jug and basin on the marble stand, trying to cool her inflamed part with the damp sponge, but to no avail. The lust that pre-occupied her was driving her to distraction. She crept out of her room, with only a towel draped round her body, and turned down the landing. Ratatouille, opposite, was already awake. She could hear him softly whistling as he performed his ablutions. Next to his room Lulu, another housemaid could be heard scrubbing her teeth and spitting into the porcelain bowl. Opening Yves' door as carefully as she could manage, she saw him lying on his back. The sheet was tossed aside on the floor. She entered on tip toe, closing the door with the smallest click, and crept nearer his prostrate form.

His chest was thickly matted with black hair, and his curly locks were in disarray on the pillow. The muscular thighs were splayed open in a wide V, and both his fists were clamped about his principal feature so tightly that the knuckles showed white. It was an entrancing sight for the Corsican maid. She dropped the towel and placed a hand to her private part, rubbing gently. The swollen stem of Yves' member twitched in his sleep, and a wolfish grin spread over his lips. He was obviously in the middle of an erotic dream as a drop of his jissom appeared at the tip of his pink glans. She touched it lightly, marvelling at its lubricity. When she lifted her finger tip away, a viscous thread of the juice came away in a luminous thread and stretched at least fifteen centimetres before it broke and fell back on to the swollen head of his rod.

Mariette's parts were now burning and wishing to come into contact with this magnificent stocky pole. She carefully climbed on the bed and placed her knees on either side of the boy's hips. With her finger tip again she spread the flowing liquid that still seeped from the orifice of the object she so desired, until the whole of the tulip shaped head was coated with his jissom. Slowly she lowered her haunches until the first outer lips of her own orifice touched the very tip of Yves' upright stem, which he still clutched, in the abandoned fantasy of his dream. At the moment of contact, as if to order, his fingers relaxed their grip and slid away from his tool. As she lowered herself even further his arms stretched wide, as if in acceptance of her offering. Mariette snuffled down until she enclosed the whole of the throbbing organ, and she sighed as it responded with a strong muscular contraction. She stayed there still, in wonderment that, even asleep, her divine bootboy could give her such thrills.

Yves stirred in his carnally inspired slumber, heaving his hips upwards, and even lifting Mariette's considerable weight. Her hot emission came tumbling down in delightful waves over the inserted phallus which had so often driven her wild with emotion, and she clutched her breasts, rolling them around in her ecstasy. Suddenly she felt a bursting shower of liquid shoot into the deepest recess of her love chamber and heard Yves groan loudly from the sheer bliss of his ejaculation. Mariette covered his mouth with her hands, and moments later, when he had subsided, with her lips, forcing him from his sleep and his glorious reveries.

The moment of awakening was divine. Light streamed through the window, outlining the shape of his plump little mistress, with her buttocks rounded over his groin. It was one of those rare moments when dreams are the stuff of reality, and life is but a dream; an elusive shadow that we are privileged to have wash over us.

Chapter Eleven

No-one was more excited than Carlotta Bombieri when it was announced that the British Fleet were soon to be expected in the Mediterranean. She realised that its arrival would mean big business for her several establishments. She had recently expanded, opening departments in Nice, Villefranche and Antibes as well as her original parlour in Marseilles. Time was short now. She had to engage many more 'artistes', as she called her girls, if she were to cope with the massive demands of the hundreds if not thousands of frustrated Jack Tars who would fly to her for relief. Telegrams were despatched to Tangier, Casablanca, Paris, and Naples, which was her birthplace. Her agents were quick to oblige, with photographs and curriculum vitae of possible candidates. When she had perused these, and taken note of any 'specialities' which the ladies offered, pre-paid tickets were sent off, marked 'urgent' on the envelopes.

Borzdoff, Rognon, Fanshawe, and Letitia's co-author James, (for he had quickly become an addict to the charms of Carlotta's bordello in Marseilles) were delighted at the news. It would be so much more convenient to have nearer facilities, they thought, and a bigger number of girls would add interestingly to the variety of possibilities. They paid their respects to the owner one evening after a hair-raising drive along the coast road.

'Ah, you have come for a little sport,' the bejewelled dwarf smiled. 'Messieurs, I don't think you will go away disappointed.' She clapped her hands and a dozen girls appeared as from nowhere. All were stark naked. It was her new policy, she explained. No-one could complain if the lady of his choice was not up to standard when she was undressed.

'How naive of the old girl,' James smirked. 'Doesn't she know that some of us chaps wouldn't dream of going to bed with an undressed lady?' He did not add, but the others guessed, that his own preference, as he was a product of the English public school system, was for a woman in the garb of a governess, or on occasion, a school matron.

Fanshawe said nothing, but he was thinking much the same; except in his case the clothing had to be black, made of leather or rubber. He had never been able to work out why.

Rognon and Borzdoff were uncomplicated in this respect. They only wanted naked flesh, as much of it as was possible.

None of the present bunch was sufficiently covered for their tastes, they said, where upon Carlotta threw off her silk boudoir gown, revealing a tight corset of flaming scarlet taffeta, laced with a black ribbon. Her dumpy legs were clad in black silk stockings, held up by a suspender belt which was decorated with crimson rose buds. Her huge breasts were hardly contained by the corset, and bulged in creamy mounds over the top. On one side, even a nipple was revealed, startling pink in colour, and extremely prominent. 'Go on, you fools, go get the booze,' she yelled at the girls, 'and put the music on.'

The gaggle of ladies dispersed, save for one who went to wind up the gramophone in the corner. By the time she had placed the needle in the groove, another returned with several bottles of Moet et Chandon in an ice bucket. Carlotta was anything but mean when it came to supplying her clients with drink.

The diminutive madame took up a pose, with an artificial rose between her teeth, on a low table, in the soft glow of a beaded lamp overhead. The effect, if not exactly electrifying, was of some small statuesque quality, bust poked forward, posterior thrust out, hands on hips, and a salacious leer on her painted mouth. The music was of the Arabic variety, wailing, rhythmic, and deeply sensuous.

Carlotta swivelled her large hips in time to the tune, circling and grinding, Fanshawe thought, like a hoofer in Minsky's,

New York. Rognon was immediately captivated and felt a familiar throb in his groin. Borzdoff was less impressed, until the champagne girl came over uninvited and sat on one of his knees, and swayed in time to the music. She had large pendulous breasts which she managed to dangle in front of his nose. Soon she took hold of one of them and pushed its nipple into his mouth.

The girl who had started the gramophone slid over and dropped her bottom on to the couch next to Rognon. It was a pleasant behind, if not as large as he would have liked, and when she placed a hand in his groin and tickled his swelling member through the cloth of his trousers, he began to think she was quite adorable.

Carlotta undid one of the suspenders, and stepping off the table, advanced towards James. She lifted a foot up to his knee, with difficulty since her legs were so short, and begged him to assist her by removing her black stocking. As he drew the silk down her thigh, James felt a tremor between the tops of his legs. The moment was akin to one many years ago when he peeped through a keyhole in his headmaster's house and saw his wife at her *toilette*.

She repeated the action, using the other leg on Fanshawe. He was unmoved until he had rolled the stocking down to her fat ankle and found that she was wearing patent leather high heeled shoes, exactly the sort of stuff that figured in his fantasies. He too felt a thrill, a ripple in his testes, followed by a distinct throb in his tool.

The girl ministering to Borzdoff extracted her nipple from his lips and reached over for a glass of champagne. After she had trickled a few drops on to the prominence, she popped it back in. Borzdoff sucked with renewed energy.

Carlotta was anything but a fool. She had noticed that slightly glazed look in Fanshawe's eyes when he touched her shoe, so she took to grinding a heel in the area of his fly buttons. There was a wicked, hurtful look on her face which seized his imagination. His rod shot to full thickness in a trice, bulging away from his pants. Carlotta seized her chance. Stooping, she removed the shoe and tapped the disturbance smartly with it, saying, 'You naughty boy, you naughty little boy. How dare you be so rude.'

The correction, mild as it had been, affected his tumescence even more, jolting it into full stretch. He could feel his glans shoot out of his foreskin.

The girl next to Rognon was no fool either. She came over to Fanshawe and pulled him back to the couch. There she opened his flies, and next, Rognon's, exposing both of their pieces, and sat between them with a swollen stamen in each of her hands, twitching in time to Carlotta's music.

A third girl entered in a matter-of-fact way. She was wearing a small maid's apron which just decently covered her private parts. After pouring more champagne and handing it round, she knelt at James's feet. As he watched Carlotta's dance progress from slow undulations to a more insistent and faster rhythm, the girl swayed in front of him, cupping her breasts in her hands. The effect was hypnotic. She watched the hardness in his trousers grow to an interesting shape, and then cupped that, before opening his buttons and lowering her lips on to the tip of the massive member she found.

A fourth courtesan, taller than the rest, with an interesting display of tattoos in the area of her groin and on her rump, idled into the room. 'You can't have two, dear,' she said to her colleague who was playing with the organs of Fanshawe and Rognon.

Carlotta danced towards the group. 'Quite, don't be greedy,' she said, and supervised the redistribution of the prize possessions between the pair of girls who both then took to sucking noisily.

The dwarfish madame began to unlace her corset, at the same time tapping with her heels on the floor like a flamenco dancer. Her dance brought her to Borzdoff, who still had his lips enjoyably at his girl's nipple, and his own hands massaging his considerable organ.

As the corset came off Carlotta's huge breasts fell into their natural place, curvaceous and rotund. She pushed the girl to her knees and, after fishing in Borzdoff's trousers, tipped her forward and introduced his thick rod gently between her lips.

Bombieri contemplated the scene with satisfaction. The four men stretched out, with their legs extended, being paid profoundly moving attention. Each had his eyes closed, so there was no need to continue her dance. But she let the music play on until the record reached its end. When she lifted the needle, there was only the sound of sucking in the room, from a quartet of experts applying that well-known technique of oral stimulation, and the groans of a quartet of clients in the throes of simultaneous satisfaction.

'I say chaps, that was a bit of all right, don't you think?' James said, breaking the silence after the satisfied grunts of the four faded away, and post-ejaculatory, smug little smiles creased their faces.

'A bit public, for my taste,' yawned Fanshawe, buttoning his flies, 'though I suppose you should try every goddam thing there is to do in this crazy world, unless it's cruel to kids, animals or old ladies.

'Speaking of old ladies, I thought you did very well, Lotty,' Rognon rather tactless remarked, wiping his piece with his silk handkerchief.

Bombieri smiled, 'That is why you come to the professionals, my dear,' she smirked, heaving her bust into place. 'Bravo girls, Carlotta is proud of you.'

The four ladies curtsied daintily and left the *salon*, with a flurry of little waves and blown kisses.

'Madame,' said one of them, Zizi by name, as she hurried back into the room, 'there are a few gentlemen in the hallway, waiting to consult you.'

Our four heroes looked up, and sure enough, framed by the beaded curtains, looped back with tassels, which hung in the archway, were three men. Their eyes were staring, their mouths open. They had obviously been witness to the foregoing scene. All had their hands over their crotches, a sure sign that they had been enflamed by what they had seen, such is the nature of the lascivious male beast of the species.

'Come in, my dears, and meet my friends,' the resourceful Carlotta cried, followed by, 'bring more champagne, you silly idle tarts.'

It was hard for the first group of clients to behave in any other way than as gentlemen and sports, once Bombieri's invitation had been made, especially as one of the new arrivals, to their surprise, was the painter Gavroche.

'Hullo, Rognon, *mon vieux*,' he called, 'you dirty old ram. I didn't expect to find you here.'

The art dealer was not too pleased by this remark. 'Why ever not, Gavroche,' he retorted. 'There's life in the old dog yet.'

'Hi,' Fanshawe drawled, 'they have a nice line in lollypopping here.'

'So we noticed,' remarked one of Gavroche's artist friends.

Introductions proper were made over drinks. Gavroche had brought his mates Gabin and Davide along for a treat, to celebrate his continued success at Rognon's gallery. The pictures based on Vladimir and his friend Ivan from the *corps de ballet*, and Josette, had been much admired and sold for huge prices, so he had money in his pocket.

'My favourite here is Josephine,' Gavroche confided to James. 'Have you tried her yet?' James confessed he had not, but was curious to know why Gavroche preferred her. 'She has a splendid way with a bottle of oil,' Gavroche croaked, quivering at the memory of his last encounter. 'It's marvellous if you like slithering about, all greasy and lubricated, and she's so supple, so athletic,' he added, his voice trailing away as a far off look came into his eye. 'Look, here she is now.'

A slender ravishing girl entered. She had a walk like a panther, proud and feline. Josephine hailed from Morocco and was of mixed blood. Her skin was golden and of silky appearance, well oiled by the attar of roses which was her stock in trade. 'Cheri,' she addressed Gavroche, sinking into his lap to sip from his glass, 'it is so long. I have been waiting for you to come back, you monster.'

Josephine was followed by Mirette who glided in brushing her long tawny hair with vigorous strokes. Gabin's backside happened to face her, so she gave it a playful couple of taps, indicating the nature of one of her specialities. He found it quite stimulating and found her high small breasts were also to his satisfaction.

Lola came next, trailing a pink feather boa which she flicked at Davide's crotch playfully, an artful smile on her lips. He found her gorgeous and irresistible.

Carlotta was pleased with her girls and offered them all a glass of champagne. The conversation was gay and witty, spiked with raucous laughter when one of the new arrivals, for instance, played a naughty little trick, or when one of the three girls gasped in mock surprise at the size of the erection she managed to induce by skilful and discreet manipulation. Bombieri judged the time to be ripe for the three couples to attend to business and tipped the wink to Josephine, who led the way, with a little nod to her chums Mirette and Lola.

Madame placed a bejewelled finger to her lips, indicating to Rognon, Fanshawe, James and Borzdoff to remain quietly in place, and when her new clients had departed for the upstairs room, led the way without a word towards a hidden door which led to a staircase. The four, with newly filled glasses climbed the treads carefully as requested, and came into a dimly lit passage on the first floor where three small panes of glass threw off the merest glow of light. They lit cigarettes and sipped their champagne in anticipation of the show that was to begin.

Carlotta breathed heavily nearby, rubbing her hands together. 'You know this will cost extra,' she whispered to Rognon, her favourite of the group.

'No problem,' he replied, giving her large breasts an affectionate cuddle. She returned the compliment with a calculated caress at his groin, lingering and delicate, causing his detumesced organ to start to life again.

Her progress down the line of voyeurs was impressively successful in arousing their expectations. 'You must be quiet,' she urged Fanshawe, 'this little secret must not get out,' and massaged his bottom seductively, exploring naughtily into the crack between his cheeks, with a little jab at the most sensitive spot. 'Do not get over excited, my dear,' she whispered in James's ear, 'nor speak out loud, or all is lost. Silence is golden,' and she gave him a rippling tickle over the ribs with a quick little squeeze at his nipples.

Borzdoff was already excited, as he had been privileged to enter the passage before and had seen some extraordinary events take place. It is curious how the love-making of others can so affect us mere mortals.

Carlotta's hand slipped into his trouser pocket. 'Ah, I see you are primed, Borzdoff, like a cannon about to discharge its shot,' she hissed, in wily fashion. '*Attends*, they are about to begin.'

The watching foursome had to admit that the three professional ladies in the adjoining rooms were expert at their trade. they watched as Josephine anointed Gavroche with a liberal amount of her precious oil and massaged every particle and crevice of his body with her long slim fingers, probing and pressing gently, then vigorously, until his stem rose vertically from his belly, thick and proud. Then she poured a stream of the unguent over the erect member and smoothed it until it was equally distributed, slapping and tickling with her palms like a milkmaid attends to a beast about to be milked.

Gavroche was in heaven, writhing with the deepest pleasure on the silken sheets and reaching up to stroke her pendulous breasts. His body was so oiled that when she lay on top of him she could roller-coaster all over him without friction. The severity of his hardness was completed so fast, and his need to evacuate his seed so acute, he slid her off his body and mounted her in one swooping movement, expelling his fluids with an impressive series of thrusts of his buttocks.

The party moved down the corridor and watched outside the small cabinet where Mirette was attending to Gabin with her hairbrush. His backside was already reddened from her light little strokes, which obviously tickled, rather than hurt badly. She turned him over and played with the same effect at his stubby organ, tapping it to one side and then the other, with great dexterity. She held his scrotum as she played on his instrument, bringing it to full extension by her dainty flicks and manipulations and was rewarded, professionally, when a stream of his juices flew out and laced across her bosom.

Lola and Davide took more time to come to his climax. Her act with the feather boa was leisurely and playful, calculated to arouse slowly but surely. The opening gambit was a long slow delicious trail of the boa from his toes to his head, and then back down the other side. Delightful small flicks at his chest and belly followed and then, of course, there was some attention paid to the limp article that lay across the top of his thigh.

Carlotta and the other four onlookers could hardly suppress a giggle at the sight of the tiny tremors which began to course through Davide's less than averagely sized, drooping pride and joy. Lola persisted, helping the situation with kisses and tweakings. Eventually there was some life in the object, then more and more until it swelled to giant size.

'Such tall trees from acorns grow,' whispered James, devastated with the laughter he had to choke back.

The resourceful Lola threaded her boa round the wavering flag pole several times and pulled the ends tightly together, obviously contributing a stimulating constriction to it, as Davide visibly began to pant and heave.

'AAaaagh,' he cried as the friction of the feathers brought him to boiling and a truly remarkable orgasm shot half way across the room.

Speaking of boiling, the four voyeurs were near to bursting themselves, but they had to hurry back downstairs before Gavroche and his mates composed themselves and returned to the *salon*, that is, if they were finished for the moment. Carlotta clapped her hands together. The remaining girls filed in to audition again, but none of the four had the patience to go through the normal processes. Blindly they each took one of them by the hand and led them upstairs to other rooms to continue the evening's sport.

It was a good night for Carlotta, especially when she held the money in her hands later, and boded well for the arrival of the British Fleet in a few days' time.

Chapter Twelve

The ballet rehearsals were proceeding space, gathering in intensity as opening night approached. International balletomanes and members of the press began to arrive in Monte Carlo, ecstatic at the prospect of seeing the new season's offerings.

Impresarios who had heard of the Ballets Russes' success on its latest tours and residences came along sniffing, looking to earn themselves a quick dollar. Borzdoff fobbed them off with his usual lack of tact, refusing them entry to the increasingly nerve-wracked practice sessions.

Rumours about the sacking of Vera Lidova were rife, and there was much speculation about the new ballerina, Rose la Touche.

'But she's inexperienced,' complained one American devotee,' and I'm quite sure she won't be able to balance long enough on her pointes for the *Rose Adagio*'.

'Old-fashioned Paris Opera trash, darling,' added another more outspoken fan, drooping his wrists with that characteristic movement that sexual deviants use when they wish to stress a point.

On stage the choreographers beat their breasts as the dancers tried to come to grips with the New Music, discordant and unmelodic compositions in which no two bars were played at the same time, rhythm or tempo. It was far removed from the splendours of Minkus, Glinka, Delibes, Strauss and all the other favourites, whose melodies were delivered in strict time; reliable old settings that did not tax the dancers in such a tortuous way.

The subjects of the scenarios also presented problems. No

longer were ballets about mice and fairies, ghosts and apparitions. The fashion of the day was for stories about real people, dramatic inventions as difficult as those being explored in the cinema. It was horror all round.

Hundreds of costumes had to be completed, and scenery painted by cubists and fauves, Art Deco maniacs and New Expressionists.

Borzdoff thought he was going crazy, and for once the dancers retired to the Hotel de la Poste without the maddening lust that normally plagued their bodies and minds.

Vladimir would go home to Angelique and weep with exhaustion, and the normally ebullient Dhokouminsky failed to satisfy Sabine.

Rose de la Touche was as tired as Paquin, and so needed none of his stimulations, and Galina, the *soubrette*, was soundly asleep by the time Polovsky climbed into her bed.

Tempers flew under the strain. Anna Galinka slapped Anton across the cheek after he dropped her from a high lift, and the *corps de ballet* went on temporary strike when the ballet master kept them in the theatre until midnight rehearsing a new work by Trotovsky.

The final dress rehearsal of the Gala opening was a disaster. The curtain came down too soon at the end of the first ballet, rendering Dhokouminsky senseless, but the flow of alcohol in his veins, plus a large brandy administered by Borzdoff quickly revived him. Scenery fell over as Rose de la Touche struggled to stay on point, ruining her balance; and an over enthusiastic *jeune soloiste* fell into the orchestra pit, ruining the timpani, when he overstretched the capacity of his elevation.

Borzdoff thanked God for a bad rehearsal, following the theatrical tradition that says a good one spells disaster, and when the curtain rose the following night he said fervent prayers. They were answered, as the glittering audience rose to its feet roaring its acclaim.

Marcel, surrounded by the ladies he had dressed for the occasion was moved to tears by the excitements of the evening, and Bernadette, thrilled to the marrow by Paquin's dancing, which was truly superb, was for once dumbstruck and silent.

Letitia, locked in James's arms in a box, vowed to seduce Anton, whose *tours de force*, wearing his revealing tights, had entranced her.

The Swedish lovelies Erik and Kirsten, who had never seen a ballet, were in a paroxysm of delight, and promised themselves to start ballet class immediately. Equal enthusiasm gripped the Contessa Lucia di Flagelli and Marcello Cerruti. Lucia determined to find out about the slant eyed Mongolian boy who had enchanted her in Trotovsky's piece, and Cerruti was even more resolved to lure Galina to the fleshpots and vice of steaming Rome.

All repaired to the ballroom of the Hotel de Paris, where a celebratory buffet, costing hundreds of francs per person, had been provided by the greedy management.

Rose de la Touche had a standing ovation when she entered. Even the affected deviant who had slandered her earlier rushed to kiss her hand in a sycophantic fashion.

Dhokouminsky was cheered to the roof, especially by Sophie who still had great affection for her ex-lover. He scoffed a large plate of prawns in garlic sauce, a plate of *charcuterie*, five thick slices of *boeuf roti*, and drank two bottles of Beaujolais before he spoke, and when he did, it was with his mouth full.

Sabine fell on his neck when he had completed his meal, groping for his omnipotent organ, which came miraculously to life, so soon after his athletic endeavours, and promised him a night of voluptuous carnality in return for his thrilling performance.

The evening represented the climax of the whirl of excitement, high jinks, larks, and thrills of the culmination of the Jazz Age. Everyone danced till dawn to the savage hot music of the fashionable black musicians who had been imported for the event.

Edith, the Charleston expert from Chicago, last mentioned for the demolition of the beach bar, rendered a few excerpts from her repertoire, by way of an impromptu cabaret.

Her costume was terrific in a stunning, sequined shade of vermilion, with long fringes and beads which twinkled and jangled as she danced, high stepping and kicking for all she was worth. Round kicks, high kicks, kicks up to the back of her head, all came naturally to the inebriated damsel. She was the pride of the football pack, the cheerleader *par excellence* who gained a reputation for lewdness by performing her wild dances in the football stadiums of the United States without her knickers.

The throbbing horns and saxophones of the band drove her to such extravagant display that she split the seams of her sparkling dress, but this was not a deterrent. On she went, thrusting and pushing her pelvis in such a riotously outrageous evocation of the social scene of Memphis and New Orleans that the crowd went berserk, taking to the floor in droves, copying her flamboyant style.

Balloons and streamers fell from the ceiling on the gallivanting crowd whose behaviour grew more abandoned as the delirium grew to climax. Men started to throw off their evening jackets and ties, and loosened their braces. The women cast off their painful tight fitting shoes, stomping and treading to the insistent beat the better for dancing barefoot.

Anna Galinka was inspired to pull her dress over her head and throw it at the handsome black singer. He gathered it up in his hands, kissed it, and threw it aside, removing his shirt as he did so, exposing his shinning black skin to the delight of the crowd.

A drunk fell down on the dance floor and was dragged out of the ballroom to be deposited in the fountain of the public garden outside and a girl wearing nothing but a pair of camiknickers climbed in and tried to revive him with half a bottle of champagne which she clamped to his mouth.

Back inside the ballroom, Borzdoff was lifted up on the shoulders of several *corps de ballet* boys, and taken on a lap of triumph round the floor. They tripped over Dhokouminsky who had passed out, and the manager fell on top of his principal dancer in an undignified, but jolly heap.

The twenties were roaring to their end, and Wall Street

was crashing. Every minute the clock moved, the era of desperate licentiousness and carnal folly was coming to an end, but the revellers continued till dawn, bare-breasted and bare-chested, slapping their thighs, slapping their butts, strutting high and low with a voh de oh doh.

Marie-Therese, the occult cellist, standing apart from the throng with a mysterious smile on her beautiful features, said to Charles, her perfectionist new lover, 'Isn't it all divinely decadent? The more I see of the world, the more I think we are driving ourselves to distraction and madness'.

Sophie, nearby, spied Bernadette and Marcel. She ran over to them, fighting her way through the crowd who still danced relentlessly on. She was breathless and giddy from her efforts on the dance floor, but still had enough energy to exclaim, 'It's heaven, I'm in heaven. This must be the centre of the earth, and we shall never be happier. The world revolves around us and our wonderful friends, and I am filled with joy.' She fell in a dead faint at Bernadette's feet, and the relentless dance went on inexorably around and over her prostrate body as a second wave of balloons fell from the ceiling.

Anton found her as he went whirling by with Angelique, Vladimir's chocolate girl. He gave her immediate mouth to mouth resuscitation. When Sophie began to come to her senses, she saw who her rescuer was through half closed eyes, and the vision caused her to pass out again, so Anton lifted her gently up and carried her through the dancing merrymakers into the fresh air outside. Ah, the sweetness of the reunion when she finally recovered close to a flower bed filled with lilies and carnations. The sight of his face again, and the intoxicating scents completed her rapture.

Edith came across Charles and Marie-Therese, holding hands in a corner. 'Hi, I'm Edith,' she called. 'So you're the one now, eh? He tires easy don't he, honey, but I guess he's cute'. With that she made a lurch for Charles's scrotum, but slipped and went careering into the band stand. The black singer hauled her to her feet and slapped her bottom playfully. 'You're cute too,' she said. Then, 'Is it true what they say about black guys?'

'Why, maam, ah jest don't know. What do they say about black guys?'

'You all got great big dongs, honey,' Edith drawled.

'You wanna see, lady?'

'Sure.' she said, eyeing his bulge with interest. 'Come up to my place, room twenty-one, when the hop's over,and ah'll give yer an honest opinion'.

'Ok, lady', the singer replied, and turned away to belt into a hot rag from Alabama.

Lucia di Flagelli finally came face to face with Vladimir, whose exotic Mongolian features had engrossed her when he took the lead in Trotovsky's Art Deco ballet. She handed him her card gravely by way of introduction, babbling away in fast incomprehensible Italian. Her devotion was so obvious that even without a word of the tongue, he got the drift of her meaning. But the contessa wanted more than that to be understood. 'Bernadette' she called imperiously, 'please to translate.' So Bernadette translated into French, and then asked Borzdoff to translate into Russian, and finally Vladimir, with difficulty all round, comprehended. Lucia wanted to steal him away to Rome. She was so rich she could give him his own company, and pay him a vast salary, provide him with a villa, and keep him in whatever luxury he wanted. It seemed like a dream to the poor ex-peasant boy. He rushed to find Angelique, and all this was relayed to her Naturally she was overcome too. She was so proud of the skinny youth and their baby. She fished in her bag and pulled out a photo of the child, and told Lucia in sign language that it was theirs. It was not surprising that Lucia excused herself rapidly. She had just decided that she really was infatuated by Vladimir's equally handsome friend Ivan.

Marcel got his arms round the Swedish siren Kirsten for a slow foxtrot and told her that he had dreamed about her after the luncheon party. Between sentences, he bit the lobe of her right ear and caressed a thigh through her skin tight dress of lame.

Kirsten loved it, and stirred her pudendum against his growing organ. 'It's so hot, just like a sauna bath,' she smiled, engagingly.

'What is that?' he enquired, adjusting his member to a more effective and comfortable uprightness in his trousers.

'Oh, don't you know?' she answered. 'At home we sit around in a very hot little hut, without our clothes, because there is so hot a fire, then we run out into the snow and we beat ourselves and our friends with twigs from the birch trees.'

'How primitive,' the elegant couturier smiled, leering, 'how deliciously primitive,' and steered Kirsten's hand to his crotch.

Marcello Cerruti had tried to prise Galina from Polovsky ever since Bernadette's lunch, with yet more invitations to Rome and several expensive presents. But she was still not sure whether the prospect of permanent corruption and immorality was quite her scene. However, she played him at the game, and even now she had her tongue down his throat, at the same time keeping a wary eye on her conductor friend. She need not have bothered as he had retired behind a potted palm with Anna Galinka, her nearest rival. Little did Galina know that Polovsky was promising to talk to Borzdoff the next day and convince him that Anna should take over her very own role in *Petroushka*.

Rose la Touche was triumphant: the world at her feet. Borzdoff was so relieved to have got rid of Vera Lidova that he was promising his new star anything she wanted, and of course, after such an ovation, she wanted everything; top billing, her own dressing room, an increase in salary, her own choice of roles, Paquin to be her principal partner, and absolutely nothing to do with the drunken Dhokouminsky. This was going too far for Borzdoff, who, being a lush himself, was fond of his old friend, the Tartar, and saw no harm in his stupid behaviour.

'Just look at the devil,' Rose complained as the gentleman was seen being dragged senseless out of the ballroom by two flunkeys who tugged at his braces, and when they had snapped, pulled him by the ankles.

'Ah, such is life,' sighed Borzdoff, gazing at his troupe with a world weary eye, imagining the shocking performance they would give tomorrow after this marathon of a party.

Outside, in the clear light of day, scores of couples lay exhausted on the grass, regardless of their expensive couture finery. The sun was warm already and all the men had thrown off what jackets remained from the ball.

Waiters from the *brasserie* opposite obliged with coffee at inflated prices and the first newspaper was already being scrutinized for its review of last night's performance.

There was a sudden huge bang which shook the very fabric of the Hotel and went reverberating round the bay. Alarmed, everyone jumped to their feet and ran to the sea wall which was the direction from which the sound came.

There in front of their eyes was a wonderful sight, the entire British Navy, lined up in formation in the distance. Destroyers, frigates, troop carriers, battleships, were arranged in order, flags and pennants flying proudly, with the Admiral's flagship in the middle, and his open launch at the ready.

Everyone cheered at the impressive spectacle, and their cries were suddenly drowned by the roar of a hundred gun salute, and then the jolly cacophony of all the sirens and hooters of the ships in the bay answering.

Borzdoff nudged James, the English don who had accompanied him with Fanshawe and Rognon to the house of pleasure in Marseilles. 'Carlotta will be pleased. Look at all those boys.' And there they were, hundreds and hundreds of bell-bottomed Jacks lined up and standing to attention on the deck of every vessel.

'What a lot of cock,' Edith breathed.

'What do the flags read?' someone asked, for the ships were decorated with lines of them from stem to stern, fluttering and waving in the breeze.

James, read out the message carefully, '*Greetings from His Majesty and the people of Great Britain to the Principality of Monaco. Vive l'entente Cordial*'.

Massed bands on the decks played *La Marseillaise* and the British National Anthem, and it is fair to say that there was joy that morning in every part of the Riviera.

The vicomtesse, for one, was thrilled. She extricated her cousin Sophie from the crowd and steered her towards the limousine which Jean-Paul had parked nearby. 'There is much to do. These British Officers must be entertained properly or else we shirk our duties as hospitable Frenchwomen.'

Sophie agreed. Many Englishmen had featured in her love life, even before she hitched up with her beloved Arthur, who was now snoring on the back seat with Marcel. 'My head hurts, I cannot think,' she said painfully when the vicomtesse started a rundown of her plans.

'And we have not done our duty by the Swedish guests, either,' Bernadette complained. 'I do hope they are properly installed.'

'Yes, I hope Erik is truly installed in Kirsten, when we come across them from the garden room,' Sophie gurgled, with a more louche tone than usual because she was profoundly drunk.

'Drive on, Jean-Paul,' the vicomtesse ordered, 'and *chere cousine*, I expect to see you bathed and dressed and sober by the cocktail hour this evening, otherwise I shall be obliged to think that you are not meeting your social obligations as a gentlewoman.' Her tone was, for once, so severe that Sophie presented herself bright and bushy tailed at the appointed hour.

The chauffeur Jean-Paul, if he has featured less in this present journal than an earlier document with which the reader may be familiar, has only himself to blame. The truth is that he had not recently been making enough attempt to brighten up his rather dull life. He saw the comings and goings at the mansion every day, and knew that the residents, their guests, and even the other employees, were having a wonderful time.

The theme of the season that year, as you will by now have gathered, was 'Change partners and dance', and the devotees of the hedonistic life were certainly that instruction.

Jean-Paul, as personal driver to the Riviera's most popular and entertaining hostess, was privy to all of this. He had access to private conversations in the back seats of the limousine he drove, knew intimate details of the times and duration of lovers' meetings, and, more telling, the deceits people used when they changed their instructions to him, and arrived at a very different destination to the one which had originally been announced.

None of this was of interest to Jean-Paul, nor the aura of expensive perfumes that women left behind them in his vehicle, or the sight of silk-clad stockings, and the occasional garter, when he assisted ladies to their seats. His sexual psyche was moved by none of these things. The stimulations that drive most men forward in the hunt for love had no effect on the chauffeur, unfortunately. It was a great pity because he was unusually attractive to women, as he exuded a masculine quality and possessed such beauty as would be envied by other men.

True, the ladies flirted outrageously with him, even though he was of the lower orders in their terms, but then females have often been known to amuse themselves with such distraction; sometimes with cruel effect. But Jean-Paul was unmoved. He answered politely, behaved discreetly, and doffed his cap with great charm, but resisted tempting invitations and tactfully steered his way through a steady career and a humdrum way of life.

Ladies would rave about him to the vicomtesse, and she would laugh and tell them not to bother, they were wasting their time bestowing their charms on him. She knew, because she had tried herself!

Little did she know, but Jean-Paul had a grave physical problem, and it was this which had turned him to a man of stone. His penis was of a diminutive size, of such smallness that he was truly ashamed. He had consulted doctors and specialists to no avail. All anyone could tell him was that all men are different. That if there were no small penises, the national average would not be the same. The figure of fifteen centimetres, at the full stretch of erection, had been arrived at only because there were many men like him to compensate for the few, the very few, who had outstanding examples.

There was no satisfaction in these statistics for Jean-Paul. He pulled and tweaked morning and night, in the bath, the shower, and in bed, but the obstinate little horror did nothing to improve itself. It merely got sore and gave him such pain that he had to deny himself the therapy for a while. His real trouble had started in school where other adolescents had hooted with glee at the sight of the minute organ in the showers after exercises in the gymnasium, and he had been seized with a consuming envy of the incredibly developed protuberances which he saw dangling from most boy's bellies. In spite of his prayers and manipulations, the tip of the hated member even when erect, barely peeped out from his bush of pubic hair. It was a disaster.

The reader can understand, then, that though he could be aroused like other men, he had developed a terror at the thought of using his organ on women who would have made contact with better things than he had to offer. In other words he suffered, to an unusual degree, that fear of comparison that is the norm in the male of the species. How often has a lover wondered if his stamen is as impressive to a lady as the last one to enter her? Equally, how many men wonder if they are long enough or thick enough to please the object of their desires? Let no man assert that he has never had cause to ponder these questions.

In truth, Jean-Paul was more to be pitied than blamed for getting embroiled in his particular neurosis, and others with the same problem will sympathise, and even take heart from how he occasionally overcame it. Last season, his ingenuity and resourcefulness had come to his rescue on two occasions. The first was when an elderly German matron, a guest of Bernadette, had signalled her interest in the attractive young man. He guessed, quite rightly, that it would have been a long time since she had seen, or been in intimate contact with, a male organ, and therefore less likely to make dreaded comparisons. The lady, in the privacy of her hotel bedroom, was so charmed by his massage, nipple sucking and digital stimulations, and even the insertion of a champagne cork to her private part, that she had been overcome with glorious orgasmic bliss to such an extent that she had not even seen or felt his diminutive stem, nor witnessed his own self-induced ejaculation. On the second occasion, a similarly frustrated lady, a rich elderly widow, came to joyous conclusion in the bath, after much soaping and fun with bubbles, and even the play of Jean-Paul's big toe at the gates of her portal. Covered by the foam, his tiny root had experienced a very interesting and extravagant emission. The memory of it kept him going for weeks, as the earlier one had.

But time had passed by, and the chauffeur's frustration needed to be dealt with. The semi-permanent erection that plagued him, fortunately did not spoil the hang of his immaculate uniform, as it was so unobtrusive; but the throb was there, most of the day, and at least half of the night when he dreamed of elderly ladies and their requirements. The only lady of advanced years, so far to be seen this Season, was Carlotta Bombieri, and she was utterly unsuitable since every moment of her time was spent in accommodating men's tools, either in her own capacious duct, or in those of her girls. But relief was in sight. Letitia's mother arrived at the coast in search of her errant daughter, with strict instructions from the family to bring her back to England and save them from further disgrace. Jean-Paul was despatched to Nice Central Station to meet the lady and convey her to the mansion.

She was tiny and bird-like, but energetic and wiry, not a lady to stand any nonsense. Widowed for ten years, she had managed the castle and the huge estates with aplomb, and was used to ordering sulky servants and dealing with grumpy gardeners. But she had no need to use her acid tones on the chauffeur. He was silky smooth and delightful; not obsequious, but sincerely charming. The duchess was totally bowled over by the handsome driver who pointed out places of interest on the way, and even pulled up at certain *points de vue* so that she could feast her eyes on the beauties of the Cote d'Azur. At one of the stops he hurried over to a kiosk and bought her an iced glass of *citron pressé* and presented her with a sprig of heavenly scented mimosa which he plucked from a nearby tree.

She wondered how such a divine man came to be in service, but just put it down to the eccentric ways of the French. In England, she thought, this Adonis would be snatched up by the aristocracy whose ancient blood lines were always in need of a fresh injection. Ah, how ravishing, she thought, to be bowling along with a boy young enough to be her grandson, but who was so attentive and generous. She noted the neat line of his haircut, his swarthy Mediterranean complexion and his beautiful brown eyes. His expensive dove grey uniform gave his slim figure distinction, and his peaked cap had exactly the right dashing tilt. Jean-Paul's suntanned hands at the wheel fascinated her. So perfectly in control of the limousine, so strong and capable. How she would love to have them around her waist. How she longed to have his thin moustache brush her lips.

Jean-Paul kept getting glimpses of the duchess in his driving mirror, and then their eyes met, smiling. He recognised in her expression that oncoming of lust that follows admiration and returned it with a smouldering glance which devastated her.

The look reminded her of a young Grenadier Guard, the last man to pleasure her. It happened a few years before in the marquee after a gymkhana and sports day in the castle grounds, on a trestle table covered with the remains of high tea. He was wonderful, and she surmised that this dark Latin would show the same enthusiasm. When they arrived at the mansion he opened the rear door and kissed her proffered hand before he helped her out, and gave here his arm to escort her up the steps. The tops of her legs had an unaccustomed dampness and her nipples were swelling with excitement. Bernadette noticed the gleam in her eye when they greeted each other, and also the fond looks she bestowed on Jean-Paul as he went to fetch the duchess' luggage from the car boot. 'Jean-Paul will take them upstairs for you,' she said, though it was normally a job for Yves. She added, 'We shall meet in half an hour when you are refreshed from your journey.'

The duchess felt not a twinge of tiredness. On the contrary she felt young and gay, and leapt on to the bed with that same jollity a child has when it arrives in a new hotel. 'You have really been excessively kind, young man,' she enthused, 'what a treasure Bernadette must find you. How long have you been in her employ?'

'Five years, madame,' the chauffeur replied.

'I can see why she wants to hang on to you,' she teased.

'I must ask the vicomtesse if I can borrow you sometime during my stay. It would be delightful to go sight seeing, and you would be the most charming companion.' Her request was granted a few days later. Entranced by the weather, the luxury of the mansion and its gardens, the delicious food prepared by M.Ratatouille, and her expectations of Jean-Paul, the duchess was radiant when she presented herself to him after breakfast. 'Take me where you will,' she said, twinkling.

'An honour, madame,' he bowed.

'And you must call me Mabel, and then I can use your Christian name also,' she insisted, climbing into the front seat in order to be next to him, though she said it was to take advantage of the better view obtainable there.

Jean-Paul drove along the Corniche at a leisurely pace. The palm trees which lined the road threw dark shadows which contrasted with the brilliant intervening patches of sun light, and troughs of garnish flowers provided wonderful splashes of colour. Along the beaches, umbrellas and canopies in gay shades added festive touches, and the careless crowds promenading from one bathing place to another created a kaleidoscope effect with their striped costumes.

The duchess was enchanted, and placing a hand on the chauffeur's knee, told him so. The minute organ gave an initial twitch, and he smiled.

'We are travelling in the direction of Cannes, Mabel,' he said. 'If there is a spot where you want to get out, let me know'.

'You're in charge today, Jean-Paul,' she answered, placing the same hand higher up is leg, with a firm pressure that spoke of her desire. 'It is a little stuffy, don't you think?' she queried. He pulled over to the side of the road and leaned across her to wind down the passenger window. His cheek touched her breast, and he heard her give out a deep sigh. When he spoke next, with his lips close to her ear, asking if it was alright now, her lips quivered, with a sharp intake of breath. 'Oh yes dear,' she breathed, and lightly stroked his hair, 'you darling boy'.

They were on their way again, and Jean-Paul now placed a hand on hers. 'There's a turning not far from here up into the hills, where it's cooler, would you like that?'

'Just as you wish,' the duchess murmured. She stretched out her legs and closed her eyes, the perfect picture of relaxed contentment, but her left thigh was pressed against him, with an urgency that could not be mistaken for casual contact. 'I had a friend like you once,' she said, 'just as nice and charming'.

'You remind me too of a lady of whom I was very fond,' Jean-Paul murmured, 'Only she was not as pretty.'

'You darling,' she exclaimed, 'I liked you the first moment I saw you.'

'Here's the road I mentioned,' he announced, and turned sharp right on to a narrow track which took them higher and higher until the whole coast was spread out below them.

'What a perfect spot,' the duchess cried, and gambolled around like a teenager. When she had taken in the wonderful view she threw herself with abandon on the grass on the cliff top they had reached and wallowed in the scents of the wild flowers that grew in abundance at that spot. 'Where are you?' she called, with a flirtatious edge to her voice.

'Coming,' he answered. He was at that moment stuffing a *boudin blanc*, which is a particular kind of pale sausage, into his underwear.

Come here, it's so lovely,' she cried, throwing handfuls of the little blooms into the air with the rapture of a child of nature. 'See, I have found a four-leaved clover.'

He fell on the grass beside her and plucked a flower. 'I see you like butter,' he said, placing it under her chin. Then with another of violet hue, he told her it matched the colour of her eyes.

She plucked a handful of grass and tickled his face with it, snuggling closer to him the while. 'This is how my friends back home in England would be—green with envy' she said, thinking how lucky she was to be out with such a nice young man whose penis was pressed so intimately into her thigh. The *boudin blanc* had made its mark. She was ecstatic to feel the thick soft flesh of it next to her leg, and gazed imploringly in his eyes.

Daringly, he made the first kiss. His moustache was heaven

to her mouth. Jean-Paul pushed his tongue as far as it could reach, reducing her to a state of complete passivity, except that her legs parted slightly and her bosom heaved.

As he pressed closer, the hidden sausage came nearer her private part and she wriggled to bring it even closer. It felt larger than any other member she could recall, and the new sensation of size gave her a frisson of such intensity that she placed a hand on it and squeezed. The solidly made piece of *charcuterie*, examples of which have satisfied many a French appetite, felt enormous. 'Gorgeous, gorgeous,' she moaned.

Jean-Paul had her skirt lifted in a trice, with his fine fingers at the duchess's private parts. smoothing and plucking mischievously, causing her to cry out softly, and when he inserted a deft finger tip she arched her back and pushed her mound of Venus, drawing it further in.

'You darling,' she cried, 'you certainly know about women.' Then his hands were at her small breasts, driving her to further distraction, with the sausage placed squarely over her pelvic bone, pressuring her most sensitive area. The movement of his hips made the most exquisite sensations arrive there, and also to his own tiny erect shaft which nestled between the *boudin* and his belly. 'I love it,' she breathed harshly.

'So do I,' he answered, his breathing becoming quicker.

In an inspired moment, he turned the duchess on to her side and tucked her knees up high, as he cradled his crotch to her rear. He could feel from the wet state of her orifice that she was desperate for him to enter. With the fingers of one hand he kept her on heat while he fished in his fly buttons for the hidden sausage, and then, when he had withdrawn it, holding it firmly in his right fist, plunged it to its depth into the expectant cavity. He lunged his whole body as he applied the *boudin*, and she returned the thrust backwards. It was a novel method for her, having been brought up as an English gentlewoman, and the more thrilling for being so foreign.

'I'm dying,' she called, and came massively, drowning the *boudin*, and did so again, after he had given her part yet another vigorous application with it. They both lay still, breathing heavily, until, groaning appreciatively, the nimble duchess reached between the top of her legs for the organ that had ravished her so delightfully. Wet with her juices, the object was silky and hard to the touch, and she was aware of the grasp of Jean-Paul's fist holding it in place. 'You are wonderful,' she murmured. 'What a huge thing you've got!

The compliment was music to his ears. Months of frustration and worry about the size of his genitals vanished in a moment, and Jean-Paul gave way to the most enormous pent-up rush of ejaculatory passion, spurt after spurt of heavenly bliss. He had proved himself at last.

Chapter Thirteen

'How peaceful and calm it is here, so relaxing after the excitements of the last few days,' Sophie sighed. 'So refreshing to get away from all the noise and the crowds in the theatre, and the tiresome chore of dressing up every evening.'

'I like that,' the vicomtesse retorted sardonically. 'You like nothing more than getting into your finery and parading in the foyer before a performance.'

The two were secreted in the garden room, late in the afternoon, several days after the ballet première, and they had promised themselves that, come what may, they were going to stay in that evening.

'But it is so chic to appear in the wonderful creations of your clever Marcel, and watch the envy in the eyes of lesser mortals,' Sophie laughed. 'Why, last evening, the Marquesa de Bergonza-Stracciata nearly choked when she saw the gorgeous ensemble Marcel designed for me. It was worth going just for that, let alone Anton's thrilling performance. How I adore that boy.'

'Yes, he surpassed himself,' Bernadette admitted, thinking of the fabulous sweep of silver lamè, encrusted with diamante, that Sophie had swaggered in wearing, turning more heads than any other outfit. 'Mine was delightful too, *non*? The purple silk, with the dyed fox stole, don't you think?'

'Captivating,' Sophie agreed, reaching for a Black Sobranie and her cigarette holder.

'I have devised a new cocktail, and I wish you to try it, darling. I am sure you will like it,' Bernadette said, shaking the mixture vigorously in the gold container. 'It contains

Cointreau, the juice of fresh peaches, crushed ice, and just a trickle of cream.'

'Delicious, pronounced Sophie, 'but I think those British naval officers you have invited will require something more to their taste. The English like warm beer, or neat whisky, do they not?'

'When they are in la belle France, they must behave in a civilised manner, not like heathens,' the vicomtesse ruled.

As they sipped their drinks, the gently fading light through the azure glass dome of the roof softened the outlines of the richly furnished room, if anything giving it even greater allure and a sense of refined costly elegance. Both were wearing new house gowns of crêpe de Chine in a delicate shade of shell pink which hung in folds over silk underwear. Sophie sported camiknickers of the palest lavender, trimmed with lace and contrasting cyclamen ribbons, and Bernadette wore gauzy drawers and a camisole in a fetching shade of parma violet, embroidered minutely with lilies of the valley picked out in white and fresh green. They were feeling rested after leisurely baths and massages from a visiting therapist, a tall negro who bore a striking resemblance to the jazz singer who performed at the party after the first night of the ballet.

'His hands were so strong, darling,' Bernadette said, 'he did me a lot of good, I'm sure,'

'Yes, he worked so hard on me he had to take off his shirt,' Sophie reminisced, recalling the rippling muscles of the masseur's torso. 'It's curious that he spoke so much about Edith, the Charleston expert, don't you think?' she added. But the question drifted on the air, so peaceful was the room, and so contented its occupants.

'So now we come to the question of the Swedish *amoureux*,' Bernadette at last announced.

'Yes, we have been singularly backward in our attentions to that pair, when you consider how long they have been in residence,' Sophie complained, and added, 'I hear they have been having a marvellous time.'

'Scandalous, I would say,' the vicomtesse smiled. 'Why they have been seen in undignified positions on every part of the Cote d'Azur. Do you know—my spies are everywhere—it was reported to me that they were seen in flagrante delicto standing at the mast of a schooner as it sailed from Toulon to Nice? And on another occasion, they were observed in coitus on a rubber inflatable mattress in the bay of Villefranche?'

'My dear, I heard those liberated Swedes even resorted to love on a park bench in Menton, until a keeper drove them off with his besom brush,' Sophie giggled, 'and what's more, they were discovered half naked under a gambling table in the Casino in Monte Carlo,'

'How thrilling,' Bernadette exclaimed. 'We stand to learn much from these unsophisticated, but charmingly unselfconscious children of the Far North. If you think how inhibited we are, *mon dieu*, and yet the French have a reputation for depravity and salaciousness. Why, erotic books are written about our so-called licentiousness.'

'It's grossly unfair,' said Sophie, who at that very moment was dipping greedily into the newly catalogued series of Japanese prints of Sumo wrestlers and geishas that Bernadette had recently been working on.

'I played a provocative little trick on our love birds,' the vicomtesse confided to her cousin. 'They came to me last night, asking for French novels to help them with their language studies. Naturally, I made up a parcel of the most intimate variety, and I also slipped in an Indian manual of sex instruction. I dare say that by now it will have come to their attention,'

'And are you suggesting, my sweet, that the stimulation of this holiday reading will spring Erik's prize possession to attention, for our amusement?' her cousin giggled.

'We shall see, darling,' Bernadette breathed, as she drew the curtain away from the two-way mirror and settled on the *chaise longue*.

Sophie tiptoed over and joined her. The sense of anticipation was superb. Never had the secret garden room seemed such a marvellous place to be, as the two excited and happy ladies settled down to watch and wait for the expected cabaret.

The Swedish lovelies had thrown off their outer garments

and were reclining on a sofa in their underwear, struggling with their French language studies. It would be impossible, here, to reproduce their excruciating accents and their difficulties with the notoriously convoluted grammar. But it amused the two ladies for a while and gave them an opportunity to admire the couple's golden skin and almost-white hair, bleached by the Riviera sun. Soon Sophie got bored with their study and went to the console to pour large gins.

The couple were bored too, and Erik threw away his tome and yawned. 'We have better things to do, Kirsten,' he said as he slipped off his underpants.

'Ya, ya, I agree,' she said, following his example.

The ladies had to admit they were a handsome pair; long limbed and slender, with fine muscular definition to their well exercised bodies. Kirsten's breasts were shapely, though small, with an upturned tilt at the nipples, and she had a flat belly and boyish rump. Erik was as finely tuned, though broader and taller. He had no body hair, it seemed, but in fact, it was so bleached it merged into the colour of his skin, giving him a fascinating naked appearance. She being boyish, and he being so good looking, without any male coarseness, the pair seemed almost androgynous. The effect they had was of a natural and outstanding beauty, as Bernadette and Sophie properly acknowledge to each other in whispers. Both of them were so engrossed in the physical perfection of the pair beyond the two-way mirror, and the thick Aubusson carpet so camouflaged the sound of advancing footsteps, that neither heard Marcel and Arthur enter the secret garden room.

The men were amazed by what they saw, and in one delighted sweep of their heads, took in the glories of the room's furnishings; the Far Eastern carvings, ancient Aztec sculptures, Indian artwork, and Roman statuary, all imbued with erotic and sensuous imagery, and chosen by Henri, the late vicomte, for their collective ability to stimulate the senses. They noted the wall hangings of fine Gobelin tapestries, scenes of Arcadian naked sports which depicted fleshly females, in the style of Rubens, being ravaged by abandoned satyrs, horned beasts of enormous strength, and the proud possessors of giant phalluses. Large bookcases held Henri's private collection of important graphics and writings, a legacy envied by many distinguished followers of the genre which captivated him throughout his life; and the centre of the room was taken up by a fountain over which presided a marble carving of an Olympian pair of lovers conjoined in an attitude of coitus which was a miracle of the sculptor's art.

Central to this vast and exceptional room was the large gilded mirror into which their wives were gazing with a rapt expression, so pre-occupied that they knew nothing of their entry until each laid a hand on his wife's shoulder. An icy chill penetrated both Bernadette and Sophie's hearts. Who were these intruders in the temple dedicated to the carnal arts? How had anyone been so devilishly clever as to divine its secrets and discover the hidden door? They turned swiftly, with terror stricken eyes, but melted when they saw their husbands.

The vicomtesse, in an almost involuntary gesture which took only a fraction of a second to execute, placed a finger to her lips; that signal that is universally understood. Marcel and Arthur looked past the women, from where they stood behind the divan, and saw the handsome couple beyond, through the darkened glass of the mirror.

They were prostrate on a large double bed, engaged in a long kiss, with their loose limbs wrapped together in a serpentine convolutedness of great charm and beauty. Sophie and her cousin looked fearfully at their husbands, wondering what their reactions would be, but were immensely relieved to see broad smiles spread over their faces, then grins and winks of mutual satisfaction.

'You deceitful, but utterly adorable creature,' Marcel whispered urgently to Bernadette. 'How long have you had this secret, and why have you kept it from me?

'All shall be revealed,' she answered. You just need to know that this secret room is my inheritance from Henri, and I was going to give you the key on our approaching wedding anniversary. Now you have spoilt my surprise'.

Marcel took his wife in his arms and rained kisses on her mouth, neck and breasts. 'My darling, we came to look for you and Sophie in the small *salon*, and we saw a narrow door ajar. It was a hidden door, *non*, that I never before suspected'.

Sophie immediately burst into silent tears, masking the sound of her weeping on account of the lovers so close by. 'It is my fault,' she moaned in Bernadette's ear, 'my hands were full with the drinks tray, and I forgot to return and lock the door'.

'*N'importe quoi, cherie,*' the vicomtesse soothed. 'Our little secret is out, but it must be fate, and anyway, will it not be vastly more entertaining having male companions to share the joys of the hidden garden room?'

Sophie dried her tears on the sleeve of her fine crêpe de Chine gown, and drew Arthur to her bosom. 'I have been the sole sharer of Bernadette's haven, Now you, my darling, are privileged to join us. It is a great honour,' she whispered.

Arthur fell to his knees at Bernadette's feet. The erotic possibilities of the room crowded into his imagination. Now he knew why she allotted the guest wing to interesting, well shaped young people. Ian and Cynthia, for example, the Scottish redheads who were newly wed. And horror, oh horror. He himself had been an occupant, with Charles for companion. He had brought the infatuated debutante Annabelle there and lost his virginity to her. The vicomtesse would surely have seen all, and been witness to his every action. He looked imploringly into her eyes and Bernadette guessed the question that was silently poised.

'Yes, indeed,' she said, with an intriguing smile,' and that was when Sophie first became interested in you, so do not complain if we had a little fun at your expense.'

'But you saw everything?' he asked his wife.

'Yes, even how you had to put on a jockstrap under your bathing drawers, because your tool, which I adore, my love, was so troublesome in the heat, and showed all day in your flannels.'

Marcel laughed, almost choking, as he had to remain silent, at this joke. As a young man, he had been obliged to take the same precaution. 'It's wondering, darling,' he said to Bernadette. Quite clearly we are going to have years of free entertainment together in this divine room.'

'You can thank my late husband Henri for that.' she replied with a wink. 'Come, let us arrange ourselves, the cabaret is about to begin.'

The four settled comfortably on the *chaise longue*, with the ladies nestled in their husbands' laps. They saw Erik reach for the Indian manual which Bernadette had contrived cunningly into the parcel of novels that she had supplied for the Swedish couple's edification.

'I leafed through this earlier,' Erik was heard to say. 'My goodness, those Indians know a thing or two.'

'Mmm, very interesting,' Kirsten said. They were lying on their bellies on the bed, perusing the erotic documents together. 'There are so many things here we have not tried, darling,' she said. Each turn of the pages brought a fresh note of surprise to her voice. 'My God, they are athletes,' she exclaimed.

'So are we, darling,' Erik exclaimed, and it was true, for the Swedish are rigorous in this respect. It is well known that they are so slavishly devoted to the cult of Health and Beauty, and to Swedish Gymnastics, that they even continue their exercises naked in the deep snows of winter, after taking the sauna baths which Kirsten had described to Marcel at the recent luncheon. 'Come, let us begin,' he said, in a businesslike manner. He placed the manual on a side table to give a clear space on the bed, and set to work.

It was clear to the four spectators that Erik and Kirsten did not feel it was necessary to bother with the first ten pages or so of the instructions, as they were obviously already familiar with the most basic positions, and therefore skipped to something more adventurous. It was fascinating to watch; calculated, professional to a degree, and quite clinically cold in approach, without excitement of any kind—and as far as Erik was concerned, without the slightest degree of tumescence, which Arthur, for one, found extraordinary.

Each pose or position briefly struck by the pair was striking, and also enlightening. Because this initial investigation was only of a preparatory nature, Erik and Kirsten were content to reproduce the basic concept, or choreography of each example, with their sexual parts coming together in close contact, but without actual entry. This would have been impossible in any case, since the concentration required in such a scientific approach sent his blood rushing to refresh his brain cells rather than to swell his organ. It was an example of that thoroughness and dedication for which the stolid citizens of Scandinavia are renowned. Readers of Ibsen and Chekhov may have noticed in those pages a certain lack of gaiety, to say the least, and wondered if the Swedes, Finns and Danes are perhaps a little serious in their approach to life, compared with the frivolous French.

But the scene was novel and entertaining to the two married couples watching from the other side of the glass, and even more so when Erik and Kirsten came to the inevitable *Soixante Neuf* at the close of the manual. As his lips closed over her blonde tufted part, and her mouth opened to receive his member, it was obvious that electric things were happening. Both squirmed in their glee and growing arousal, as did the four spectators.

'My goodness, they're enjoying that.' Sophie whispered.

'About time too,' said Arthur, for even though there had been no great carnality so far, the spectacles of the naked bodies in so many suggestive positions had already moved him to such a degree that his hardness was clearly felt by Sophie's buttocks.

What they could see of Erik's appendage, for a considerable amount of it was hidden in Kirsten's mouth, quite clearly thickened in dimension and showed off the blue veins that ran along the stem. His tongue worked at her entry, burrowing and lapping delightfully.

'God, what a hard-on, I've got.' Marcel hissed.

'You will just have to wait.' Bernadette said firmly.

Suddenly Erik tore himself away from his enjoyable occupation. 'I shall be finished if I am not careful,' he yelled, running into the bathroom.

Bernadette revealed to Marcel the peephole in the carved screen which allowed sight of that room.

'Poor man, he is trying to calm the beast with cold water'. Marcel reported.

Sophie pushed him away, in order to take a peep.

'Enormous, just like you, darling,' she said to Arthur. 'I hope he can do as well with it as you do with yours.' She squeezed Arthur's rampant organ with affection. That very morning he had laboured divinely with it before going off riding with Marcel, presenting her with countless opportunities to climax, and she was intensely grateful.

Erik returned. There was no visible change in the conformation of his member that they could recognise, but they surmised that some of the threatening heat must have fled, as he approached Kirsten calmly. His pole was almost vertical to his belly, twitching with muscular throbs. She lay expectantly, with her legs wide open, but he turned her over and entered her from behind. He glanced at the manual as he did so arranging the placing of his hands and legs as that particular page instructed. When he was satisfied with the grouping, gave ten slow thrusts, pushing in up to the hilt and then withdrawing so that the tip of his stamen appeared free from her moist entrance. To the watchers' amazement, he counted from one to ten as he gave these delicate plunges, and when they were over, he dismounted and casually referred to the book of instructions. A veil will again be drawn over much of the detail of Erik and Kirsten's investigations. To report accurately, photographs or drawings of each example of the cunning Indian suggestions would be necessary, and since these are not available, the reader must draw on his own experience to guess the variety of interest that precipitated that evening, both in the guest suite and in the adjoining hidden chamber. Suffice it to say that the thorough Erik never allowed himself more than ten strokes, whatever position he and Kirsten were in, in spite of her protests, for she was now most anxious to come to climax, and each perfunctory set of ten insertions, followed by the inevitable frustrating withdrawal, increased her frustration.

'Don't go away,' she cried. Or, 'For heaven's sake, Erik, get on with it'. Once when he came to the end of his self-imposed ration in a coitus of extreme interest, with Kirsten standing on her head, her legs open in a wide split to the sides, she screamed, 'Oh Erik, ram it in. I'll go mad if you don't.'

The four onlookers were inflamed themselves by now.

Kirsten's open legs and moistened part, her lovely breasts, and her beseeching demands to Erik, in whatever position he arranged her, according to the manual's instructions, drove them heady with desire. The husbands clutched their respective wives and pressed their swollen members at them, rubbing their breasts, and fingering them through the legs of their delicious camiknickers. The wives were delirious also at the vision of Erik's steaming penis, glossy with love juices, making these deliberate and titillating entrances and exits; his swollen glans exposed from his foreskin, and the massive size of his scrotum. The prospect of love upstairs in the privacy of their bedrooms added to the voyeuristic pleasure, and both sought their spouses' bursting stems through their fly buttons

'May I borrow the book, when it has been returned?' Sophie gurgled. 'I'm not sure I shall be able to remember all these exquisite variations.'

'Don't worry, darling, Arthur will,' Bernadette whispered.

Erik and Kirsten were now at about the sixtieth variation. In order to comply with regulations as set out, in the book he piled pillows at the foot of the bed, to bring his pelvis higher from the floor. His back was arched impressively, as his head was much lower than his hips. Kirsten, after study of the particular page, placed herself by his right thigh. He gave her a hand to help her to balance as she bent slightly and hoisted up her right heel.

The spectators watched as the Swedish athlete pushed until her right leg was so stretched upwards that her foot was much higher than her head. The pose was exactly like one of Vera Likov's incredible preparations at ballet class.

Erik wriggled a little until the knob of his member was directly underneath her wet orifice. He stretched up a hand and took hold of her elevated leg. 'Now, bend,' he urged, and as Kirsten's supporting knee flexed, her part opened and slid over his rod, enclosing it completely in one fell swoop. Of course, in this position, Erik had less chance of the usual ten firm strokes, but Kirsten compensated, giving thanks for her severe athletic training as she did so, by jerking her knee from bent to straight the required number of times. It was a magnificent display of gymnastics.

The effect on Erik was substantial. Through the next eight variations his admirably controlled sets of ten strokes started to disintegrate into uncounted, frenzied thrusts, leaping from one pose to the next with little of his earlier regard for clinical accuracy. Red faced and perspiring, with his body wracked from the innumerable sensations it had received, he drove himself recklessly on. Kirsten lunged her part at his organ with rapacious lust, and screamed each time he withdrew, fingering herself when he briefly consulted the instructions.

Now they were at number sixty nine. Kirsten licked her lips at the prospect, and lay to receive him, lasciviousness streaming from every pore in her body. Erik barely made it in time. By the time the tip of his bursting stem reached her lips, the first gush of his fluids had spurted from his orifice, but before the rest emerged, his red, fiery glans was completely inserted. At exactly the same moment, his thrusting tongue brought Kirsten to the ravishing conclusion that had so far evaded her.

The spectators, in other circumstances, would have burst into applause at such a happy outcome, and such devotion to study, but they crept away, and you can imagine that their admiration for the sexual gymnasts they had witnessed spilled over to admiration of their own efforts in the privacy of their own apartments.

Chapter Fourteen

The day the first party of British ratings were given leave to go ashore turned out to be a day to remember. The Admiral of the Fleet himself told the lads what was expected of them. He listed good behaviour and perfect manners, forbade drunkenness and swearing, advised them to stay away from filthy French wine and stick to beer, and reminded them that each of them, in his own way, was an ambassador for the beloved mother country. He also gave strict instructions that they were to refrain from entering houses of pleasure, and to resist the charms of certain freelance ladies who might lure them into the back room of a bar. Other things to be avoided were garlic, snails and frogs legs; filthy things that would only give them diseases and render them incapable of carrying out their duties to the Crown.

The bell-bottomed boys gave him a lusty set of three cheers and threw their caps in the air. The Admiral was delighted. The spontaneous action reminded him of his favourite moment in the Gilbert and Sullivan masterpiece, H.M.S. Pinafore, whose captain he had modelled himself on. Tears sprang to his eyes as he watched the open launch take the first batch ashore. By nine o'clock there were several hundred matelots wandering around Monte Carlo on a spree.

A considerable number discovered a party from the Ballets Russes sunbathing and swimming on the rocks below the Opera House. As it would have seemed churlish, or against the spirit of *entente cordiale*, not to participate they speedily threw off every vestige of clothing and joined in the fun. It never ceases to amaze how quickly friendships can be forged by the simple adoption of nudity, especially when people are immersed in water. It must be that splashing about in the waves induces memories of innocent childhood, a time before the onset of worrying problems such as self-consciousness.

As we know already, the ballet had no inhibitions about displaying their ravishing bodies, and the British sailors, having been aboard for months, were only too keen to do so as well. The boys of the troupe did not mind at all, so long as their own particular girlfriends were not involved. Carefully steering those specimens out of the way (and it must be remembered that in a ballet company, there are comparatively few men), they left lots of spares for the English lads to play with.

Ah, it was carefree and jolly, with lots of bare bottoms bobbing up and down in the briny, and much flirtation going on below the waves. Some of the more enterprising boys, when they could bear to tear themselves away, got dressed quickly and ran into town to buy booze—that well known aphrodisiac—and returned to the fray with gusto.

Edith spied the party and launched herself off a rock with aplomb. The British party knew instinctively from that moment on that, if all else failed, they would be alright with that lady. Mentally she was adding up how many pounds of British flesh she had encountered in the water as she went from one lad to another, trying them for size and hardness. It was a jolly jape they appreciated in their frustrated condition, so much better than scrubbing decks, and silly things like coiling ropes.

The first tar she took advantage of was a massive lad from Sheffield who gave her what she wanted on a slippery rock in a tiny cove. She groaned as he tried to control their fierce action on the slime of covering seaweed, and gazed up at the burning sun as he poured his pent-up fluids into her. She was desperate for more and joined another lad, who was a strong swimmer, enjoying the swell a hundred metres out from shore. He slid into her lubricated interior with ease and ravaged her deliciously; each penetration timed to the rise and fall of the waves. Charles passed nearby, in a yacht he was demonstrating to a potential client. He concluded that the closeness of the partnership indicated one thing only, and was relieved he was not the male involved in her pleasure.

On the rocks the remaining tars were learning to speak Russian with more avidity than was usually reserved for their studies, and some had gone so far as to draw towels over themselves and their tutors for more privacy and concentration. At the end of the morning more than a few were invited back to the Hotel de la Poste for a little lunch and post-prandial exercise, and the remainder went in search of other amusements, accompanied by Edith who had determined to lavish her talents further on them with a display of the corrupting Charleston.

They met up with another party who. after flirting outrageously with Angelique in the chocolate shop, had repaired to the Café de la Colombe for drinks and now were enjoying the company of Gavroche's mistress and model, Josette. She sang saucy French songs accompanied by Gabin on the guitar and received a heart ovation from the boys.

The merry sounds attracted a few of the *jolies filles* of the district who had rents to pay and were glad of a little business. Madame *la patronne* was also happy. Her corkscrew had not been so busy in years.

Camille was spotted by another gang further along the boulevard and followed for about two kilometres, and during the walk she enjoyed several transports, arriving at her apartment in need of a change of underwear.

It was raucous and heady. The day was magnificent and happiness rolled around in great lumps, almost a tangible sensation.

At the mansion Sophie and Bernadette were entertaining a group of officers. The important ladies of the town had arranged to split the gentlemen between them in groups. Bernadette's lot were of the stuffiest kind. Even when they got drunk on her peach cocktail they made no advances, which was not very flattering, to say the least. The vicomtesse put it down to their public school education, though Sophie reminded her that her darling Arthur had gone through the same system, to which the vicomtesse asserted that one always had to have an exception in order to prove a rule.

Jean-Paul was unavailable to drive any of the gentlemen back to the port when it came time to leave, for he had taken Mabel, the Duchess of Rotherham on another outing. Today's seduction was a simpler affair than the previous. He had conducted her to Grasse, the centre of the perfume producing district where, in a field of intoxicating lavender which stretched as far as the eye could see, he had devoured her private parts with such efficiency that she invited him to England with the promise of a situation, a lodge of his own, and all the vegetables he wanted from the castle gardens. They had a blissful day, and at its end, when Jean-Paul escorted her back to Nice Central Station, she wept into the bunch of lavender he had picked for her, and promised to place it in her underwear drawer, as she handed over a most expensive gold watch and a pair of cufflinks that would do him proud.

At another of the parties given for the officers, namely a buffet lunch provided by the Marquesa de Bergonza-Stracciata, the lady who had so envied Sophie's new outfit on the first night of the ballet, Lucia, la Contessa di Flagelli, had more success than the vicomtesse and her cousin. Two wildly frustrated young officers, inflamed by the wine, and by her imperious beauty, took her to a nearby hotel when the reception was over, and enjoyed her jointly. She was delighted. It was the first time since she had left Rome with Cerruti that she had been subjected to this kind of lovemaking. It reminded her, as the two gallant officers strove to possess her simultaneously, (it was their first experience of such an orgiastic adventure), so dearly of the eternal city, and its favourite practices.

The Season was rolling inexorably to its end. Over the next few days other tars and officers came plundering, until almost the entire fleet had tasted the heady joys of the Riviera.

The ballet had done their last electrifying performance and received their final bouquets. Angelique packed her trunk and prepared to join the wardrobe department on tour, with her beautiful slant-eyed baby who had become the company mascot.

Marcel shut his salon, and Arlette, the chief *vendeuse* went off to Tangier for a well earned holiday with Francois.

M.Rognon closed his art gallery, regretful of the incident with Vera Lidova that had cost his wallet so much, but revelled in the success he had enjoyed with Gavroche's inspired oils based on Fanshawe's ridiculous tales.

Charles tied up the yachts and left for England with Marie-Therese who was to be subjected to the family inspection, and Edith returned to the United States in time for the fall season of American football, as she was required to perform her onerous duties as cheer leader *par excellence* for the Chicago team.

Lady Letitia and James moved on to the Greek Islands to commence their research for the next book on the Graeco-Romano empire, after James paid a last visit to Carlotta Bombieri's establishment.

Frederick was installed in the house of safety with a ream of paper and a typewriter, with a guard and two Alsatian dogs to prevent him from leaving before he had completed a novel, and Lucia and Cerruti went back to their Roman fleshpots with some alacrity, anxious to pick up where they had left off.

The sad-happy day when the Ballets Russes resumed their peregrinations suddenly arrived. They embarked at Marseilles, for a trip first to Athens where they were to perform in the ruins of the Acropolis, and then on to Alexandria, as they were to dance under the stars before the pyramids of Ancient Egypt. By ironic chance, the liner on which they were to be transported across the Mediterranean belonged to the line owned by Constantine Vossoudossoulos, the millionaire who was presumed to have seduced Paolo, Letitia's young lover.

The ancient vessel was already crammed with tourists and culture seekers from all parts of the globe. They were astonished to see the riff-raff of the Ballets Russes swarm up the gangplank like so many demented lemmings. Most of them were drunk, having come from a final Charleston party on the beach; especially Dhokouminsky who was supported by his amour Sabine. She was still smarting from the embarrassment of an incident during the afternoon when, in the throes of a thrilling coitus in a bathing tent,

Dhokouminsky's abandoned wild behaviour had resulted in the collapse of the tent, and the entire beach full of holidaymakers had been treated to the sight of them in flagrante delicto.

Angelique waited until the wild rush of the *corps de ballet* was over before ascending the gangplank proudly with her baby, the slant-eyed beauty she and Vladimir had christened Marguerite, after the flowers which grew on the balcony of the tiny attic apartment where she had been conceived. Vladimir carried the canary in a willow cage covered by a shawl. Angelique had cried when the moment of parting came, and the Mongolian was so moved he determined to smuggle the little bird on board and take it on the tour.

Anton and Paquin were delighted to spot Bernadette, Marcel, Sophie and Arthur on the quayside. They had so much luggage with them they were obviously coming along for the trip. Both of the ladies looked up and waved, with alluring smiles, and the boys waved back, fantasising about nights at sea with the ravishing pair.

Such thoughts had occurred also to the vicomtesse and her cousin. They had been in a turmoil for days since the decision to go on holiday had been made, and thought of the frustration that would undoubtedly arise in the close confines of the ship, in tantalising proximity to such desirable men.

'How on earth can we play, with our husbands on board?' Sophie wailed. It really is too bad that they are coming.' But, as in all human comedies, coincidence came to the rescue. Erik and Kirsten announced their intention to join the party. 'The Swedish goddess will occupy Marcel very nicely, I think,' Bernadette pronounced, 'and that will leave me free to be entertained by Monsieur Paquin.'

'But what about me?' Sophie demanded, with lascivious thoughts of hot nights on the Nile in the arms of Anton.

'You must have noticed, darling, that Arthur is absolutely besotted with Rose la Touche, Paquin's girl friend. If we organise things properly, he will be involved with her while I am involved with Paquin, which will leave you free to enjoy yourself with Anton.'

The logic of all of this evaded Sophie, but as always she

trusted in her cousin and came to the embarkation in a happier frame of mind.

The night drew darker as the remaining passengers boarded, and the band on the quay struck up a lively tune. Expectation, thrill, and glamour were in the air. Assignations were made, and a hundred promises of undying affection.

Polovsky clutched Galina to his chest and swore to marry her in Athens, but the *soubrette's* imagination took her to Rome and the expensive fleshpots that Cerruti had seductively described.

Paquin managed to steal a kiss on Bernadette's cheek, and Anton passed a sly hand over Sophie's rounded rump, while Marcel and Kirsten spent a few magic moments together, and Arthur helped Rose la Touche carry her baggage down to her cabin.

A tear came into Borzdoff's eye as he clasped Dhokouminsky and Sabine to his breast. 'We are to following in the steps of the divine Isadora Duncan.' he said. 'It was in the moonlight on the steps of the Parthenon that she find her first inspiration.' Such an artistic consideration evaded the giant Slav's interest, as he groped at Sabine's hidden sexual parts through her skirts. 'And when we to perform before the triangles we shall be to following the traditions of the ancient temple dancers of the Pharoes,' continued Borzdoff, but his remark went unnoticed as Dhokouminsky was entirely occupied with a new sensation that had come to his attention.

As the ship's siren sounded and fireworks went blazing into the dark sky, the Slav found a wonderful vibration in the brass rail of the deck. It emanated from the engine room of the staid old vessel and rumbled through every panel and timber until it thudded into Dhokouminsky's groin as he leaned over waving to the people on the quay. The shuddering thrill ran into his testes and throbbed into his ever willing organ, causing it yet again to swell in the old familiar way. He tipped the wink to his friend Paquin, who passed the message on to Anton, and by a wicked, conspiratorial kind of semaphore, the word got round to all the boys of the ballet, who naturally took with glee to pressing their crotches against the brass rail, in order to take advantage of the free and unexpected, titillating throb it transmitted.

Streamers and balloons went cascading into the midnight air as the antique liner galvanised itself into action and slowly drew out of the port to begin its journey to exotic places. The last fireworks fell from the sky as the stewards rang the bell for dinner, and while the ship's siren sounded its lugubrious and haunting sound, the ladies moved as one towards the dining saloon, leaving the men to enjoy the resounding throb of the old engines in their most sensitive parts.